Private Listing

Watch Me

C.S. Berry

AI was not used in the making of this book or cover artwork.

Cover design by Opulent Design

Author Note

Dear Reader,

If you're related to me, please stop reading right here. Seriously. I'm not ready to look across a table and have you ask me so have you ever. . . Because no. Now go read something less spicy and don't talk to me about it.

Everyone else, I hope you're ready for this. Private Listing started out as just an idea for a serial and it built itself into a four book series. These books are meant to be read in order and there will be cliffhangers.

Don't worry. There is plenty of group spice, but beyond just sex, she develops personal relationships with each of her guys.

PRIVATE LISTING is very much about consensual play.

While I tried to be as conscious of proper play within BDSM, please remember this is a fantasy. While everything might be possible, always go to a more trusted source for information than my book

This story launched me into a new genre and brought me so many fans. If you want to connect with me, my Facebook group is C.S. Berry's Spicy Executive Suite. You can also follow me on Instagram, but I generally post about the stories that are ongoing on Vella (which may contain spoilers). While there are new scenes in the ebook, you can always continue in the Vella, if you need to know now and can't wait for the next book to release. The chapters coordinate with the episode numbers.

For a list of content warnings, please visit my website csberry.com.

XOXOXO,

C.S. Berry

Chapter 1

The Interview

Madison

"Madison Harris, here to interview at Morrigan Technology Group." I manage to get that out without so much as a tremor of desperation in my voice. This is my fourth interview since graduation out of fifty resumes sent. If I don't find something soon, I'll be forced to move back to my parents' farm and give up my dream of living and thriving in New York City.

The woman working at the front desk gives me a once-over before pressing a button and holding her finger over her earpiece. "A Madison Harris is here." A brief pause. The woman looks me over again. "Yes."

Shit, did I do a button wrong? I check my white blouse's buttons are done properly and that my pencil skirt hasn't rotated around. Sure, one of the buttons on my blouse is a little strained over my breasts, but if I want it to fit everywhere else, that's the way it has to be. I can't afford to buy all new clothes or have them tailored. Yet.

Someday, yes. Right now, I'm lucky I have enough money to buy a subway pass for next month.

I doublecheck my heels are the same color. Never again will I buy the same pair in both black and navy. Both shoes are currently black. Everything looks fine, so what was that look about?

"I'll send her right up." The woman gives me a plastic grin and holds out a swipeable card. "Go to the far elevator. You'll use this to access the top floor. Make sure to return it to me when you leave."

"Thank you." I take the card and head toward the elevator. There are several elevators with bunches of people getting on and off, but no one else waits at the one she told me to go to. I take a deep breath and press the button.

I glance toward the lobby with all the people coming and going. A brief spark of excitement races through me. I could be one of these people. Heading to work. Going out with the girls after work for a drink at the bar on the other side of the lobby.

Of course, I'd need to find girls to go with, but that shouldn't be hard. In a company this size, there should be plenty of women my age or a little older who don't mind hanging out with a twenty-two-year-old. The elevator arrives and the doors open.

This is it. I swipe the card, and the elevator heads up. I can do this. I can get this job. Sure, my experience is a little lacking, but that's why I need a job. God, I hope I get this job.

Of all the postings I applied to, this is the one I hoped I'd get an interview for. Morrigan Technology Group is a cybersecurity company that works with all the top businesses in the city. This job is working with the top executives as their executive assistant, but there's so much more to it. It could be the training ground I need to help me get to the next level.

The elevator dings its arrival. When the doors open, I try to swallow my awe. It's gorgeous. This floor drips with elegance, purpose, and structure. Glass, dark wood, and marble fill the space.

I step forward onto the marble tile. My heels clicking on the surface is the only sound. A desk is situated in the center of a semi-circle of four offices with a conference room along one side. The door to the conference room is open, and I can see the tops of the surrounding buildings out the windows.

Straight to the top. A little rush goes through me.

"Ms. Harris." A deep voice resonates down my spine and makes me turn. My gaze lands on a well-built chest wrapped in a suit that fits to perfection. Tipping my head back, I lift my gaze to his clean-shaven, strong jaw, full lips lifted in a friendly smile, aristocratic nose, light blue eyes accented by long black eyelashes, and dark hair perfectly styled in a bun. He's beautiful.

A pulse of heat kicks through my system, making me forget what he just asked me. I'm so screwed if I work for this guy. Every piece of paper will have drool on it, and I'll have to train myself not to stare at him as if he could be my last meal.

He holds out his hand, and I snap out of it. I need this job. I brace myself for when our hands touch, but bracing isn't enough. Swallowing, I manage to thwart the gasp that tries to escape at the desire that pools low and heavy in my belly. I force my lips up into a smile.

His dark eyebrow lifts, and his smile ratchets up to gigawatt brilliance. That should be illegal. "I'm Cooper Graham, the chief technical officer."

"It's a pleasure to meet you." My heart kicks up a notch as I try not to say more than that and release his hand. My brain keeps teetering around pleasure and those gorgeous lips. Something positively stupid is bound to slip out of my mouth with this god of a man before me.

He holds his hand out toward the conference room. "If you'll come with me."

I most definitely would love to come with him, on him, for him. Fortunately, he turns away, giving me a moment to draw a ragged breath, and I follow him into the conference room. When he holds out a chair for me, I drop into it. A smile teases his lips as he rounds the table and sits.

"You'll have to forgive us. The others will be in. They got caught up in a meeting that ran over." Cooper folds his long fingers together on the table.

I'm going to hell because all I can think about are those fingers on my body. I want to drop my head and beat it on the table until rational thoughts come back to me. This is an interview for a job I'm not sure I'm qualified for, but the phone interview with Blake Wagner went so well he was willing to overlook my obvious lack of qualifications, knowing I was young and eager to get as much experience as possible. I assured him I was a quick learner and wouldn't let him down.

Technically, I have all the qualifications, just not as much work experience as they were looking for, even with my internships. This job is a stretch, a pie in the sky, and if I get hired, it will set me up for future success.

Cooper smiles. "Why don't you tell me about yourself while we wait? It shouldn't be long."

I cross my legs and lean forward slightly. I will not screw this up because of a minor attraction to one of my bosses. Surely I'll get over it quickly.

"I graduated summa cum laude with my master's in business from Fletcher University. I spent my summers interning with various businesses around New York."

He holds up his hand. "Why aren't you working for a company you interned with?"

This question comes up all the time. I have yet to find a diplomatic way to phrase my answer. "The companies had a different direction they wanted me to take. I don't want to crawl my way up from the bottom—though I'm not averse to hard work. I just want something more than a computer and eight to ten hours a day. I need more stimulation than that. I want to do more than reports and making coffee. However, I do make an excellent pot of coffee."

"Good to hear. I'm definitely a beast before I have my first cup." He leans back. His gaze wanders down my body.

Goosebumps rise along my skin in the wake of his perusal. Yeah, I'm going to have to lock that down. Though I'm glad I'm not the only one having trouble concentrating.

"Sorry we're late." That sounds like Blake Wagner's voice from the phone, which I'll admit I could listen to all night. His voice is a smooth and rich baritone.

Standing, I turn to greet the new men. My knees almost give out. This will not be an easy job. Before me are three men who belong on the cover of *GQ*. All tall, all gorgeous, all as well-built as Cooper. I'm lit up like a pinball machine on the inside.

"Seth Hart, chief executive officer." The one with blond hair neatly cut short and dark blue eyes that I can't seem to drop my gaze from steps forward and holds out his hand.

His eyes are the richest shade of blue I've ever seen. I resist the urge to fan myself and swoon before confidently holding out my hand to take his. A bolt of desire spreads through me from his touch, warming my entire body as his large hand firmly engulfs mine.

"A pleasure to meet you," I force out. Like an out-of-body experience, I can see myself greeting him and I want to yell, *Stop thinking with your hormones. You need this job.*

Power seems to emanate from him. His smile is tight and controlled as he backs out of the way so the others can greet me.

A larger, muscled man with dark hair steps forward. His green eyes sweep over my body, pausing on all the highlights—legs, ass, waist, breasts—before meeting my eyes. There's a mischievous sparkle in his, but it quickly disappears. Did I only imagine it?

"Blake Wagner, vice president. We spoke on the phone."

Yup, I'd recognize that voice anywhere. I hoped he was closer to fifty, but I'm not even sure he's thirty yet. He has one of those chin dimples that begs for my tongue to dive into it.

When I take his offered hand, my insides melt. Something about him makes me want to seek shelter in his arms. I need to stop checking out these guys. I just have to get through this interview, focus on my goal: Get the job. When they're my bosses, the flutters in my stomach will dissipate in time. Hopefully.

"It's good to meet you in person," I say without sounding completely breathless.

His smile is plastic kindness. He moves to sit next to Cooper.

The final guy seems younger than the others, maybe because his dirty blond hair is playfully messy and his brown eyes are soft, but he's just as solid as the rest of them. And still probably a few years older than me.

"Noah Burns, chief financial officer." He holds out his hand. The fluttering double-times as I take it. His dark eyes hold mine with a quiet intensity that has my knees nearly giving out.

I smile, and all I have left is, "A pleasure."

He squeezes my hand gently and releases it. I almost want to hold my arms up in triumph for not drooling or swooning over any of them in real life.

My knees are grateful as I sink into the chair across from this quartet of gorgeous men. At least if I end up hating my bosses, they're pretty to look at. If I can stop ogling them long enough to nail this interview.

"Morrigan Technology Group is one of the top cybersecurity firms in the nation. Over the past six years, we've worked tirelessly to make it to that distinction. We help protect our clients' information systems from internal and external threats, including disaster recovery." Seth's voice is rich and almost melodic as he speaks. "We need someone who will go the extra mile to take care of our needs."

I swallow against the image that pops into my brain unbidden: me, spread out on the conference table as a feast for these four men. Definitely willing to fulfill whatever they need. Ugh, I can't keep my brain on track.

I smile and nod because that seems like the easiest thing to do right now rather than admit that maybe I'm not the correct person for the job, not because I don't have the experience, but because I want to experience something more with each of them. Any of them. All of them.

My cheeks heat, and I cross my legs.

"You'll be required to work potentially long hours to help us." Blake's green eyes hold me in place. "Keep our schedules. Attend meetings to take notes. We'll expect you to be a liaison with important clients and later take on projects as you gain knowledge of the company. But there will also be filing and the like."

Which is exactly why I want this position. Blake leans forward, and his muscled arms strain the fabric of his suit. What would he look like naked, unconfined by those clothes? My cheeks have to be reaching nuclear levels of heat.

"We aren't always easy to work with, but we compensate for the work we need. Unfortunately, we are rather demanding and require access to you day and night."

I swallow the piece of me that wants to tell them anything they want they can have and give him a nod of acknowledgment instead.

They all give each other a look like they're talking without speaking.

Noah taps on a piece of paper in front of him, drawing my attention. "Our compensation package includes a corporate apartment, a phone, access to the corporate fleet of drivers, and a generous salary with benefits."

My eyes must be wide as he slides the paper across to me. The mentioned benefits already exceed what I expected. I take it and glance over the numbers. There are way more zeros than I figured. It's more than I could imagine needing. I take a deep breath and release it. This is the job I want, and it's the job I need. It would set me up nicely for my future.

"I would be working for all four of you?" My eyes catch on Noah's smile.

"Yes," he says. "Some of the work will be specific to each of us, but there will also be some general work that needs to be done. We've had trouble keeping someone in this position. Especially with privacy concerns."

Privacy concerns at a cybersecurity company?

"We tend to be very private people." Seth taps his long index finger against the polished wood table. "We require a lot from our executive assistant, but you can see that you will be fairly compensated for those requirements. We generally run a trial period of a couple of weeks with new hires before we move them into the apartment. Of course, we'll also require a signed NDA."

My heart beats really hard. My breath catches in my throat.

Does this mean I have the position? This doesn't even feel like a formal interview. They haven't asked me a single question. I have to play this cool because I want this job. Almost as much as I want the guys sitting across from me. Of course, as I get to know them, I doubt that initial attraction will last. I've found that most men don't live up to my expectations.

"Would I be working alone with you?" As soon as the question leaves my mouth, I worry about the implications. I shift in my seat. There have been men I absolutely didn't want to be alone with in my internships, but I'm not getting that feeling from these men. "I mean, will there be other staff working with us?"

"For the most part," Cooper says, "it will just be the five of us up here. The apartment is on the floor below, accessible only by the card in the elevator, so it's perfectly safe."

"Have we scared you off yet?" Noah asks with a crooked grin.

I meet each of their steady gazes. "No, I think this is the perfect opportunity for me. It allows me to work with each of the officers and gives me experience in different areas. I like a changing schedule, for each day to differ from the one before. A lot of office positions can become monotonous. I love a challenge. That's part of why I didn't take the job with my internship."

And I'm babbling. I press my lips together before I tell them again that I like variety.

Seth draws my attention by leaning back. "One other question, Ms. Harris."

"You can call me Madison," I say automatically.

He gives me a tight smile. "We've had some issues with jealous boyfriends with previous assistants. The hours. The demands on your time. Would we need to worry about that with you?"

It's as if they all inch forward slightly and suck the air out of the room. That's definitely not a typical question. My cheeks burst with heat as I think of all the things that have skittered through my mind since meeting them. All of them inappropriate, but would be worse if I actually had a boyfriend. "Um, no. It's not currently an issue you'd have to worry about."

In fact, it's been a while since I last dated anyone, choosing to focus on school and then my career rather than men. Which may explain why I'm practically drooling over my future bosses. My last year of college was brutal, with little time for any socialization.

I'm so close to my goal that I don't want to have a guy who needs my attention constantly. I want something larger than even this job. To be the boss myself one day.

"Excellent." When Cooper rises, they all stand with him, ending the interview. I collect my things.

Lord, they're tall. I feel like I'm standing in a den of lions. Hungry lions who've caught the scent of something good as each of them takes my hand again before following me out to the elevator. My hand buzzes from the sparks each of them lit within me. Finally, I shake Cooper's hand.

"We'll be in touch soon, Madison."

Chapter 2

A New Start

Madison

As I climb the stairs to my third-floor apartment, I can't help but wonder if that really happened. They told me about the position and the compensation package. Dare I hope that means I have the job? They didn't ask any actual interview questions, but that makes some sense since Blake spent almost an hour interviewing me on the phone.

The only thing they did was meet me. Could that really be all? Or were they disappointed and they've already written me off? Fuck, I hope that's not the case.

How soon is soon? Because I need work now.

Of course, after meeting my bosses, I'm going to need to be on my best behavior and try to keep my fantasy life off work-related men. I'm pretty sure my dreams won't receive the memo, though.

"Hey, Madison!"

I clutch my heart at Robert's loud voice. "You startled me."

My neighbor has a few inches on me, and while he isn't toned, he has some muscle and enough weight behind it to be intimidating. His brown hair is long and shaggy, and his brown eyes follow me wherever I go.

When I first met him, he creeped me out, but he hasn't done anything bad.

I finish the few steps to our floor and dig my keys out of my purse. I definitely won't miss the stairs if I get that job and the apartment.

"How did your interview go?" Robert follows me to my door and stands a little too close, but I've gotten used to it. He's harmless, just a little lonely. It still makes me wary.

"It went well." I unlock my door but don't dare open it yet. Robert has followed me in before, and getting him back out is a hassle I don't want to deal with tonight. He doesn't seem to understand boundaries.

"We should celebrate." Robert's brown eyes widen, and he gestures for me to come with him to his place. "I have a cake we can eat. I picked it up special today."

Even though cake sounds good, and I've only got a package of ramen noodles waiting for me inside, I still don't feel comfortable going into Robert's apartment. Even in my apartment, he made me uncomfortable. He may feel harmless, but something holds me back from being too friendly with him.

"I'm exhausted, Robert. But maybe another time." I open my door and slip through without opening it wide enough for him.

It's almost shut when Robert says, "I'll bring you over a piece."

Closing the door, I lean back against it and engage the locks. I've lived in this building for the past two years. It's cheaper than living on campus and gives me a space to call my own. Well, mostly my own.

I have a roommate who is sometimes here, but most of the time she's gone, giving me a larger apartment all to myself. I set my purse and bag in my room and head to the fridge. I'm running low on funds, so the fridge is pretty bare.

I have some back-up cash saved, but I don't want to touch it if I don't have to. It's just enough money for bus fare and food on the way back to the Midwest. It's my get-out-of-jail-free card, in case the city becomes too much or I just can't cut it.

I pull out my pan and put water on to boil. I've made ramen so often, I don't even need to measure the water anymore. It would be great if this position actually comes through. With the extra income, I could eat whatever I want every night. I have a couple more interviews next week. There's still the offer from Taylor's, one of my internships. The offer would barely let me continue to scrape by here, but it would mean not having to leave the city.

It would also mean having to work with Hunter Adams. He's a good-looking guy. I'll admit I thought he was attractive more than once when I first met him. But just because he's good looking doesn't mean he's nice. He bullies the other employees and harasses the women.

Remembering the day he cornered me in the copy room makes me shudder. I got away from his inappropriate touching, but if I work there again, he'll keep coming at me. Hunter is untouchable. How do you tell the boss that his son is making unwelcome advances?

I shake Hunter from my head and think about the interview today.

Four very hot men. I don't know their personalities yet, but if they're anything like Hunter, I'll have no problem cooling my thoughts toward them.

After dumping the ramen into the pot, I stir it. I have to admit, at least to myself, if one of them backed me into the corner of the copy room, I might not be inclined to get away. In fact, combining that with my earlier fantasy of all four of them and the conference table might be what I get off to tonight.

There's something about them that draws me. Maybe it's just attraction. There was never a spark with Hunter, just this feeling of needing to stay away from him. But these men... They make my heart pound harder and set off butterflies instead of alarms.

Tonight, I'll let the fantasy run its course one time before I get the position and have to maintain my composure so I can be the best professional executive assistant I can. It'll be my new focus.

When I add the seasoning and pour my ramen into a bowl, my phone rings. Expecting it to be my mom, I answer it without looking at the caller ID.

"Hello." I set my bowl on the table and stare down at the noodles floating in the broth. Suddenly my appetite isn't quite there.

"Ms. Harris?"

I almost drop the phone when I hear Mr. Wagner's deep voice on the line. Did he know I was fantasizing about him?

"Yes?" I reply breathlessly. Did I get the job? How do I play this cool if I got the job?

"We wanted to extend an offer to come in for a trial run, starting Monday. If you're still available?" His voice is smooth and flawless and drags against my skin in a very unholy way.

"Yes, I'm available and would love to work for you." I want to jump up and down, but I need to keep it together until I get off the phone. Suddenly my ramen doesn't look so bad, knowing I won't have to stomach it much longer.

A knock at the door draws my attention.

"Good. There are some forms we would like you to fill out beforehand." Mr. Wagner rustles some papers in the background.

The knocking continues. I walk to my door, trying to contain my excitement, and look out the peephole. Robert stands on the other side with a piece of cake on a paper plate. His fist pounds on my door.

"Of course," I say.

Robert knocks again and shouts, "I brought you some cake, Madison."

"Could you come by on Friday? We can give you your access card at that time."

"I'm sorry, Mr. Wagner, but my neighbor is at the door. Could you hold for one moment?" I feel like I'm shooting myself in the foot. But I can't concentrate with Robert pounding on my door. Experience tells me, once he knows I'm in here, he won't go away until I deal with him.

"No problem."

When I open the door, I point to the phone. Robert nods and holds out the cake. I take it and shoo him away.

"I hope you get the job," Robert whispers loudly.

He grins and gives me two thumbs up. I close the door and roll my eyes. At least he's excited for me.

"I am so sorry for that," I say again. "Yes, I can come by Friday. What time?"

The smell of the chocolate cake makes my stomach rumble. I lock my door awkwardly with the cake in one hand and the phone against my shoulder.

"Does around four work for you?" His voice seems a little more curt.

I straighten and set the cake down. "Of course, whatever time works best for you. I'm available all day."

"Ms. Harris?" His strict tone does naughty things to my insides.

I bite my lip and say, "Yes, Mr. Wagner?"

"Call me Blake." His voice is stern. "Is the neighbor going to be a recurring problem?"

What? What is that supposed to mean? Butterflies launch a full-scale assault on my stomach as I wonder if I've done something wrong. But he wants me to call him Blake. That's a good sign, right?

"I don't understand." I'm not sure what he wants me to say. Whatever it is, I'll say it.

"Does your neighbor frequently come to your door unexpectedly?" he asks.

I shake my head. "No. He's just a lonely guy who's looking for a friend."

"Are you?" Blake asks.

"Am I?" This would be easier to follow if his voice didn't make me feel all warm and gooey inside.

"His friend?"

I glance at the wall my apartment shares with Robert's. The question from the interview about a boyfriend pops through my head. Maybe they worry about me being distracted.

"Not really. I'm nice because we share a wall and I have to see him every day, but we don't have long conversations or hang out, if that's what you want to know." I stride across the room to my table and sit down in front of my meager meal. "I can assure you, Blake, that my focus will be on my job and on you four and no one else."

"Good." His voice is like satin again and that warmth floods my system. "We'll also have a signing bonus available for you on Friday if you agree to certain conditions of your employment."

"Signing bonus?" Inside, I can't help but wonder what conditions. I know about the NDA, but what else don't I know about?

"We have some nonstandard conditions we would like to offer and agree upon before employment. Whether or not they're acceptable won't affect your job at Morrigan Technology Group."

"Is there something you can send me ahead of time to review?" I have a weird feeling about this. Not weird like Robert weird, but weird like something that's going to change my life weird.

"We'd rather explain it to you in person."

We? As in all of them again? My brain might short circuit and go to fantasyland. Maybe I should be honest about my attraction up front. Because I'm going to say something awkward, or blush when they say something that could be taken the wrong way, and accidentally flirt, and get fired. I can tell them that I never intend to act on it. But if they wanted to...

"Friday at four?" I say instead.

"See you then."

Friday seemed forever away on Tuesday night, but now at three forty-five, I stand at the same desk with the same judgmental woman behind it. Hopefully, she doesn't realize I'm wearing the same skirt. Everyone here seems so fancy and well put together.

I'll get there after a few paychecks, but until then, she'll just have to deal with me wearing the same skirt a few times this week.

"Madison Harris to see Blake Wagner." Not even a slight quiver in my voice.

She holds out the access card and gestures toward the elevator as she talks into her headset.

Okay, I know the drill apparently. I walk over to the bank of elevators and hit the button on the far one. As I step inside, I hear someone call my name.

"Hold the elevator, please." I think it's Noah's voice.

I press the button to hold the doors open, and Noah rounds the corner into the elevator and gives me a broad smile.

"Thanks," he says.

"You're welcome," I reply and swipe my card as the doors close us in.

"You've decided to join us?" Noah's voice is deep but almost scratchy. His dirty blond hair is particularly messy today. Almost begging me to run my fingers through it to tame it. His brown eyes meet mine. He smells like the outdoors on a sunny day.

I want to lean into him and feel his warmth.

"Yes, I'm meeting with Blake to go over some paperwork." I clasp my hands behind my back. This guy is about to be my boss, even though he can't be much older than I am. And on second viewing, he's still very attractive. "I start on Monday."

"I'm sure the others will have tons for you to do, but I have a few special projects for you to work on." Noah dips his head a little and gives me a smile that makes my breath catch and my heart quicken. His brown eyes never leave me.

He slips his hand into his pocket, and I barely resist glancing down at the front of his pants. My cheeks heat as the elevator reaches the top floor. That would have been so inappropriate. He holds his other hand out when the doors open to allow me to go first.

Thanking him, I walk into the office for the second time and breathe in. I'd hoped it was just the first meeting with my heightened nerves that made me so attracted to them, but apparently not.

I try to focus on my new workspace. It's just as gorgeous as I remember. I'm going to work here. I can't wait.

Noah's hand goes to the small of my back as he draws me forward. His touch floods me with sparks. "Blake's office is this way. And please call me Noah and not Mr. Burns. I always feel like the old man from *the Simpsons* when someone calls me that."

I smile. "I can't imagine anyone comparing you to him."

He flashes me his dimples when he smiles. My heart skips a beat. His hand barely touches my back, but I can feel the heat of him through my clothes, seeping under my skin.

When he looks away, I resist the urge to fan myself. If I'd met him in college, I would have flirted and invited him back to my place.

After knocking on the door, he turns to me. His eyes darken as his gaze drops to my lips. "I hope everything goes well, Madison."

"Me too, Noah." My heart ratchets up a beat as he dips his head slightly. My lips part in anticipation.

The door opens, and we both turn to see Blake. It feels like we've been caught doing something we shouldn't, but Blake doesn't seem put off.

"Early," he says. "That bodes well."

Noah touches my arm, and little ripples surge under my skin from his fingertips. "I'll see you Monday morning."

I nod, still a little breathless. "Okay."

I watch him walk to the next office and disappear before I turn to Blake. He's taller and thicker than Noah. His expression is less shy numbers guy and more commanding.

He gestures for me and says, "Come in."

As I pass him and the door closes, his hand goes to the small of my back. Sparks of awareness float through me. His touch makes me weak in the knees. My eyes widen at my reaction. He leads me to a chair, and I gratefully drop into it. If they're going to continue to touch me, these men will be hard on my knees.

I understand these guys are attractive, but usually I'm not attracted to a whole group. One usually stands out, but there's a spark with each of them.

Blake rounds his desk and sits. "You have our offer sheet, of course. All of that will remain the same unless you want to negotiate?"

"No, it all looks great. Far more than I could imagine. I'm just so happy to have a job to look forward to on Monday. I've been going a little stir crazy around the apartment without school or work to keep me occupied." *Shut up, Madison.* I can't seem to keep myself from rambling.

Blake just smiles. "Two-week trial period and then we'll move you in downstairs. After we go through the paperwork, Cooper will show you around the apartment. On Monday, you'll have orientation, and I'll show you around the office."

"That sounds amazing." Keep it short and sweet. That's my new motto.

"To get things rolling, we have a few things for you to fill out. All this is normal paperwork you've probably filled out for your previous employers." He holds out a stack of papers. "We want to digitize it, but it seems better for some things to be on paper, just in case."

"Of course." I take the stack and hold it on my lap.

"Seth wants to talk to you himself about the other matter I mentioned."

My heart pounds noisily as I recall the CEO and those blue eyes. I'm not sure I'll hear what he says when that deep blue enraptures me and becomes my primary focus. "That sounds good."

I look down at the papers in my hands.

Blake stands and comes around the desk. "I'll set you up at your desk to fill this out. Then Cooper will take you on the tour. Seth will see you afterward."

It all seems so neat and tidy, but what could be so important the

CEO needs to explain it to me? Unless they're worried that I won't be professional. Have they noticed the way I look at them? Am I going to get a lecture before I even start?

Maybe they'll distract me so much I won't be able to do my job. This isn't normal for me. If I have an itch, I see something I like and I scratch it. I haven't always chosen the best people for sex, but it's also never consumed me the way it does around these men.

Whatever is happening, I need to get myself under control and focus on what's important. Getting to the next level in my career. This is just a stepping-stone, and it should give me a real leg up. I can't fuck this up with something as trivial as sexual attraction.

Chapter 3

The Apartment

Madison

As I sit in the center of everything trying to fill out my paperwork, I feel really exposed. Which doesn't make a lot of sense given that I'm the only one in this space and all the doors are closed to the guys' offices, except for Blake's. I cross my legs and finish the last form.

I lean back in my chair and look around. I'm all alone out here. Blake's low voice murmurs in conversation, but otherwise it's quiet. I'm not sure if I should go to his door or wait for Cooper. I don't want to interrupt his phone call, so I wait.

My desk is beautiful. A sleek combination of glass and dark wood. Absolutely no clutter litters the surface. Even the computer monitor is sleek. I inhale and exhale. This is mine. This is happening. I can do this.

"Madison." Cooper's voice sends warm shivers down my spine to pool between my legs.

I have to get this under control. I turn in my chair to see him striding toward me. His dark hair is pulled back. How long is it when it's down? His sky blue eyes focus on mine, and that smile of his should be illegal in forty-eight states.

"Are you ready for the tour?" He holds out a hand.

"Yes, Mr. Graham." I brace myself for his touch. As I slide my hand into his, sparks burst through me. He helps me stand, drawing me close to him. I close my eyes at the sensations rippling through me for a second. When he doesn't immediately back up, I dare to open my eyes and tip my chin to meet his gaze.

"Cooper, please."

His cologne has a clean and crisp scent, and my knees try to betray me once again.

I fall back a small step—space is needed—and smile up at him. "Of course, Cooper."

His eyes darken, and his gaze drops to my lips before he clears his throat. "I get the pleasure of showing you the apartment."

He hasn't released my hand. Instead, he repositions his so we're holding hands as he leads me to the elevator. I'm going to be wrecked if these men keep manhandling me. I shouldn't like it, but my body isn't listening to my feminist brain currently. No, my body is too focused on the feel of his skin against mine and wondering if he is as commanding in the bedroom.

After we step into the elevator, he swipes his card and releases my hand.

"Did you have any issues with the paperwork?" he asks, one hundred percent the professional while I'm over here panting because he touched my hand.

"No."

The elevator ride is quick, only one floor down. He gestures for me to precede him out. I step out on similar marble floors. It's a small hallway with the elevator and five doors, one in front and four down the hallway.

Cooper moves to the first door and slides his access card into it. "This apartment will be yours if these two weeks go well."

I follow him in. Immediately, my attention is drawn to the floor-to-ceiling windows along one wall. The ceiling is at least twelve feet tall. It feels like I can see the entire city from up here. Considering my current view from my apartment is brick walls, this is definitely an upgrade.

"All the apartments share this space." Cooper's hand goes to the small of my back as he leads me into the room.

"All?"

I tear my eyes from the leather sectional and the huge flat-screen TV next to the fireplace in the corner. At the other end is a large table with ten chairs surrounding it. The chandelier glitters and sparkles as it dangles over the center of the table.

"The four of us live on this floor as well. The bedrooms are all separate and have their own access code, but the living space is shared." Cooper leads me into the kitchen area.

It's huge, with marble countertops and stainless steel appliances. It's so much bigger than my kitchen. I can't resist running my hand over the smooth, cool marble. This is like a dream.

"Part of your duties will be to order groceries and be here for the deliveries once a week."

I smile. Maybe they require a housewife, not an administrative assistant.

"Do you cook?" Cooper leans against the counter as I walk around the island.

"Probably not to the level you guys are used to, but I know how to follow a recipe." There's a huge farm-style sink. Everything is pristine and perfect.

"We aren't all that particular." Cooper closes in on me.

My breath catches in my throat as I peer up at him.

"We also won't require you to cook for all of us unless that's something you'd like to do." He reaches out and tucks a stray hair behind my ear.

My insides turn to liquid as I try to stay focused on the work and the apartment and not this dangerous attraction.

His smile is a little predatory, but in the next instant, it softens and he steps away. "Still more to see."

My heart is trying to take off at the rate it's racing. I blow out a breath and follow him.

He opens double doors into what qualifies as a study or a library. Books line wooden bookshelves from floor to ceiling. A rolling ladder rests in the corner. Low leather chairs in small groups fill the space. A library table with five chairs sits close to the window.

I long to trail my fingertips along the spines of the books to see what these men consider worthy of their presence. This can't be real life.

What bosses ask their assistant to basically live and work with them twenty-four seven? Especially these men. Maybe I can understand the convenience, but when they said an apartment was part of the package, I figured it would be just me in a small studio, which I would have been grateful for.

"We try not to keep working after business hours, but sometimes we're forced to work on some projects into the night. Otherwise, this space is just a quiet area to read. Noah prefers it when we're watching TV." Cooper turns his gaze on me. "Do you read, Madison?"

Heat rushes my cheeks at his attention. "I usually just read on my phone when I have time. It's been a while since I've gone to the library to get actual books."

I don't add that some of what I like to read gets pretty dirty.

"You are welcome to read whatever you find here." Cooper's smile turns sly. "You might even find some inspiring works of fiction."

I choose to ignore the teasing tone. See? I can be professional.

"This is amazing. I can't believe I might live here." I can't contain my grin. A freaking library. I would have been happy with a studio apartment. Maybe a one bedroom with a galley kitchen, but this... I don't even have words. Am I stepping into a very pretty trap?

"Let me show you to your room." Cooper reaches for my hand, and without thinking, I take it. He leads me to one side and stops in front of a door. "All the other bedrooms have a door to the hallway, but this is the largest room, and has the emergency door in case of fire. It leads directly out onto the stairs."

He turns the knob and pushes the door open, letting me lead the way in. The first room is a sitting room. Hardwood floors are everywhere throughout the apartment, but a light cream area rug makes this space a little more homey. There's a white couch, a tall wingback chair and another flat-screen TV, not as big as the one in the living room, but bigger than any TV I've ever owned.

A bar area sits off to the side with a small refrigerator and a microwave.

Cooper gestures to it. "If you don't want to journey into the shared space."

This room is already bigger than the living area in my apartment. To say this would be a step up is an understatement.

I nod and continue to explore. I open the bedroom door and gasp. The bed is bigger than king-sized with more room than I'll ever need on my own. The covers are a pale peach with so many pillows I could bury myself in them. A low pile, light gray rug covers the floor.

"The room dictated the size of the bed." Cooper straightens his tie as he moves past me to the wall opposite the floor-to-ceiling windows.

Instead of following him, I walk to the windows and take in the view. At least on this side, this is the tallest building. Cooper's warmth reaches me before I hear him behind me. He stands so close his suit jacket brushes my shirt.

Sparks dance along my skin.

I want to lean into him and take in all his warmth. Feel his hands sliding up my sides, dragging the satin of my top against my skin. Pressing me against the window as he reaches down—

"Quite the view, isn't it?" Cooper's breath flutters through my hair.

I swallow as shivers trickle down my spine. "Gorgeous."

"The windows are all shielded. They allow us to look out, but no one can see in. Plus, it keeps the temperature from spiking from the sun." He steps into me lightly, and I hold my breath, waiting for anything more.

My professionalism took a walk as soon as I met these men. Working with them? Living with them? I'm going to need to invest in rechargeable toys to keep me from jumping them.

"Let me show you the bathroom and the closet." His fingers trail over my wrist and hand before interweaving with my own.

I bite back the whimper that wants to escape and turn to follow him past that huge bed that could definitely use some messing up. If I start dwelling on fantasies, I'll get confused about where real life begins and the fantasy ends.

As attentive as my new employers are, they haven't said anything to make me believe they want more than an executive assistant. If anything, they've pointedly touched me to see if I react, or maybe they're just trying to get me used to them.

No one's made an obvious move on me. Maybe I'm reading too much into the touches. I need to take my mind out of the gutter and put it back in the boardroom.

"This is your bathroom." Cooper's voice echoes in the large space. He releases my hand to let me explore.

Everything is Carrara marble and white tile. The shower is big enough for me and the four of them... but I won't be thinking about that. I turn to the white slipper tub. It's deep and wide, perfect for a soak. Before my mind can go there, *alone*. A soak alone. The vanity has two sinks and there is a water closet off to the side.

Cooper opens a door and gestures for me to come to him. I go without hesitation. Beyond the door is an enormous closet.

"It would take me years to fill this," I can't help saying. My stuff would fit in a small corner of this closet.

His lips press tight as his gaze trails over me. I shouldn't have said that out loud. Now he'll see how cheap everything I have on really is, or well-worn if I found it at the thrift store.

"I take it most of your money went to college?"

I nod, unable to face him and find that look of distaste that accompanies the realization I'm not in the same league as these men.

"If you need help filling out your wardrobe, I know a few places that will have things in your size for good prices."

What? I turn and meet his light blue eyes. No disdain, only thoughtfulness. "It'll take me a few paychecks before I'm able to take you up on that offer."

His smile is wide. "Don't worry about it. We'll sort it out as time goes on."

He steps out of the closet and closes the door. As we pass by the bed, I resist the urge to run and jump on it. Though I promise myself that if I get to this part of the job, I will most definitely do that. He leads me back through the mini apartment, out to the shared living space.

"What do you think, Madison?" He stops in the center of the space and turns toward me. One of his dark eyebrows arches. "Do you think you could live with the four of us? Work with us day and night?"

If I can get over lusting after them, then yes. "Of course. This is perfect. I'd be lucky to live here."

Away from creepy neighbors and absentee roommates. It truly seems like a dream come true, but I can't help but wonder if the other side of the coin is waiting for me in this meeting with Seth.

Chapter 4

Consent

Seth

My palms are clammy. Maybe we should go about this differently. We all agreed to this, but it's not exactly the best idea. This could blow up in our faces. Again.

There's this window of opportunity. If we broach it too soon, they run away. If we wait too long, they feel foolish. This time, I decided to be upfront. That means entrusting this woman with a lot of information when trust hasn't been earned yet on either side.

We're strangers to her, and she's a stranger to us.

A knock on my office door makes me stand. My door opens, and Blake walks in without waiting for my say-so. We've worked together for so long that we're usually good at reading each other's mood, but I can't tell if Blake is as nervous as I am.

Fuck, I'm never nervous, but this has me tied in knots.

"Cooper is finishing up the tour." Blake glances over his shoulder as if they will appear there at any moment. "Are you sure you want to do this? She could get to know us better. We can wait and see how the two weeks go before scaring her away."

Tuesday, I studied Ms. Harris closely during our interview. Her blue eyes were wide but far from naive. Her blond hair fell loose around her shoulders. The clothes she wore didn't fit her quite right. Definitely not tailored. The shirt was stretched across her good-sized breasts but wasn't too big around her small waist. Her skirt, though, showed the curves of her ass nicely and gave enough glimpses of her thighs and her well-shaped calves for me to want them wrapped around my waist.

As she met each of us, her full lips parted and her cheeks flushed. Her pupils were blown with desire. She might be hesitant to take what we're offering, but where there's a spark, we can coax it into a flame.

I lower myself into my chair and lean back. "We'll take it slow. A trial run before she moves in with us is best. We may decide she won't suit our needs."

"She's young." Blake raises an eyebrow.

Just out of college, starting out. It was one reason we pulled her resume. We need someone fresh to do this job. Someone who's ambitious. Who wants to do more than just sit at a desk and give us reports. She's driven, graduating in four years with an MBA and doing internships at the same time.

Her resume looks like ours would have.

"We aren't that much older than her." Yes, we have a company we built from the ground up. But we're all in our upper twenties. Only Coop has already turned thirty. Blake and I were a year behind him in school, while Noah was a year behind us, but he skipped a grade early on, so he also got his degree the same year Blake and I did.

"Twenty-nine is a long way from twenty-two." Blake snorts and glances over his shoulder again. He steps in closer. "NDA first. God knows, if she spreads this contract business around, we could all be toast."

"I haven't forgotten how to do my job." I straighten and walk around the desk. "We all agreed we want her, so what's this about?"

I rest my hip on the desk and cross my arms. We all want her. Probably too much.

It was an easy decision, and surprisingly, everyone was in without any convincing.

"I don't want to fail again." Blake always needed to be the best at everything. Throughout high school and college, there were athletics and academics, but in the real world, it's more difficult to figure out how to be the best.

Our company is almost number one. Almost. Our industry is super competitive and being ranked that high is amazing. Which is why we push ourselves so hard.

Blake takes failure a lot harder than the rest of us.

"She hasn't even started." I lower my arms. "We'll know up front if she's interested in pursuing the contract or not. She'll still make an excellent executive assistant. She's got the brain and hunger for it."

He nods and leaves.

He's not wrong. The last time we tried this, we lost an outstanding executive assistant. We all weren't into her, though. Madison has something that draws even me. This had better work, or I'll be taking a lot of cold showers.

Movement at my door captures my attention. Madison stands there with her fist up, preparing to knock on the open door. She's tucked her blond hair into a bun. Little tendrils escape to dance around her shoulders. Her cream shell top goes well with her black skirt.

She smiles tentatively as her blue eyes meet mine. "I didn't want to interrupt, if you aren't ready for me."

When her arm drops to her side, I wave her in and gesture to the chair before me. Her floral scent wafts by me as she sits.

"Have you ever signed a nondisclosure agreement before?" I go to the door and close it. Much as I want to stay near her, this conversation might be easier if I sit behind the desk.

"Yes." She crosses her legs.

"We deal in a very specialized field, and you'll have access to proprietary information."

She nods seriously.

"We are also very private men, and as you've seen the apartment, you'll be privy to our lives. We expect discretion in all of this." I pick up the agreement from my desk and move it over to her.

She pulls her chair closer to the desk and turns it to face her.

"Before we can talk any further, I need you to sign the NDA." I recline in my chair.

"I can do that." She reads over page after page.

It gives me time to study her and wonder if this will actually work. It almost worked once before, but issues we couldn't have foreseen popped up. Not just on the personal side, but on the business side as well. Andrea got greedy and not in a good way. She threatened to post her story online unless we agreed to a payoff.

There's still talk, but we've made sure it doesn't affect our business. It could have destroyed our reputations. I'll do whatever I can to prevent that from happening.

"Do you have a pen I could use?" Madison's light voice draws me back to the present.

I take the pen from my inner pocket, the one my father gave me on graduation from high school. I use it in all my business deals. It hasn't failed me yet.

She signs her name and dates the NDA. She offers me the pen back and sits upright in her chair. Crossing her legs, she runs her hands over her skirt.

I pick up the contract and slide it into my drawer for later. I center the other papers on my desk and exhale. Here we go.

Madison

"Blake told you there was another offer we had for you." Seth's blue eyes are just as intense as yesterday.

I manage to keep my breathing stable even as my heart races in my chest. I have no idea what this is about, but Seth seems so serious.

Does he ever really smile? What would he look like smiling and relaxed, without the weight of the world on his shoulders?

"We're very busy men. As our business continues to expand, our careers take up most of our time and probably will for years to come." Seth rests his interlaced hands on his desk as he meets my eyes.

"Yes, sir." That's clear from them working and living in the same place and the type of hours they expect from me. I'm fully prepared to give them whatever they need of me. The salary and experience are worth anything.

He looks down at the desk for a moment before lifting his eyes back to me. He seems nervous almost. That doesn't help my own nerves.

"I want you to understand that you have this job as the executive assistant, whether or not you agree to the next conditions. They will not affect your employment." Seth takes a deep breath and releases it.

Suddenly I'm not sure I want to know what these conditions are. I clasp my hands in my lap to keep them from trembling. I mean, it can't be anything too bad, right? This isn't like the Mafia where it requires blood to get in. Right?

"I'm doing this all wrong," he mutters. He walks around the desk and sits in the chair beside me. The sensual fragrance of sandalwood mixed with his unique scent penetrates my senses.

My pulse throbs as he's close enough for the heat of his skin to warm mine. I bite my lip and try to settle down this overwhelming attraction. What if they know and want to make sure I won't try to slip into their rooms at night?

I can't lose this job. I can't go work for Taylor's and deal with Hunter's groping. Going home is out of the question. I'll never be able to pay off my student loans.

"Madison."

I lift my gaze to meet his eyes.

"This is where things get a little weird." He rubs his hand over the back of his neck.

"Weird?" My knee starts bouncing slightly.

He chuckles, the sound a little harsh. "First off, anything said here stays between you and me. If this doesn't sound like something you're willing to try, then that's as far as this goes. If at any time you decide this isn't working, it ends."

I shift in my seat so I'm facing him head on. That sounds reasonable. But I can't imagine what he's going to ask that could make this man nervous.

"We all want you to be more than just our assistant. So, what I need to know from you is, are you attracted to us?"

What? My breath catches in my throat.

"Is this a trap?" I bolt up from my seat. Did he honestly just ask me if I'm attracted to them? Not just him. Them? All of them? This isn't a normal question employers ask before you begin a job.

He stands slowly and holds out his hands to calm me down. "This is why we want to discuss this. Please sit down, Madison."

I narrow my eyes at him as I lower into the chair. This still feels like they're trying to make me admit to being attracted to them. For what purpose? I don't know. It's not like I'd act on it.

He sits and loosens his tie. "We're busy men, as I've said, and dating takes away from our careers. We've all discussed approaching you with this as an alternative. You are a very attractive woman. We would all like to share you, if you want."

My brain stalls out. This doesn't happen. Not in real life.

Do I want? I can't stop thinking about it. Fantasizing about it. I have to stop myself from shifting in my seat as my pussy throbs for it. But this still seems like something that should get me in trouble. Sleeping with all four of my bosses?

I can't find anything particularly wrong about what he just said, but I don't want to give away anything either. They find me attractive? My heart flutters, and warmth flows through me.

Who wouldn't find them attractive? I'm surprised they need to ask me. How many women would gladly drop everything to be with just one of these men?

"The two-week trial is just that. We'll focus on training you for your career here at Morrigan, and you can decide whether you want to explore more with us." Seth undoes the button at his collar, his fingers pulling at his shirt like it's choking him.

"Let me see if I understand." I take a deep breath, trying to make sense of this. "Please correct me if I'm wrong. All four of you want to enter into a sexual relationship with me because you're too busy to go find single women to hook up with?"

"No." Seth jerks like I hit him. "Not because we are too busy to find single women. We don't want to just hook up with someone. We're attracted to you and want to explore that if you're open to it."

I lick my suddenly dry lips. I can't believe I'm actually considering this. "Let's say, for argument's sake, that I find all of you attractive too. And may be open to a sexual relationship. Maybe. What exactly do you want from me?"

He runs his hand over the back of his neck and then leans forward on the arm of the chair. "You would fill out consent forms for all of us. We would sit down and discuss a contract of behavior that suits all of our needs. We're not paying you for sex, but we would give you a signing bonus for signing the consent forms, as they protect us from future litigation of sexual harassment."

This sounds very methodical and clinical. But just talking about it is turning me on. "And if I want to withdraw consent?"

"You can do so at any point. No questions asked. This would be a consensual agreement between adults." Seth relaxes a little. "You keep the bonus even if we never actually have sex."

"How many women have you offered this to?" Curiosity gets the better of me. It's not a sticking point, but I'm curious. How many women have turned this down? Unless the sex sucks, I'm not out yet. Or if they turn out to be jerks. These guys have haunted my dreams for the past few nights. If they are half as good as they were in my sleep, I'm all in.

"This particular deal? You're the first. But to be transparent, we've tried this before. We only got to the sexual part of the deal with one assistant."

Heat burns my chest as I think of that woman having these men. I swallow the frog in my throat. "What happened?"

His smile doesn't reach his eyes. "She blackmailed us for money."

"Oh." That's not cool. I'm not naive enough to believe everyone has good intentions, but that had to sting, to give that much trust to someone and have them throw it back in your face. "Are there rules?"

"Ones we all will agree to." He nods. "These first weeks will be a trial run of the actual job. We'll focus on work while you're here, but I can't guarantee we won't pursue you at all. Which is why we want to lay this all out now." Seth takes a breath and pulls over the other papers on his desk.

"When will we discuss the contract?" I cross my legs against the pulsing there. Obviously, that part of me is all on board.

"At the end of the trial period, we'll decide as a group whether we go forward with that step." Seth reaches out and brushes a stray strand of hair behind my ear. His touch leaves sparks in its wake. His eyes meet mine as his hand retreats.

"What if we can't wait two weeks?" I arch my eyebrow.

"Hypothetically?" He mimics my eyebrow arch, and I can't contain my smile.

"Of course."

"We will all likely touch you during the two weeks. It's inevitable in the course of a day."

They all touched me today. Blake and Noah touching the small of my back. Cooper taking my hand to lead me around. Seth brushing my hair from my face. I can't help being greedy and longing for more. "But these two weeks will be all business?"

"Yes." Seth smiles. "Unless you initiate."

They're giving me the power. My insides melt a little further. They're trusting me, and in return, I'll have to trust them, which is scary, but exciting too.

"I'd have these two weeks to consider this offer even if I sign those forms and take the signing bonus?" I want this, but what if they're assholes, like Hunter? If he had a form like this, he would have taken advantage of me from day one. He never would have let me say no.

"Yes, you could take the signing bonus and then withdraw consent at any time. But I would hope that you wouldn't go into this just for the money." His eyes narrow on me as if trying to read if I'm that kind of person.

"If I decide to withdraw, I wouldn't feel comfortable keeping the money," I assure him. "Even if it's for this signature and not for whatever type of relationship we have."

"Good." His eyes darken.

My breath catches. "Where do I sign?"

Chapter 5

Orientation

Madison

The weekend dragged until Monday morning. My first official day of work.

I have copies of the consent forms they asked me to sign. Seth clarified these forms were just the initial paperwork. If and when we decide to move forward, that's when we'd all sign a contract.

The signing bonus allowed me to go out and buy new clothes for this week. Everything on me is new, from my pencil skirt and blouse to the expensive underwear and garter belt holding up my silk stockings. Seth said things would be normal these first two weeks, but I can't help the anticipation curling in my stomach. My new clothes make me feel decadent and sexy.

I made sure not to spend too much money, only enough that I know my paycheck will cover it. Just in case this doesn't work out. I'd feel bad about taking their money just to sign some forms to say I wouldn't come at them with sexual harassment charges for consensual sexual advances.

Especially when I really want those sexual advances.

A giddy feeling bubbles up within me as I step into the lobby with all the worker bees. The first day of my career.

Instead of talking to the receptionist, I walk past her to the elevator with my ID/access card. My big splurge clicks along the tile floors. I've never owned a pair of shoes that cost more than my usual monthly grocery budget, but these make me stand taller, straighten my shoulders, and feel like I can take whatever this day throws at me.

When I step out into the top floor lobby, I head for my desk. My desk. My office. Maybe even my men, if things work out right.

The doors are all closed this morning. I'm a little early, but I couldn't wait any longer. I sit down and open a lower drawer to put my purse in. After I flick on the computer, I look through the other drawers in my desk. Pretty typical stuff. Pens, paper clips, a stapler, binder clips.

I lift a set of keys out and recognize some as drawer keys, but there are a few that look big enough for a door. I'm sure they'll let me know what these are for.

"Early again. That's good." Blake's voice drifts like a caress against my skin.

I turn in my chair to see him leaning against his office doorframe, watching me intently with those green eyes. My chest tightens.

"I'm eager to get started," I say, pushing my hair behind my ears. This morning, I curled it and left it down, but I brought a few things to put it up as the day goes on. I kept my makeup light and natural.

Blake's eyes darken before he nods. He steps forward. "We can start with a tour, and then each of us will have you for an hour to discuss what we expect of you."

I swallow at the innuendo hiding in that statement and smile. Seth promised these two weeks were to get acquainted with the job and each of them, without the other duties to start. But my insides melt at the thought of spending one-on-one time with each of these men who admitted they want me.

I stand and straighten my skirt. My gaze locks with Blake's as he stalks toward me. He's thicker than the others. Not heavy, just more built. My heartbeat races. His lips press into a fine line. I'm not sure I've seen him smile for real.

"We'll start on this floor and work our way down." He holds out his arm toward the conference room, and I step in that direction.

His hand lands on the small of my back, sending a scatter of sparks licking along my nerve endings. His heat engulfs me as we walk side by side. The perfect blend of spices mixes with his natural scent, making me want to lean into him.

"This is our conference room. We hold executive meetings on Wednesday afternoons and touch base on Friday before the end of the day. For outside vendor meetings, we use the conference room on the sixth floor."

"Do I attend as well?" I ask as my gaze gets caught on the skyline out the windows.

"Of course." Blake leads me away from the conference room. "Seth's, mine, Cooper's, and Noah's offices. Please knock and wait for an acknowledgment before walking into any of our offices."

He turns me down a short hall I hadn't noticed before. Probably because I was too busy checking out my bosses. I feel heat swell in my cheeks.

"Our kitchen is in here. You're welcome to bring lunch if you'd like. We'll also go out to eat or order in frequently. You can always order in with us and work through lunch if needed. If we are going out, it's usually with a client and you are expected to attend. Those will be on your calendar."

The break room/kitchen is neat and organized. A fresh pot of coffee sits in the coffee machine. There's a small dishwasher.

"First thing in the morning, unload the dishwasher and start the first pot of coffee." Blake shows me where everything goes and then guides me out of the kitchen to the elevators.

"The top four floors are the most important for you. This floor. The apartments. Coop told you about groceries, correct?"

I nod as I step into the elevator. "Order and receive."

"A list should be on your computer, including acceptable substitutions, and will be updated every Monday by three. Groceries should arrive by four. Your ID badge will allow you onto the floor and into the main apartment so you can put away the groceries. You'll meet the delivery person on the first floor and ride the elevator with them to and from delivery."

I inhale, wishing I'd brought a notebook along. This is a lot.

"No one besides us is allowed alone in the apartment or on the top floor." Blake's eyes blaze down at me.

"Of course," I manage to get out, feeling a brief rush of fear and desire combine within me. He's so large and in charge and intimidating.

"Good." He nods as the elevator doors open. "This elevator is only for our use. Never let anyone ride with you in it unless you have express permission. You have to have an access card to use it."

Okay, that's a little weird, but I can do that. He shows me around the lower levels. We breeze past people working, and he never stops to introduce me to anyone. I see some women my age at the end of the hallway and give them a smile.

A tall brunette gives me a once-over and sneers before turning to whisper something to the others. I take a breath. Okay, not the group of girls to hang out with. I'm sure there will be someone else. We continue walking, and I'm already regretting wearing my brand-new shoes without breaking them in, but I don't pause or plead for mercy.

Blake stops before a woman about my age with her brown hair pulled into a bun and glasses sliding down the end of her nose. When she startles and looks up at him with big blue eyes, she swallows. "Mr. Wagner?"

"Hope Williams, this is Madison Harris."

I hold out my hand to shake Hope's. Her eyes flow over me, but not like that other woman's did. Hope just looks curious.

"I'll need you to train Madison on the computer systems." Blake stands with his arms crossed over his chest, all intimidation.

Hope nods. "Of course. What time?"

"Around four thirty. Can you work late?" Blake's eyes never leave Hope's. "You two can get started and then work on it tomorrow morning as well."

"Yes, sir." She swallows again and then turns to me and gives me a genuine smile. "Here's my card with my direct line on it. Call me when you're ready, and I'll meet you at the elevator."

Smiling, I take the card. "Thank you."

Blake gives her a nod before he leads me down the hallway, listing off dozens of names and positions. I definitely need a directory for this place, and a map.

He seems determined to show me the entire building before we return to the top floor. I rest against the back wall of the elevator and lift each of my feet up off my shoes for a moment.

"Questions?" Blake settles against a wall and watches me closely.

"No, I just need to write a few things down to remember them."

His gaze trails over me before he gives me a curt nod.

Maybe the contract isn't his idea. Maybe he's just going along with it and doesn't really want me. An ache forms in my stomach, which is ridiculous. Before Friday, I was determined not to pursue anything with my new bosses. Now I'm upset because one out of the four hasn't tried a thing with me over the past hour.

Greedy much? I try to shake off the hurt.

This week is about getting comfortable with the job, not trying to get four guys into bed with me. My brain stalls on that image. I'd been thinking one at a time, but that huge bed waiting for me brings to mind another picture of all of them touching me at once.

The elevator stops and Blake looks at me expectantly. Fuck me.

I shake off the naughty images lingering in my mind and head toward my desk. When I lower into my chair, I almost sigh in relief at being off my feet.

"Cooper will be out in fifteen minutes to begin his hour with you." Blake stops beside me, close enough that his pant leg brushes my knee.

I lift my gaze to his green eyes. "That sounds good."

"Noah is after. Then we have lunch with a new client and would like you to attend." His eyes catch mine and my heartbeat quickens.

"Of course, Blake." I can't look away as he searches my eyes.

His hand clenches into a fist, and he releases it as he looks away from me. "This afternoon you'll spend with me first, then Seth."

Released from his spell, I nod and pull the notepad I found earlier over in front of me before I notice he hasn't left.

"Is there anything else?" I bite my lower lip as I hold my breath. I don't know what I've done to him, but he seems to be fighting something.

He shakes his head. "Make sure you stay on time."

Shouldn't be a problem. "Yes, Blake."

His hand clenches as he walks to his office. I take in the line of his broad shoulders and narrow waist. His suit jacket covers most of him, but it strains against his muscles. His door closes, leaving me alone again. His unique blend of spice lingers around my desk. I inhale it and can't help picturing more from him.

I'm not sure he wants me, but I know I want him. His deep voice whispering in my ear all the filthy things he wants to do to me. His large hands digging into my hips as he thrusts inside me.

Closing my eyes, I take a breath. I need to focus on getting to know these guys, making sure they aren't jerks. Not dropping my panties on my first day of work.

Shaking my head, I write what I learned this morning and where everything is that I might need in the coming months. I'm sure most of the information will be repeated until I know it by heart. At least, I hope so.

Hope's card goes beside my phone. If groceries get here around four, I should be able to make it down there at four thirty. I wonder how late Blake expects both of us to work.

I also need to invest in a pair of comfortable shoes to wear for when we walk everywhere. I didn't realize these would take getting used to or that I'd need to break them in before I wore them. Lesson learned, but I'm stuck with them for the rest of the day.

"My turn." Cooper's deep voice literally sends shivers throughout my body.

Chapter 6

Intro to Tech

Madison

Turning in my chair, I'm caught by Cooper's sky blue eyes. His black hair is slicked back into a bun again. My fingers itch to tug it loose and see how long his hair actually is.

He's gorgeous. They all are, but there's something about the lightness in Cooper's eyes that tugs at me.

He holds out his hand, and without a thought, I slip mine into his. Helping me from my chair, he draws me in close to him. His scent is sharper than Blake's, clean and crisp. Even with my new heels, he towers over me. I can feel each breath race through me as we stand there. Eyes locked. So close to touching, but not quite close enough.

"Come on, Madison." When he steps back, the air returns to my lungs. "We'll talk in my office."

I quickly grab my notebook and pen before following him. He guides me by my hand through his door and then shuts it. The click of the lock startles me, and I glance over my shoulder at him.

"I only get you alone for an hour." He raises his dark eyebrow. "Please have a seat."

His hand indicates one of the chairs in front of his desk. His desk echoes mine. Wood and glass, almost delicate in form. I drop into the chair and set my notebook on my lap.

Once on the other side of the desk, he sits and rests his elbows on it with his long fingers intertwined. For a moment, he just studies me.

"New clothes?" He leans back in his chair. Everything about him is elegant and smooth as he moves with the thoughtless grace of a cat.

"Yes." Warmth floods to my cheeks. The money I used means I'm open to a relationship with all of them. That I gave my consent to sexual advances from these men.

"How has your day been so far?" He strokes a finger across his lip.

My breath catches as I wonder how soft his full lips will be against mine. Is kissing even part of it? I clear my throat. "It's been good. A lot of walking. The building is amazing."

"Good." Cooper stands and walks around his desk before leaning on it before me. "I want to play a game if you're open to it."

"A game?" I rest against the back of my chair to meet his mischievous eyes.

"I need to give you a lot of information about our company, but I also want to learn more about you. So for each piece of information I give you, I'll ask you a question in return. Fair?" His lips quirk into a half smile.

"Okay." I lift my pen.

He rubs his hands together and then takes the seat next to me. Without any hesitation, he explains what the CTO does and tells me about the engineering team that works under him as they develop new technology for their clients. This is the core of what they do for cybersecurity. He's also in charge of the in-house network and team of IT guys.

Listening, I take a minute to write the key information I'll need. When I lift my gaze to him, he's watching my hand write.

When I stop writing, his gaze lifts to mine before he asks, "This arrangement is unusual, to say the least. Did you agree to it just for the money?"

I blink twice and am pretty sure my mouth is opening and closing like a dying fish. I clear my throat and shut my mouth. Taking a breath, I set my pen and notebook on his desk and turn to face him.

"No, it's not about the money. Yes, the money is nice, but if things don't go well, I don't know if I would feel comfortable keeping it."

He opens his mouth, but I rush ahead. "I know it's for signing the forms, but it still feels odd. Like I just signed for the bonus, which isn't my intention."

Cooper nods and shifts right back into work mode. "Things I'll need you to do: Handle my schedule and calendar. Book all my travel. Some filing and a few projects as they come up. You'll also come with me to meetings, when I'll need detailed notes."

When he finishes talking, I stop scribbling in my notebook and look up at him, expectantly. I know he's waiting for me to meet his eyes before he asks a personal question.

"You're attracted to all of us. Do you understand how demanding four men in the prime of their lives can be?" Cooper's eyebrow lifts.

I tighten my crossed legs at the throb between them. *God, I hope so* probably isn't the answer he wants. I raise my eyebrow back at him. "Are you worried I won't be able to handle it?"

"I have no idea what you are capable of, Madison." His lips twitch into an almost smile. "Yet."

"Let me assure you, I'm willing to devote myself to you four as much as I did my studies. I worked tirelessly to get internships every year while taking summer classes. I maintained a 4.0 GPA and worked on-campus jobs throughout my time at Fletcher. In those four years, I not only earned my bachelor's but also my master's."

Cooper leans back in his chair. "Impressive."

That information is all on my resume, so he already knew that. I take a deep breath before I reveal this part of my life to a man who, while I'm attracted to him, is still a stranger to me. But if I expect to have a relationship with each of these men, I'll need to give something of myself. More than just a willing body.

"I barely lived during school, but I was determined to finish and find the perfect job. I really believe Morrigan Technology Group can satisfy my need to be productive and train me to be the type of worker and executive I want to be someday. As to the contract we have yet to work out..." I pause because I'm not sure how he'll take the next part. "I missed out on being experimental during college. I had a few brief flings to scratch the itch but nothing spectacular."

I didn't have a regular fuck buddy situation because there wasn't a guy I wanted in my life like that. One-night stands seemed to be the less messy way to go forward, but only when I needed it. Otherwise, I took care of myself.

"That's a shame." Cooper gives me an almost feral smile.

"It is." I tuck my hair behind my ear as I meet his eyes. "When I met all of you, I knew I'd be in trouble because I felt an instant attraction. To all of you. I worried that I'd have to fight against it every day, but then you all offered me the keys to the kingdom."

"I hope you truly are as curious as you sound." Cooper's voice deepens as he leans toward me. His finger trails along my knee to the edge of my skirt. "We're all demanding in our own ways."

I struggle not to uncross my legs to give him better access and to maintain my breathing. For now, work hours mean work. Until one of them tells me differently, that's the only line I'll hold on to.

"Are you shy, sweetheart?" His voice is intimate. His fingers slide beneath my skirt and tease along my silk thigh highs. "Or are you bold and take what you want?"

Meeting his eyes, I uncross my legs and stand to face him with my ass pressed to the desk. My legs slightly apart, I lean on the desk in front of him, bracing my hands behind me on the wood. His fingers return to my thigh as he watches my eyes. His blue eyes hold mine while his hand slips beneath my skirt.

"I'm whatever you need me to be," I say softly as his hand reaches the ends of my garter belt.

His fingertips touch my bare skin above the stocking, and I resist the urge to clench his hand between my thighs. His eyes flare with heat as his touch scorches my flesh, leaving me aching and even wetter. He removes his hand and stands in front of me.

"I like to play games." Cooper's warmth floods my body. He doesn't touch me again, though. Our bodies are close, but not against one another. "I like to have fun in the bedroom, but I have to be strict here. When we are in the office, we're at work."

"Of course, Cooper." I keep my eyes on him and don't retreat. I want to be his. However he wants me to be.

"If I tell you to do something, I expect it to be done." His gaze dips down to my breasts before lifting back to my eyes. A wicked glint lingers in his eyes. "You and I will have a lot of fun."

I smile, even as I ache for more. "Yes, Cooper."

For a second, I think he'll lean in and kiss me. Meanwhile, my imagination already has me bent over his desk, skirt around my waist, panties tugged to the side, his cock notched against my entrance. I press my thighs together against the ache.

Two weeks. I'm not sure I'll last two weeks before I do something drastic.

"I need to show you what reports to run and what days to run them on." He steps away from me and heads around his desk to sit before his computer.

I take a breath, grab my notebook from his desk, then go to sit in my chair.

"Not there."

My questioning gaze lifts to Cooper.

"Come here." His voice is soft and dark, and the look in his eyes... Fuck, if I could bottle that, I'd be rich.

I go to drag the chair around the desk.

"Leave that." His eyes sparkle as he wets his lips.

I walk around the desk, excited about standing next to him but dreading standing in these heels. My feet just started to feel a little better. When I stop beside him, I set my notebook on the desk.

"Sit." He rolls away from the desk and leans back.

I glance at the desk.

"On my lap, Ms. Harris."

Well, that escalated quickly. I move in front of him and lower myself onto his lap. His hands grip my hips to guide me. My panties dampen as I feel his hard cock beneath me. I'm beginning to wonder if Cooper is the reason for the consent forms. Or if they'll all be like this.

He slides us under the desk. His arms come to either side of me as he goes through the Monday reports he needs. Knowing I won't remember any of this, I take detailed notes and try not to rub on his lap like a cat in heat. He's one hundred percent focused on teaching me the reports, though.

Every day a different report needs to be run first thing in the morning and on his desk by nine. I wonder how many requests like this will come from my other bosses.

A knock at the door startles me as I finish my notes. Cooper helps me stand and then rises behind me. His hands settle on my hips. He pulls my ass back against his erection, if I weren't already soaking wet, that would do it.

He dips his head beside mine and says softly against my ear, "I can't wait for my next time alone with you, sweetheart."

I glance over my shoulder with my pulse throbbing. Waiting is going to be hell.

Chapter 7

Playing by Numbers

Noah

Madison's cheeks are flushed when Coop opens the door for me. It wouldn't surprise me if Coop took her for a test run instead of filling her in on her duties for him. I smile at Madison as she stops before me. Her eyes are eager as she looks up at me expectantly.

She's gorgeous. Her blond hair falls in gentle waves past her shoulders. Her blue eyes capture my attention. Intelligence and curiosity spark in them.

Today her outfit fits her in a way that shows off her curves. I follow the line of her skirt down to her shapely calves and high heels. As I watch, she shifts balance from one foot to the next. I almost shake my head.

Don't get me wrong. The heels are hot, but not if she's going to walk around in pain all day. I'd rather she wear slippers or go barefoot.

"We'll be working in my office this morning." I lead her to my open door.

"I didn't get a chance to talk with you long on Friday," she says. Her eyes dart to the leather couch with a couple of chairs in front of it, then to my desk. It's a large piece of furniture, and unlike Cooper, I prefer function over style. My dual monitors sit on the desk with one turned ninety degrees.

I take a breath and gesture toward the couch. My stacks of documentation wait on the coffee table in front of it. "I'm not as eloquent with words as the others. I stick to numbers."

It's the truth. I'm also not as good as they are at picking up women. Skipping a grade in school meant I was too young for my classmates and out of sync with my peers. I'm lucky the guys took me in as a friend. Even though they were a grade ahead of me, they stood up for me against some of my classmates that didn't appreciate someone ruining all the grading curves.

They kept me safe from the older kids that wanted to teach me a lesson. They gave me friends when I didn't have any. We stuck together.

In return, I helped them build some wealth through investments during college. Joining with them to form a company after graduation had been a no-brainer. But women are still a mystery to me. The other women we've tried this arrangement with didn't entice me. There was a spark, but nothing amazing.

But with Madison, I burn to touch her. It might have started with her resume. Of all the people who applied for the job, she stood out as intelligent and driven. Her experience with internships gave her another notch up. And then, when she showed up for the interview, I was a goner.

She lowers herself to the couch, and the tension in her face eases.

"Take off your shoes."

I sit next to her on the couch. Far enough away to make her comfortable, but close enough that I can smell her soft floral scent and feel the warmth radiate off her body.

"What?" Madison glances at me almost nervously.

"Take off your shoes while you're in my office." I grab my tablet/laptop off the coffee table. "I appreciate how the heels make your legs appear longer. If I had a foot fetish, I'd love them. But they also look uncomfortable, and I'd prefer you to be comfortable in my presence."

The lines around her blue eyes fade, and she gives me a genuine smile. As she slips off the shoes and sets them beside the couch, she says, "Thank you. I thought they'd make me feel powerful, but I didn't know I'd be walking around the entire building in them."

I tap on the screen to bring up the first report. "I like what you're wearing, but if it makes you uncomfortable, you don't have to wear it."

Her gaze drops to the shoes with longing. "I do like them, and I know I'll get used to them. Eventually."

I shrug. "I'm the youngest of the group. At first, I tried to keep up with the others in everything, but at some point, I realized what mattered to them didn't matter as much to me. I needed to focus on what I wanted and not what they wanted."

Her lips press together as she nods thoughtfully. She clears her throat discreetly before saying, "Do you... not want to be part of the other arrangement?"

If she knew how much I wanted her, would it frighten her away? I take a breath and set the tablet down. When I turn to face her, her blue eyes go wide, and she scrunches her forehead in worry.

Without thinking, I lift my thumb to her forehead and smooth out the tight muscles. She inhales at my touch and I drop my gaze to her lips.

"There's very little in this world that draws me." I cup her cheek as my thumb trails over her lower lip. "Books. Numbers. Logic. I don't do well in conversations." When her lips part, I force myself to continue. "I've been with women before, but none of them made my heart pound or my chest tighten like you do. I know we need to focus on work this week, but is it okay if I kiss you?"

I know it's crazy to ask, but maybe it will help me focus, because all I want to do right now is kiss her pink lips.

Her head starts to move up, and that's all the confirmation I need. I lean in and claim her. This kiss is unlike any kiss before it. Warmth bursts through me as fire licks at my flesh. She opens beneath me. She tastes like mint and a hint of creamy coffee.

As my tongue caresses hers, she whimpers and presses against my side. I grab her hips and pull her onto my lap. I may have difficulty having conversation, but when I want something, I have no trouble taking it. When I've been with women before, I've always stayed in control. Able to think rationally and take into consideration all the variables, but something about Madison pulls at something wild within me. A need that throbs relentlessly through me.

Her skirt rides up to her hips as she straddles my lap and presses against my hard cock. I thread my hands through her hair as I devour her mouth. We should get back to work. But when she grinds down on me, making both of us moan, I can't find a reason to stop right now. I've wanted to do this since we met.

On Friday, I barely held myself back in the elevator, but now to have her here in my office. Alone. And she wants me. Fuck. My normally high IQ takes a nosedive into burning desire.

I can't get enough of her mouth, but I need more. I leave her lips to press kisses along her jawline.

"Noah," she sighs as her hands latch into my hair to press me against her neck.

My cell phone vibrates in my pocket. I pull back.

"Oh." Madison straightens in surprise. Her normally light eyes are blown dark with desire. Her lipstick is smeared. Her hands lower to my shoulders.

I'm sure I'm not faring any better. Lifting my hips, I reach into my pocket for my phone.

Madison starts to slide off to the side, but I grab her hip to keep her there. I'm not nearly done with her.

"Not yet." I give her half a smile before answering my cell.

Seth's voice comes through the phone. "We're leaving for lunch in thirty minutes. Will you be finished by then, or will you need more time with Madison this afternoon?"

Madison's lips quirk up into a smile, and she covers her mouth. Her cheeks tinge pink. I barely resist leaning back in to taste her joy.

I clear my throat and arch an eyebrow to get her to behave long enough for me to talk to Seth. "We might need a little more time after lunch."

"Special project?" Seth's voice almost sounds bored.

Definitely a special project. I thread my hand into the back of Madison's blond hair, and she softens at my touch. Her gaze drops to my mouth, and she bites down on her lip.

"I'll make sure not to monopolize her."

Her hips roll against me, and I choke down a moan. I have no doubt by the end of the day Seth will know exactly what everyone does with Madison today, but I don't need or want his reminder to go slow right now.

"Right. Well, I won't keep you." Seth ends the call.

Wrapping my arm around Madison's waist, I lean forward with her still against me to set my phone on the coffee table. I lift my gaze to hers. "Where were we?"

Her fingers latch into my unruly hair, and she pulls me into another all-consuming kiss. I've never had such a potent attraction to anyone before. I want more from her. I want it all.

I roll her until her back rests on the couch and press down over her.

When I trail kisses down her neck again, she pants out, "I don't think I'm learning much about what you do as CFO."

I lift my lips from the pulse in her neck and stare down at her. Her face is flushed. Moving my hand to her top button, I raise an eyebrow for permission.

She bites her lip and nods. Her thighs press into my hips.

"I assume you took a basic accounting course both in undergrad and to get your MBA?" I flick open a button and kiss the skin I expose.

"I did." Her answer is breathy.

I reward her with another button loosened and another kiss. "And we already know you had a perfect score in every class?"

"I did."

Two more buttons released, and I pause to appreciate her lace bra with a front clasp. I lower my forehead to rest against her chest as I try to focus on what she needs to know and what I want to do to her in the next thirty minutes. Her fingers ruffle through my hair.

"Fuck, you're full of surprises." I lift my head to see her grin.

"Good ones, I hope." Her eyes are soft and her smile warms my insides.

"The best." I flick open her bra and watch her eyes as I push open her shirt and bra together to see her breasts. "Perfection."

"I took a few other accounting classes besides the basics." She gives me a hopeful look.

"Well, then I can't teach you anything you don't already know." I lower my head to her breast and kiss the hardened tip.

"I'm sure we could make quick work of it this afternoon. Cooper showed me the reports system. Hope will teach me the computers. I'm a very fast learner," she assures me. Her legs wrap around mine.

"We will." The tip of my tongue traces the edge of her areola before I drag it across to her other breast.

She arches against me and practically purrs when I trace her nipple with my tongue. My cock throbs, hard and ready. When I slide my hand between her thighs to feel how damp her panties are, she whimpers.

So fucking wet.

"What do you want, kitten?" I blow across her wet breast.

Her hands tug my head down against her chest. I open my mouth and suck on her hardened nipple. She cries out softly, but I don't care if the others hear. I press my fingers against her damp heat, stroking her through her panties.

"Noah," she moans.

"Tell me what you want." I switch to her other breast, lavishing it with attention, wringing little noises from within her. I need her to tell me what she wants. I need her to tell me she wants me.

"I want you to make me come. I want you, Noah." Her neck arches as she presses her breast into my mouth and her hips into my hand. "Please make me come."

My chest fills with warmth, and I rise up to reclaim her lips with mine. I shove her panties to the side and thrust two fingers into her wet pussy. I swallow her cries as she follows the thrusts of my hand with her hips.

I move my thumb over her clit and rub. When she tightens around my fingers and gasps her release, my cock hardens painfully, so close to the edge myself that just feeling her come on my fingers almost tips me over. Breathing in, I keep thrusting my fingers into her convulsing pussy as she rides the waves of her orgasm. When she finally collapses onto the couch, I draw my fingers out and smooth and straighten her panties.

When her satisfied eyes watch me lift my hand to my mouth and suck her wetness from it, my aching cock twitches. She tastes fucking fantastic. Everything about her is amazing.

"Thank you." She sits up next to me, one leg behind me and the other on the floor beside mine. Her hand wanders over my shirt. "How much time do we have until lunch?"

I glance at my phone screen. "Ten minutes."

"Can I..." She licks her lips, and her hand drops to my erection, rubbing my cock through my pants. She leans in and kisses next to my ear before whispering, "Please."

Fuck it. I release my belt as she slides to the floor between my knees. Her eager eyes watch as I fumble with my button and zipper. Gently, she pushes my hands away and reaches in to lift my throbbing cock out of my boxers.

"Hold my hair?" She arches an eyebrow at me with a smile that makes precum drip off my tip.

I do as she asks and gather her hair into a ponytail with one hand.

When she licks the wetness off my cock, I suck in a breath. It's been too long. I don't know how long I'll last.

"Should I let you know when—"

Her grin turns mischievous. "Surprise me."

Fuck. I think I'm in love.

And then all rational thought leaves me as she lowers her mouth over me and licks along the underside of my cock. Her hand wraps around the base to pump while the other teases my balls until I forget my own fucking name.

She strokes and sucks and licks until I thrust my hips to keep up with her. Using my hold on her hair, I press her farther down onto my cock. She lets me push deeper into her throat while she swallows my dick and curls her tongue around it.

I can't hold back any longer.

My release shakes through me, and she keeps sucking and licking until I'm completely spent. She sits back on her heels and tucks my cock back into my pants before fastening everything. She straightens herself, doing up her bra and buttoning her shirt while I just watch.

Fuck. I want more. I want her naked and strapped to my bed, aching for me.

When she holds out her hand, I help her stand. She moves to my side and collapses onto the couch next to me.

Unable to resist, I grasp her chin so our faces are aligned. I capture her lips in a soft kiss. She leans into me in response.

"Honestly, I had a whole plan to get through." I glance at the stack of papers and then return my gaze to her soft blue eyes. "That got away from me."

She laughs and leans her head on my shoulder. "Me too."

I have a feeling things will always get away from me when it comes to her. I'm looking forward to it.

Chapter 8

Business Lunch

Madison

I'm not going to lie, but I feel a little awkward as Noah and I make sure we look proper before walking into the lobby to meet the others. I'm pretty sure they'll all be able to tell we haven't exactly been behaving in a business-appropriate manner.

Fortunately, Noah's attached bathroom had a spare toothbrush, which I gladly used. I wiped off the rest of my lipstick and figured I'd reapply after lunch.

"We didn't get much work done." I smile shyly up at Noah as he fixes my hair behind my ear. His hands curl around my neck. I don't regret a single second we spent together, but I know this can't become a habit. Work has to come first.

"Call it a stress reliever. First day jitters." He captures my lips in another searing kiss that has me throbbing between my legs again. I don't think the two of us can be left alone, because I already want to pick up where we left off.

I just shake my head and straighten his collar. "What's your excuse then?"

"First day jitters." His hand goes to my lower back, and he leads me to the door.

I breathe in and release it. This is what I signed up for. What I agreed to. Even though we haven't finalized everything, Noah seemed so unsure of himself. I couldn't let him feel like I didn't want him when I do. He definitely didn't hesitate or worry during. One thing led to another, and it all felt really, really fantastic.

The rumble of male voices comes through the door when Noah opens it. Silence falls as we step into the center where my desk is. When he focuses on my now bare lips, Cooper's eyebrows almost meet his hairline.

I fight to keep from blushing, but then I turn to Blake. His lips press together as his eyes dip to my lips, then down at my shirt. Afraid that I missed a button, I glance down and reach up to fix whatever he saw, but everything is in order.

Shit, if I didn't look guilty before, I probably do now. Sandalwood teases my nose as I look up into Seth's blue eyes. There's a hint of a twinkle in them as he offers me his arm. I don't hesitate before I wrap my hand around his elbow.

"Oh, wait." I turn, but Cooper is already holding my purse out to me. I give him a grateful smile and say, "Thanks."

"Anytime." Cooper winks at me as I take it.

He turns and claps Noah on the shoulder. Noah shakes his head at Cooper, but he can't seem to stop the small smile on his face.

Something settles in my chest. I put that smile there.

"You ready?" Seth asks.

"Yes, thank you." I glance at him as he leads the others to the elevator.

As the doors shut, the men surround me as their gazes watch the numbers go down. My pulse rockets and I squeeze Seth's arm nervously. I don't know what their intentions are once we pass the two-week mark. But I'm definitely not averse to them all around me.

The heat of them penetrates me. They make me feel small and

sheltered within their ranks. My heart races at their imposing energy flowing over me.

"We're meeting a new client." Seth tilts his head my way as he speaks. "Normally, you'll have all the information before one of these lunches and be expected to take detailed notes. But as it's your first day, we thought you might just observe."

I nod my head. I can do that. This afternoon, I'll keep my focus on work and not on the front of Seth's pants. I seriously have a problem if I can't keep my mind from circling to other things. Maybe once we get into the arrangement, I'll be able to focus better on actual work.

Until then, I need to keep my head in the game.

When we reach the basement level, we step out into the parking garage, and two black cars with tinted windows wait idling for us. Noah and Cooper go to one while Blake and Seth lead me to the other.

Blake gets into the front passenger seat. Seth holds open the back door for me and walks around to slide in on the other side. Two men dressed in suits walk out to take the drivers' seats.

"How has your morning been?" Seth asks quietly.

Heat rushes to my cheeks, thinking about Noah. I shake that off. "I saw most of the building. Cooper showed me the reports system and some of the daily reports I need to run."

While I sat on his lap.

"And Noah?"

I can hear a hint of teasing in Seth's tone and turn to catch his slight smile. "Noah..."

I pause and swallow. My gaze drops to my hands in my lap. They all are supposed to want me, so it shouldn't be a surprise, but today I should be focused on learning my job responsibilities.

Seth captures my chin and lifts my face so I meet his eyes. "We'll use the time we have with you as effectively as possible. I don't blame Noah for wanting a taste."

His gaze drops to my lips, and I press my legs together from the ache his darkened eyes cause. I want his lips on mine. To allow me a taste of him.

"We will try to focus on work." His thumb ghosts over my lower lip before he draws his hand away. "But don't feel guilty about what you do with any of us. Or feel you're wasting company time. With the hours we keep, the work will get done."

I press my lips tight, trying to piece together what I want to say. I understand what he's telling me, but I also need him to know my thoughts.

"I don't want you to think I'm taking advantage of the situation. I'm here because I think this will be an amazing career for me. The other part of the arrangement is a bonus." I shrug. "But I don't want it to take over."

"We'll find a balance," Seth assures me with a faint smile.

I relax into the seat as he lifts his phone to work. When I glance up, my gaze meets Blake's green eyes. His visor is down and the mirror reflects his intensity. I offer him a smile, and he closes the mirror. The rejection stings.

Thankfully, the drive is short. When Blake steps out, he opens my door and offers me his hand. I keep my smile on my lips, but he remains stoic. I follow him into the restaurant and past the hostess back to a private room.

Noah and Cooper are already here. Blake pulls out a chair for me, and I drop into it. He sits to one side while Seth sits on the other.

"The other reason we felt you wouldn't need to be briefed on this new client is you worked for them." Seth stands as the door to the room opens.

Curiosity fills me. I had a lot of internships, so it could be any number of previous employers. I stand with the rest of them and watch Hunter Adams and his father, William Adams, walk in. My heart skips and my hands go clammy. I force myself to remain smiling as they haven't noticed me yet. Seth's large body blocks me from their view.

The men all exchange introductions.

Hunter is undeniably handsome with windswept blond hair and sky blue eyes. His chiseled face makes him popular with most women, but that doesn't stop him from wanting everyone to fall at his feet. Including me.

William notices me first. He reaches out and takes my hand between both of his. "Madison! What a pleasant surprise. So glad you found a good place to land. Though it's definitely a loss for Taylor's."

Hunter got his looks from his father, though his father is more mature, and his blond hair is more white than blond. William is kinder too. There's no predatory glint in his eyes. If Hunter didn't exist, I would have seriously considered working with William.

William releases my hand. I brace myself as Hunter steps too close and takes my hand. My instinct is to jerk away, but this is business. My heart flutters wildly as the need to flee this predator fills every inch of me.

"Madison. It's disappointing that you didn't come and work for us. We made so many plans on how best to use your skills." Hunter's blue eyes capture mine like I'm a bird he's caught in his hands and would rather kill than free.

"I'm sure taking the position at Taylor's would have been a good fit, but I couldn't resist working at Morrigan after the interview." I draw my hand back.

Hunter's smile is anything but happy. "Wish you would have told us they made an offer. We would have countered."

Blake touches the small of my back, and I retreat gratefully to my chair. I don't dare return my gaze to Hunter's. I don't want to see what he thinks of the guys touching me. He's a possessive asshole.

Everyone settles around the table as Seth talks with William about what Morrigan can do for Taylor's. I'm just happy to focus on my salad while I listen and take mental notes.

The whole time, the weight of Hunter's stare on me is stifling. He tried so many times to corner me after the copy room incident, but I avoided him until my internship ended. It would have sucked to tuck my tail and return there after graduation. And I know he wouldn't have let me escape from him again.

Focusing on William and Seth helps me get through the salad course. Our meals must have been preordered because the main course comes out promptly. There's a small portion of steak and fish on the plate along with some sautéed vegetables and rice pilaf.

My gaze strays accidentally to Hunter's. He watches my mouth as I eat. The primal look on his face makes me a little sick. I glance around to see if anyone else notices.

While almost everyone participates in the conversation between Seth and William, Blake's gaze falls on Hunter. His brows are knotted. I'm tempted to slip my hand over his under the table to let him know I don't want Hunter's attention. I never have and never will.

But Blake seems so distant. If he were Noah, it would be a no-brainer, but Blake doesn't seem to want me that way, and I won't force it on him.

When the conversation switches to more personal matters rather than business, I clear my throat. I need a break from Hunter's feral gaze.

"If you'll excuse me?" I lay my cloth napkin next to my plate.

Seth nods at me, and all their gazes follow me as I walk out of the private dining room. When I close the door behind me, I take a breath and head to the restroom. After going and washing my hands, I stand at the mirror and reapply my lipstick.

Lunch is almost over. I just have to go back out there and pretend my skin doesn't crawl when Hunter shakes my hand as they leave. Easy, right?

Fuck. He is not ruining this job for me.

I straighten my shoulders and leave the bathroom.

Hunter stands in the hallway across from the ladies' room. His smile is wide as he says, "Hello, Maddy."

Chapter 9

Harassment

Blake

Something is definitely off about the way Hunter stared at Madison during lunch. Madison is so tense I'm surprised the fork doesn't bend in her fingers. The others watch her walk out the door to the restroom, but I watch Hunter's gaze follow her.

He's more interested in her than in our talks about the future of security at his business. The business he'll supposedly take over someday. I'm not surprised when he excuses himself a few minutes after Madison leaves.

I need to protect my friends better than I did with Andrea. No one knew she'd blackmail us. We never suspected it. I never suspected it. I let them down.

If something is going on with these two, I'm going to find out. I touch Seth's shoulder to let him know I'm going. His brow furrows for a second before he gives me a slight nod.

We did a background check on Madison. No red flags came up besides her lack of money, but with what we pay, that shouldn't be an issue. It's also why I suggested the bonus to help her get on her feet.

I follow Hunter discreetly and move to the side when he lounges outside the women's door. His grin is way too pleased with himself. I need to see how Madison handles this because I'm not about to let us get trapped in a similar situation again.

Noah is smitten. Cooper is already into this woman too. Even Seth has issues keeping his hands off her. I need to make sure she isn't stringing us along. I need to protect my family.

"Hello, Maddy." Hunter's smug voice draws my attention.

Madison pales, and her gaze flicks around, looking for an escape. Or making sure no one else is around. "Hunter."

He doesn't move from his position on the wall. "You didn't really think you could escape me, did you, little bird?"

"I don't know what you mean." She straightens even as she edges toward the dining room.

"You were supposed to be a good little bird and come work for me." He steps away from the wall, closing in on her. "We would have had a good time. You and me."

She swallows. Her gaze is almost wild as she looks for an escape. Or am I seeing what I want to?

"I already told you I'm not interested."

"Ah, but now you don't have the excuse that you work for me. Do you, Maddy?" He closes in on her, trapping her against the wall.

"Hunter, this is inappropriate." She tries to sound stern, but it comes out a little panicked.

I can't hold back anymore. I stride over to them. "Madison."

Her shoulders relax as Hunter steps back with a slightly pissed off smile on his face.

"We're about ready to go." I meet Hunter's blue eyes as I reach out a hand for her.

She slides her trembling hand into mine and steps beside me. I don't bother looking at Hunter again as I lead her back to the dining room.

"Ah, Madison." William smiles as we return, and I help her sit. "You've always been so brilliant. It's no wonder you want to work with these fine young gentlemen."

Her cheeks are still a little pale, but she gives him a warm smile. "I'll always be grateful for the experience I gained working at Taylor's."

"Our offer still stands. If you ever need a job, you call me." William stands as Hunter returns.

Hunter's gaze falls on Madison again. "We definitely would love to have you back."

I don't know what game Hunter is playing, but I also wonder if Madison is playing one in return. Maybe this is part of their game. I can't trust my instincts on this one, because I want her and that complicates everything. Maybe she's not into him. Maybe she is.

I need to know for sure. I make a note to run a more thorough background check on Hunter Adams.

"We're happy to have her on our team and hope to keep her satisfied with us." Seth smiles as he says the words, but there is a little bite in his tone.

"Of course, of course." William smiles, but Hunter's smile drops a little. "You can't blame us for trying. Madison is one of the best interns we've ever had. Wish we could have offered her more to come to work for us, but we have to stick to the budget."

"I'll call you later this week to schedule a follow up." Seth rises and holds out his hand to William. After they shake, he turns to Hunter. Hunter's smile doesn't reach his eyes as he shakes Seth's hand.

"A pleasure doing business with you." Hunter's eyes find Madison.

I'm not about to let him get his hands on her again. Even if she wants it, I don't want to see another man with his hands on her. We may share with each other, but not outside of us.

The others step forward to shake hands, but when Madison gets to her feet, I steer her away and out of the room. She doesn't hesitate to keep up as we make our way out to the waiting car.

I won't question her now, but later, I'll definitely be looking for answers.

Madison

I breathe a sigh of relief as we return to the office. The men are all quiet as we ride the elevator up.

Noah leads me into his office and closes the door. "Okay, let's actually talk about your job this time."

He gives me an easy grin. The tension from the confrontation with Hunter eases out of me. We settle on the couch and talk about what all he needs me to do. He has reports for the morning to be run and emailed to him. A little filing. He shows me the cabinets in a room close to the break room.

After a half hour, he reluctantly stands.

"I really enjoyed this morning." He reaches for my hand and helps me stand before him.

"Me too." It feels so long ago after Hunter almost trapped me again. I thought he couldn't do anything in a crowded restaurant. Shame on me for underestimating him. It won't happen again.

I lock those thoughts away as I focus on Noah's dark eyes and remember his kiss, the feel of his fingers inside me, and his hot cock on my tongue.

He presses a kiss beside my lips. Butterflies take flight in my stomach.

"I look forward to getting to know you better."

Smiling, I squeeze his hand. "I really like you, Noah."

He softens and draws me into his arms. "If I could keep you all day, I would, but I have to share."

He pulls away and brushes my hair behind my ear, causing a shiver to course down my spine. Leaning in, he presses a kiss to the other side of my lips. I melt.

When we step into the inner office, Blake is waiting for me.

"She's all yours." Noah grins as he passes me off. He's not subtle when he adjusts his cock in his trousers, sparking the flames hotter between my thighs. Will I get to taste him again this week, or will that brief sneak peek be all I get?

Blake gestures for me to follow him into his office. I clutch my notepad and pen to my chest. I'll need to take a few minutes later to review my notes and type them into my computer.

The door shuts behind me, and Blake gestures to a chair. I still get the feeling he doesn't like me, or maybe he just doesn't trust me. It's a little sad, because I want him so badly. Even if he doesn't want me, would he at least consider some phone sex?

When I take my seat, he rounds his desk to sit on the other side.

"Like the others, I have reports I need first thing in the morning. Filing and the like, which we'll get to. Since it's Monday, we need to turn in the grocery order so they can deliver. The first delivery I'll walk through with you and help you put away everything."

I release the breath I didn't even realize I was holding. "That would be great."

He leans back in his chair and stares at me for a moment. Those green eyes taking me all in. "Did you enjoy working at Taylor's?"

Fuck, I kind of hoped we would skip this whole thing. Hunter trapped me in that hallway, and Blake probably wonders why. But I also don't want to seem like someone who would cry sexual harassment, since these guys had a previous lover who tried to blackmail them.

"Taylor's was a good experience for me. They allowed me some autonomy with what I worked on and made sure I learned more of the business and not just small sections, like some of my internships." I manage to keep the smile on my lips.

"Do you have a history with Hunter Adams?" Blake raises his eyebrow.

"Did I work with him? Yes." I'm not sure what he wants from me, and I'm not answering unasked questions.

"Were you sexually involved with him?" Blake leans forward. His face is like stone.

"No. Never." My heartbeat quickens.

"Are you planning on being sexually involved with him?" Blake's eyes are hard.

"No, definitely not." I push out a breath before lifting my gaze to his. "Hunter kept trying to make something happen between us, but I have never been and will never be interested in him like that."

Frankly, he creeps me out, but I won't tell my boss that about our potential new client. I'm treading a fine line here. I'm new and Hunter is now a customer. I don't know these men, but I know they've been blackmailed by a woman claiming sexual harassment. Blake seems the most unsure about me and I don't want to give him any reason to dislike me.

"Good." Blake relaxes and spends the rest of our time together showing me how to place the grocery order, what documents are important on my computer, and anything else he needs me to do.

Unlike the others, Blake barely touches me and doesn't even give me so much as a heated look. He seems less than impressed with me. I can't help but feel a little rejected by the time we stand to go back to my desk.

When he leaves me alone to wait for Seth, I decide to go refresh the coffee and get another cup. Today is going to be a long day. I need a little burst of energy to get me through the rest.

I've just started a new pot when Cooper comes into the break room.

"How's your day going?" Cooper's blue eyes pin me in place as they trail over my figure. That heat that's always on simmer boils to the surface. He manages to sweep away the cold bits Blake left behind.

"Keeping up. Need a little caffeinated help." Smiling, I gesture to the coffee brewing. "How's your day?"

"Not as fun as this morning." He stalks toward me. I catch my breath in anticipation. His arms cage me against the counter, and he studies the coffee machine, which begins sputtering. His finger comes up and traces my bottom lip. Sparks light up beneath his touch.

My pulse races as my eyes meet his.

"What should we do while we wait for coffee?" He lowers his head toward mine, and I nearly go up on my tiptoes to meet him. I grip his solid biceps. His mouth brushes mine briefly before he dips down to kiss me behind my ear.

My breath bursts out of me as tingles race along my veins. His hands remain on the counter, trapping me in, but I like this feeling. I like *him* stalking me and pouncing. His tongue trails down the side of my neck.

"Put your hands on my hips, sweetheart," he murmurs against my skin.

I follow his instructions and pull his hips against mine. His hard cock presses against my stomach, and I grow wet from the solidness of him. He chuckles against my throat, sending waves of need through me.

His lips close on the spot where my neck meets my shoulder. He sucks and nibbles and bites me there until I'm a hot mess beneath him. The coffee stops brewing. He lifts his mouth from my neck to hover over my lips, so close but not touching. An ache pulses between my thighs.

"Time to get back to work." He grabs my ass in his hands and pulls me against him one last time before releasing me and filling his cup of coffee.

Heat swirls through me. Desire is thick and heavy in my belly as he holds the coffee pot toward me like he wants to pour for me. He's going to be dangerous to my sanity. Always teasing. I take a deep breath and grab my cup to hold out for him.

He pours and sets the coffee pot back. His smile is feral as his gaze roams my body once again. I follow him out of the break room, tempted to follow him into his office and strip down for him. Beg him to take me against his desk or in his office chair.

He stops at my desk, though, and taps on it. His dark eyebrow raises. "Seth is expecting you soon. Better get on that, sweetheart."

My eyes widen, wondering what Seth might do with me.

Chapter 10

Boss's Orders

Madison

While I await Seth's summons, I sip my coffee at my desk. I'm all keyed up and desperate to come, but it can wait until I get home tonight. I have plenty of fantasies to get me there.

"Madison." Seth's voice sends shivers racing down my spine. I gather my notepad and pen and take one last draw from my coffee mug before heading to his office. He gestures to the chair I sat in on Friday and settles behind his desk.

"How are things going so far?"

I blush at the question, almost what Cooper asked before he kissed my neck. My fingers itch to trail along the line his lips took. "Good. I'm learning a lot and can't wait to be more productive."

Seth's blue eyes are intense as he looks me over. "My needs will be a little more complicated than the others."

Fuck, that shouldn't sound so hot. My thighs clench against the ache between them. I need to focus on work. His work needs.

"I refuse to give in to my baser urges during the day." He leans forward on the desk and arches an eyebrow at me. "But I like testing my willpower if you're willing to help."

"Whatever you want." I cross my legs against the throbbing. I want whatever he'll give me.

"Good." He leans back. "Reports. I'm sure you've got a list already, but here's what you need to add for me."

I take notes as he tells me which reports to run for him first thing in the morning.

"Slip off your shoes."

My head jerks up. He hasn't moved, but maybe I misheard him. "Sir?"

"Slip off your shoes, princess." His low voice resonates through me. "I like it when you call me *sir*."

I slip off my shoes and set them to the side. My stockinged toes curl against the wood floor. The coolness feels nice against my sore feet.

"Now, filing. I assume someone has already shown you the file room." His voice goes on as he discusses the filing he'll need me to do.

I feel a little exposed without my shoes, but maybe he's into feet. Even though he probably can't even see them from where he sits.

"Take off your shirt."

My gaze lifts to his, and he gestures with his hand.

"You heard me, princess." He rocks back in his chair and steeples his fingers against his lips.

"Yes, sir." My fingers tremble as they slip each button from the hole until my shirt is open. I take it off and shiver a little at the cool air on my heated skin when I place it on the chair next to me.

His darkened eyes are like a caress against my skin as he takes in my lacy bra. My nipples harden beneath his gaze. I gasp at the tightness. My panties are already soaked, and he hasn't even touched me yet.

"Meetings and schedules."

Lifting my notepad and pen, I take notes of the important weekly meetings, and his preferences for when and where he wants other meetings scheduled. When he pauses, I raise my gaze to his in anticipation.

"The skirt, please."

Holding his gaze, I stand and unzip my skirt before lowering and stepping out of it. My lace panties match my bra and my garter belt. His heated gaze roams over me, lighting me up and making me self-conscious about sitting on his chair.

As wet as I am, I'm likely to leave a mark.

As if sensing my dilemma, Seth nods to the door on the side of his office. "Grab a towel, princess."

I walk across his office in my underwear and step into his private bathroom. Grabbing a towel from the stack, I unfold it to cover the seat of my chair. When I sit, I cross my legs before retrieving my notepad and pen.

The corner of his lips twitches. What I would give to see a genuine smile on this man's face.

"At the end of each day, I expect notes from the meetings you attend to be in the following network drives."

My chest heaves as I take notes nearly naked. This isn't normal office protocol, but maybe it will be here. I clench my thighs together.

A knock at the door startles me, and my wide eyes meet Seth's. He lifts an eyebrow as Blake comes in without waiting for acknowledgment. He closes the door when he notices my state of undress.

"We need to get the groceries soon." Blake's green eyes drag over every inch of me, sending heat flooding through me. His eyes are smoldering as they meet mine.

"We're almost done here." Seth leans back, rocking again. "Take off your panties, princess."

I'm even wetter, knowing Blake is in here. Watching. Waiting. He leans back against the door and crosses his arms over his chest. My heart ricochets in my chest as I stand. I glance over my shoulder at Blake before meeting Seth's dark blue eyes.

I unhook my garters before my fingers hook into the sides of my panties. After I lower them and step out of them, I straighten and set my panties on the other chair. I can't believe this is happening, but I'm loving every minute of it.

I'm not shy. My body might have flaws, but swimming keeps me in shape. Toned but not hard. I keep my pussy waxed for swimming and enjoy the feel of it bare.

"Come here." Seth slides away from his desk and waits.

I walk around his desk and stand in front of him. The edge of his wooden desk presses into my ass. Anticipation of his touch rolls through me, making me tremble.

"Fix your garters."

I reach down and refasten them, glancing back to see Blake still watching. The bulge in his pants is impressive. My core clenches in anticipation. Straightening, I lock my gaze with Seth's.

"Sit on my desk."

He's cleared off the space directly in front of him. When I ease up onto the cool wood, I suck in a breath and try to keep from messing up his desk with my wetness.

He rolls his chair closer. "Put your feet on my thighs."

I do as he asks. I'm exposed to him in this position. My pussy hot and wet and on display for only him. It makes me want to moan, to beg him for more, for his touch.

"Blake." He gestures.

Blake rounds the desk, and his green eyes capture mine as he leans on the window behind Seth and resumes his stance. Blake's eyes roam all over me until his hot gaze locks on my wet pussy.

He wants me. Awareness fires through me out of control.

So turned on, I take a shuddering breath and return my gaze to Seth's. He rocks back, and his lips twitch a little toward a smile, but not all the way.

"Slide your finger against your pussy."

My breath catches. He's going to make me touch myself for him and Blake. Heat rises up my neck to my cheeks. My core clenches. I'm sure if I said I was uncomfortable with this, he would stop.

But I don't want him to. I've been needing another orgasm. If he's going to give me one, then I'm all in. Even if I have to do the work.

I slide my finger over my wet clit, rubbing in a circle. Seth watches my fingers with heated eyes. I let out a whimper as his hands close around my ankles. His touch is scalding and makes me want so much more.

"Can you use both hands, princess?" His gaze lifts to mine for a second.

I nod and slide my other hand between my legs, slipping one finger inside me while still circling my clit with the other hand. I moan at the hungry look in his eyes.

My gaze shifts to Blake and his intense gaze lingers on my pussy, watching me stroke in and out. Oh, god, I want his cock sliding in and out. The thickness dragging along my sensitive insides.

"Add another finger to your greedy pussy." Seth's words draw me back to him.

I pump two fingers in and out while winding myself up by circling my clit. My breath comes out in pants.

"Do you want to come, princess?"

"Yes, sir." My tone is breathless, and I don't know if I can hold back much longer.

"Not yet."

Groaning, I try to slow my fingers a little.

"Add a third."

I do as he says, stretching myself as I pump in and out while these two men devour me with their eyes. It's almost too much. I can feel the quivers chasing my fingers with each stroke.

Blake clears his throat. "It's almost time, Seth."

Seth's lips twitch into that almost smile. His gaze lifts to mine.

"Finish, princess." His fingers tighten on my ankles. "Come like it's my cock spreading you wide while my finger teases your clit. Come while Blake watches you take it, knowing he wants to be next to fill your hungry pussy with his cock."

"Seth." His name bursts from my lips as his words tip me over the edge, spiraling out of control and gushing for him. My fingers still as my core clenches around them. My shoulders shake from the adrenaline.

"Good girl." Seth strokes his hands up my calf. He nods to his bathroom. "Go get cleaned up and dressed so you can do your job."

I slide my fingers from my core and lower my feet to the ground to stand between Seth's legs. He takes my hand and holds my gaze captive as he sucks each one of my fingers into his mouth, causing an aftershock to rake through me.

He backs away and gestures. I gather my things and glance up at Blake once. His darkened green eyes hungrily take in every inch of me. At least now I know he wants me, even if he doesn't want to want me.

After I put myself back together and clean up, I follow Blake out to the elevator. We ride down to the ground floor and meet a guy around my age. He's cute and gives me a wicked smile.

"You're new," he says as he loads the groceries into the elevator.

"This is Madison. She'll be taking deliveries from now on." Blake leans against the back of the elevator, doing something on his phone.

"Nice." He flashes me a flirty smile. "I'm Fox."

I give him a tentative smile. I don't want to encourage him to flirt with me, especially after the situation with Hunter. My gaze flicks to Blake. I want his approval so badly. Even after coming on Seth's desk in front of him, I'm not sure he's really that into me. I mean, I was basically free porn. What guy doesn't like free porn?

Fox finishes loading the elevator and gets in. "So, did you just start?"

He seems undeterred by the brick statue in the corner of the elevator with his arms crossed over his chest.

"Today's my first day." I blush a little. Fuck, today is my first day and already Noah's gotten me off. I gave Noah head. I masturbated for Seth and Blake. And Cooper kissed down my neck, turning me on while waiting for coffee. Somehow, I don't think things are going to slow down from here.

I kind of hope they don't.

"This has been my route for a while. I've got the hang of it now. Right, Mr. Wagner?" Fox's brown eyes turn to Blake. His grin is huge.

Blake grunts, which seems like approval.

Fox beams and leans toward me conspiratorially. "That's the most I've gotten out of the guy. He's a hard nut to crack."

I give Fox a little chuckle before I glance at Blake. His green eyes are on me once again, like he can't figure me out. Honestly, I'm an open book. I'm happy to work hard and play hard. And more than happy to do both things with them.

We reach the apartment floor, and Blake gestures to me to open the door. I slide my access card. For a brief second, I worry it won't work, but it unlocks. Breathing out in relief, I hold open the door for Fox and Blake to carry in the groceries.

When they finish, Blake grabs the door from me, and I meet his eyes.

"Take Fox back down and come put the groceries away."

I nod, and Fox follows me into the elevator. When the elevator starts down, he glances over at me.

"You're younger than the others were." He tugs on the hair that covers his eyes.

"Oh?" The others. The ones that didn't work out? What did they do wrong and how do I avoid doing that?

"Yeah, they were just as hot, but older than us by a few years, you know?" He leans against the elevator wall like he's trying to be as cool as Blake. Fox isn't unattractive, but he's not like my new bosses. They are gorgeous and exude confidence and power.

"I didn't know any of them," I say, waiting for the elevator to reach the ground floor.

"You know, if you want, I can—" The elevator doors slide open.

"Nice to meet you, Fox." I hold the side of the elevator, trying to discourage him from asking me out or continuing that train of thought.

"See you next week, Madison." He waves to me with a wink.

I wave as the doors close and sag back against the wall. It's been a long day, and these heels are still killing me. When the doors open on the apartment floor, I let myself in. I walk into the kitchen and Blake has all the groceries unpacked on the counter.

I slide my heels off before joining him. He just saw me play with my bare pussy. He can deal with me in no shoes.

"Okay." I smile and stop beside him. "What's not obvious about putting away groceries?"

"Not much." Blake shrugs. "You just need to learn our way of organizing."

We start with the refrigerated items and what goes in which drawer or what shelf and why. Noah likes his apples cold, while Seth prefers his in the bowl on the counter. The freezer is organized and so are the cabinets.

"I'm never going to remember all this." I slide in the last box of pasta.

"It'll become second nature soon." Blake washes his hands in the sink and dries them on a towel.

I follow suit and dry my hands. He glances at the time on his phone.

"You have ten minutes before you need to work with Hope." Blake doesn't move from beside me.

He's warm and so big compared to any other man I've been around. I don't fight the urge to stay close to him. Isn't that the point of this arrangement?

"Hope's number is on my desk," I mention, but make no move to head to the elevator. I'm still not sure he wants me. I don't know if he will be part of this whole thing. But I want him.

Heaven help me, but I want all of them.

"We should head upstairs." Blake finally breaks the fragile bond between us, moving toward the door. I follow him to the elevator and up to our offices. When the elevator doors open, his hand returns to the small of my back to lead me, which settles the turmoil a little for me.

At my desk, he pauses for a second. When I tilt my face up to his, his green eyes capture mine.

"You did well today."

My insides warm from the praise. I'll do anything he wants for more of that.

Chapter 11

Drinks

Madison

"Hi again." Hope's wide blue eyes and friendly smile make my shoulders sag in relief. She joins me in the elevator. "I don't get to come up here often."

"Hi." With our heels, I'm about five inches taller than Hope's petite stature.

She grins up at me and fidgets with her hands. "They usually get women who are snarky and barely tolerate me, but you seem nicer." She peers into my eyes like she can see into my brain if she stares hard enough. "You are nice, right?"

I chuckle lightly. "I hope so. Sorry, I've been around men all morning and almost forgot what it's like to talk with another woman."

"And what men they are." Hope's eyebrows lift. "If they weren't so intimidating, I would have put in for a transfer when the job opened up again. But I'm pretty sure I'd cry before the end of day one working directly for them."

"They aren't that bad," I automatically defend them. I've enjoyed working with them, among other things. Heat stains my cheeks.

She smiles. "I know. I'm just a crier, and I don't think they'd appreciate it. So, where did you come from?"

"Fletcher University. I just graduated with my MBA."

Hope's eyes appear even bigger, as if that could actually happen. "Right out of college? Wow, they *are* going a different route this time."

"How long have you worked here?" I ask as we step off the elevator. All the doors are shut, and it feels like my own office. Someone even dragged another chair over beside mine behind the desk. I smile at the thoughtfulness.

"A few years." She glances at the doors. "The women they usually hire for their assistant are polished to a gleam, with sharp claws and even sharper words. I could tell you were different when Blake brought you by."

Huh, maybe they craved something different because I'm definitely not polished or mean.

"Well, good. I hope I am." I sit in my chair and wake up my computer. "Where should we start?"

We spend an hour going through basic queries and reports on the system.

"I'm not sure how late Mr. Wagner wants us to work tonight." Hope glances at her phone and then at the closed doors. "I mean, it's your first day. You're probably exhausted."

"No one told me how late I should work." I worry my bottom lip with my teeth. I don't want to overstay or leave too soon.

"I guess I get to decide." She perks up and smiles. "I think we should call it quits before your brain explodes with knowledge. We can start again fresh tomorrow morning."

Hope stands and gestures for me to get up. I glance at the doors. I'm not sure who I should tell, but I should check to see if they want me for more.

"I should—"

"Come with me to get a drink?" Hope's never-ending smile

spreads wider. "Why, I thought you'd never ask. If we don't leave now, you might be here all night. And no one wants that."

She tugs my arm, but part of me does want that. To be with them all night. I just had a taste of what could be between us, and I want so much more. If I stay here, maybe that could happen. After hours.

But I also want a friend, and here is Hope trying to be a friend to me. I have one chance at a first impression with Hope and many days and nights to spend getting to know the guys. Decision made, I smile and grab my purse. "Just one minute, okay?"

She shakes her head but holds up one finger.

I go to Seth's door and knock on it. I wait until I hear "Come in" before I open the door. Seth looks up from his desk and I blush, remembering sitting right there in front of him. His eyebrow cocks and that corner of his lips tries to lift again, like he knows exactly what I'm thinking.

"I was going to head out with Hope for the night." I gesture lamely over my shoulder.

"How was your first day?" He leans back in his chair. "Does it seem like a good fit?"

My pulse races. "Yes, I think I'll really enjoy working here."

"Good. Have a good night. We'll see you in the morning." Seth's gaze returns to his computer screen.

"Good night." I pull the door shut behind me and turn to meet Hope. We ride the elevator down, and I start toward the bar in the lobby.

Hope grabs my arm and shakes her head. "Oh, no, the mean girls hang out there after work. I know this bar next door that has much nicer people in it."

I shrug and follow her. I notice the woman from earlier who sneered at me on the tour heading into that bar. She definitely didn't give me friendly vibes.

The bar Hope brings me to is light and bright, with pretty fairy lights surrounding the liquor on the shelves. The bartender greets Hope by name. He's a large guy, probably the same size as Blake, but with tattoos covering his arms and what I can see of his chest. He has blue eyes similar to Hope's, but his head is shaved bald.

Hope orders us two daiquiris from the bartender. "Thanks, Jason."

"So, how was your first day?" Hope turns on her barstool toward me.

"It was good. There's definitely going to be a learning curve, but I think I'll be able to hack it."

The bartender sets our drinks in front of us and gives Hope a wink.

"What's your story?" Hope asks innocently and sips her drink.

"Story?"

"Where are you from and how did you wind up here?" She sits back and stares intently at me.

"I grew up in a rural community in the Midwest. My parents have a farm. We raised cows and pigs and grew corn and alfalfa. I did well in school, so I got a scholarship to Fletcher University and spent the last four years of my life grinding through coursework and internships so that I could wind up here at Morrigan Technology Group."

She nods. "That's a pretty straight life."

I give her a small smile. "Left little room to color outside the lines."

It's what draws me to these four men and what they can do to me. I've never been as turned on in my life as they made me today. I want to experience it all, and I hope they end up feeling the same.

They could always decide this won't work for them. Then I'll have to tame myself enough to act like I don't want them every day I work for them. Day in and day out. And at night go home with them and maybe see them bring home other women who will suit their fantasies better.

I definitely don't want that. I drink my daiquiri.

"What about you?" I ask Hope.

She smiles. "I'm a pretty straight case too. Though I grew up here. My brother owns a bar near where I work, so that makes life good."

"Jason is your brother?" I glance at the huge guy and at her petite stature.

"I took after Mom, and he took after Dad." She shrugs. "It's nice to have family close by and no one bothers me here. I've been working at MTG for years now. But the bosses know I'm a hard worker, so they give me extra assignments from time to time."

"So you know about their past assistants?" The daiquiri loosens my lips. My curiosity gets the better of me. I want to know about these other women that either gave up on these men or weren't a good fit.

She laughs. "Okay, the last one was Tiffany. She wore sky-high heels and short little skirts and cared more about her nails than she did getting them the reports on time. I'm pretty sure she was a temp, and they fired the agency after letting her go."

"What about before her?" I sip the last bit of daiquiri through my straw.

"That would be Rachel." She nods. "Rachel seemed nice at first. She worked hard and actually got the guys what they needed."

"What happened with her?" My heart speeds up.

"She gave her two-week notice suddenly and after a week just left, ergo Tiffany the temp." Hope waves her hand in front of her. "There was nothing wrong with Rachel. She did her job and kept her head down, but I don't think she was happy about the live-in arrangement."

"You know about that?" Does everyone know? Is that why the receptionist gave me the cold shoulder and the other women didn't even smile at me? Are they jealous? Do they have cause to be jealous?

"It's a big deal to get your own apartment in the building." Hope nods. "It means they can have you on call night and day, but really, the bosses seem like reasonable men. Have you seen the apartment?"

I swallow and nod. When I saw that enormous bed, I'd fantasized about having them all in it, but maybe that's the plan. All of us. Together. In one bed.

My face heats. I try to drink more daiquiri to cool me down, but I'm out. How many other women have they had on that bed, though?

"I've heard it's like a nice two-room apartment. Everyone is always super jealous of the bosses' assistant since she gets the apartment for free, but I don't know if it's worth the extra hours." Hope raises her hand to her brother for two more. "They'll be able to ask you to work late and on the weekend. I enjoy having nights and weekends free."

Okay, it doesn't seem like the rest of the office knows about the arrangement with the guys. They did have me sign an NDA before even mentioning it, so maybe no one can talk about it.

"Andrea was a bitch." Hope takes the fresh daiquiri and pushes the other to me. "She was a few before Rachel, and she lorded it over everyone in the company like she was a fucking queen because she was their assistant."

My throat swells. She's the one they did everything with. Maybe my first day was exactly like hers. With Noah. My heart squeezes.

"I don't think they liked her very much though, because security escorted her from the building like an embezzler when she got fired." Hope reaches out a hand and puts it over mine. "I'm sure you'll do better. You picked up the system super quick."

I return her smile. "If all these women were bitches to you, why did you invite me out?"

She taps the side of her head. "Because I know brains when I see them, and you've got them. Besides, you're too young to be jaded yet."

"I could be jaded. I'm not, but I could be."

Hope and I laugh together. We get to talking about TV and movies, which is basically Hope telling me all the shows I ought to watch or that I'm missing out on. When the daiquiris are done, we switch to water and keep talking.

We talk a little bit about dating. Hope has an online dating profile. She always meets guys at this bar. If they are too much, she introduces them to her brother and never hears from them again.

Having an older brother sounds amazing. I had to rely on myself for protection from guys who wanted to fuck me in college. No big brother to help out, just me. There were some guys who got clingy, but I couldn't have that. Getting my MBA in a year made dating steadily impossible.

I'm lucky I made it through the last year without losing my mind. Remembering Noah's touch makes a shiver race through me. It's been way too long.

"You should come with me to the next speed dating thing." Hope grabs my arm and shakes it excitedly.

"I don't think so." At least, not until I know whether the guys and I are moving forward with their plan or not. I don't think dating outside will be allowed given the questions about boyfriends and Blake's question about Robert. But maybe that's just for me?

If it only applies to me, I might have to ask for no outside dating. Because even if this is just sex, I don't think I could watch one of them get ready for a date and wait up at home like a creeper to see if he sleeps with her.

For Hope though, I say, "Maybe once I get settled in my new job."

Because if this doesn't work out, it might be fun to hang out with Hope while meeting potential guys. My insides twist. I don't want to think about this not working out.

"Good call." Hope nods. "That first blush of lust can really divert a girl from everything, and you need this job because you have to stay here and be friends with me."

I smile. She listened when I told her a little about being a poor college student to explain why I didn't have a TV or go to movies. I didn't mention I was basically a social recluse. I want to be her friend. Maybe we can go see some movies together.

I glance at my phone and notice the time. "It's late. I should get home. I need to start early tomorrow to run all the reports."

"Okay, oh, maybe we can have lunch sometime this week." Hope gestures to her brother. I figure she's going to pay the tab and start getting out money. She shoves my hand back in my purse. "Please. This is my brother's bar. I get my drinks for free."

Jason stops and gives me a once-over. I see interest light in his eyes.

"Nope." Hope shakes her head. "Hands off. This one is going to be my friend. You can't screw my friend."

He winks at me and shrugs.

"I'm not sure about lunch," I say as we head out onto the street. A car pulls up, and I move out of the way, expecting someone to come out and get in it.

"It's okay," she says. "We can get drinks after work again some night."

The back door of the black car opens and Noah steps out. "Come on, ladies. Your chariot awaits."

My eyes widen. "What?"

"Your car." Hope shakes her head and drags me forward. "I called because I figured you'd forget. One of your perks is not having to ride the subway, and an unexpected side perk of being your friend is Noah said I can get a ride home too. Thanks, Noah."

He smiles at her as she ducks into the backseat and slides over. I meet his dark brown eyes. "Come on, kitten. Enjoy the high life."

He takes my hand and helps me into the car before he shuts the door and climbs into the passenger seat. After Hope gives her address, I give mine.

The car stops at Hope's apartment building. She hugs me. I'm not sure what to do, so I pat her awkwardly on her back.

"I'm an affectionate drunk. Just go with it," she says.

Noah gets out and opens her door for her. She climbs out and waves before ducking into her apartment building.

He slides into the back with me and those tingles from earlier ripple through me. A partition comes up between us and the driver.

Noah moves closer and I can make out his intent in the flickering streetlights.

I smile as his head lowers and his mouth claims mine. He's the only one who has kissed me so far. It's like fireworks burst inside me. Our tongues tangle and caress. We make out for the ten minutes it takes to get to my apartment building.

When the car comes to a stop, Noah lifts his head with a sigh. Our breath shudders in and out like we ran the entire way here. My panties are damp, and I'm tempted to invite him upstairs to finish what he started.

His thumb traces my cheekbone. "I'd ask to come up, but it's too soon."

I open my mouth to protest, but I also know my apartment isn't anything like what he's used to. He kisses me briefly and then gets out. Leaning down, he reaches his hand in to help me out.

"The car will be here for you tomorrow at seven," he says.

"Okay, thank you."

He kisses me again and then walks me to my door. "I'll see you in the morning."

Smiling, I let myself in. My feet feel like they barely touch the ground. I turn and he's still standing there, a frown between his eyebrows as he takes in my apartment building. It isn't much, but the doors lock.

It's hopefully only for two more weeks.

When his eyes meet mine, he smiles and waves before returning to the car. I sigh as I climb the stairs.

My lips still buzz from him and that taste of mint. I want more. I know I need to be patient, but today was amazing.

Robert's door opens as I pass. My shoulders tighten.

"Hey, Madison." He steps out behind me.

"Hi, Robert. It's late and I have an early start tomorrow." I don't even turn back as I approach my door. There's a paper on it. I stare at it, not comprehending.

"The landlord stopped by earlier. I told him it must be a mistake."

Eviction Notice is stamped across the top in huge letters. Removing it, I read down the paper. Nonpayment of rent. What? I paid the rent this month.

"It's a mistake." The words fall from my lips.

"You can go to the office tomorrow morning. I told him you would be able to figure this out." Robert beams at me.

This can't be right.

"Good night." I unlock my door, still in shock.

"Hey, if you can't fix it, you can live with me. I've got a great couch. Do you want to come see it?" Robert starts toward his apartment, gesturing for me to follow him.

"Not tonight, Robert." A slice of anxiety winds through me.

He keeps asking me over and I keep saying no. I want to think he's harmless, but I know he's more powerful than me.

I slip inside my apartment and lock the door. My eyes go to my roommate's bedroom. I haven't seen or heard from her in over a week. If she didn't pay... fuck. I could barely afford my half of the rent this month.

The apartment office opens early. I should be able to take care of it before going to work.

Eviction? Shit.

Chapter 12

Rent Problems

Madison

"You only paid half the rent." The office girl looks me over like I'm beneath her.

I'm dressed just as nicely today but went for kitten heels over my killer heels to give my feet a rest. I lean in and ask, "How much is it short?"

"A thousand fifty." Her eyes roll and she shrugs. "If you want to stay, you have to pay that plus one hundred dollars for the late fee."

Fuck. That is almost all my remaining bonus. I tighten my lips. I have to live somewhere. "Fine."

I pull out my checkbook.

She holds up her hand. Her fingernails are an inch longer than her fingers and painted hot pink. "You'll need either a cashier's check or bank transfer."

Fuckity fuck. I don't have time to go to the bank with my new job. I shove my checkbook back into my purse and release my breath. "How about Venmo?"

"Oh, sure." She slips me a card with the apartment building

information on it. "Just note it's for late rent and not prepayment for next month."

Nodding, I stick the card in my purse. I need coffee, and a lot of it. My roommate Valerie was a Craigslist find. It's worked for years because she needs a place for her stuff and somewhere to crash when her boyfriend breaks up with her for a week every few months. Normally, I don't have to worry about her.

I texted her last night but didn't get an answer. I shake my head and walk outside to wait for the car. It's early, but traffic is picking up, and I can hear honking from a block over. Usually at this point, I'd head to campus to work in the library before my first class of the day.

Not having homework feels odd, but I've been getting used to it since graduation.

The car stops. It's the same driver from last night, but only him.

"Is it okay if I sit up front?" I don't know the protocol for these things.

He nods, and I slide into the front seat and strap on my seat belt. We head to the office in silence. It's slightly awkward, riding with someone I don't know.

"Um, I'm Madison. Can I know your name?"

The driver tilts his head my way. He's dressed in all black, and his short brown hair is under a cap. He's got a little extra weight on him, but I wouldn't call him chubby.

"Tim." His voice is gruff and doesn't really encourage further conversation.

"Nice to meet you, Tim." I know he's just doing his job, but it doesn't kill me to be nice. "Have you been doing this job long?"

"Five years."

Huh. I wonder if he's picked up the other women. Maybe he knows Andrea, Rachel, and Tiffany. Maybe not Tiffany. They wouldn't send a car for a temp, right?

Hopefully, I can say that I've been working here for five years at some point. I'm just hoping to make it past this week. I pull out my phone and send money via Venmo to the property management firm for the rent.

I have to live there at least another two weeks, then either I'll be moving into the corporate apartment or packing my things and going to my parents'. I won't be able to pay back the money the guys gave me as a signing bonus, though. It would take longer than a week or two now to pay them back and still be able to survive.

I check my texts to see if Valerie answered me, but there's nothing. It took me a while to fall asleep last night, worrying about everything.

When I close my eyes for a few seconds, the car stops. I open my eyes to see the building before me.

"Thank you, Tim." I grab my purse and head into work.

I bypass the apartment floor and the elevator opens to the offices. The doors are all closed. I set my purse on my desk and head for the break room to start the coffee. While I wait, I unload the dishwasher.

I grab a cup of coffee and head to my desk, where I follow the instructions to run and email reports. I check through each of the guys' schedules and make notes of where I have to be and when in my schedule.

Then I instant message Hope to let me know when she's ready to keep training me on the computer system. The floor is still quiet. I don't know if they are in or haven't even come up to work yet. I spin in my chair and study the doors to see if I can tell.

When the elevator dings, I turn back in my chair. Cooper comes out with a smile on his face and his black hair tied in a bun.

"Good morning, sweetheart," he practically purrs. He stops at my desk. "Did you sleep well?"

Not really. "Yes."

I've never been evicted before. I didn't know if someone would just show up to throw me out. Paying the extra thousand for the month is still cheaper than going to a hotel, and better for my credit.

"I had the sweetest dream."

I meet his dancing, light blue eyes. I can't help the smile that cracks my face. "Oh, yeah?"

He circles my desk and squats in front of me. His fingers toy with the hem of my skirt. "You were in it. Tied to my bed, spread wide, knees bent, while I licked and tongue fucked your pussy until you came all over my face, and I kept doing it over and over again until you begged me to fuck you."

His eyes lift to meet mine, and I suck in a breath. He's temptation personified.

"When are we going to have sleepovers, sweetheart?" His fingers trail over my knee.

"Two weeks?" My breath is quick. I don't want to wait that long, but those are the parameters of our arrangement.

He takes my hand and brings my knuckles to his lips. "Maybe we'll take a personal lunch sometime."

I've seen his schedule. Smiling ruefully, I shake my head.

"Coffee break?" He looks hopeful, but then his face falls. "Not enough time. Damn, why did I waste my hour yesterday?"

Sighing, he releases my hand. "Guess I'll settle for coffee to get me up this morning."

He winks at me as he heads down the hallway. I take a deep breath to stop the quivering inside me. Potent men.

HOPE:

Here now.

ME:

I'll come get you.

Cooper comes back around with his coffee. His eyes are hot on me and they make me a mess inside.

ME:

Maybe I'll come down there this morning.

HOPE:

Sure. I'll pull over a chair.

I grab my notepad and realize I didn't put my notes in last night. I'll do it when I find time. *If* I find time. The schedule today is full.

I open an instant message to all the bosses.

ME:

Heading down to work with Hope. Anyone need anything?

Cooper comes back out with a phone in his hand. I raise my gaze to his.

"This is yours. It's all set up and has all the company information in it. It also links to instant messenger, so you don't have to worry about missing something from us." He holds out the phone.

I rise and take it. "Thank you."

My conversation with Hope is on it, as well as the group conversation I started.

"We want access to you, Madison." His knuckles trace my jawline. "As much as we can have. The sooner the better."

Heat fills my cheeks. Nodding, I head down to Hope's desk. I pass by the mean girls from yesterday. I still give them a smile because I will not stoop to their level. The brunette sneers at me again, but I just keep going until I reach Hope. Her eyes follow me the whole way. I'm tempted to turn back and look at the brunette to let her know I'm aware of her animosity. But I resist.

"Good morning!" Hope practically buzzes with energy. She pats the chair next to her. "We need to get you trained up so I don't waste any more of your time."

"You couldn't waste my time, Hope." I smile at her and nod to the computer. "Let's do this."

I glance up to find the brunette still watching me with an almost calculating gaze. Yeah, that one is not going to be my friend. But that's okay. I settle in beside Hope, and she grins before opening the program. I'll start with one friend and see where I can go from there.

The week flies by in a whirlwind of meetings and notes and learning what to do. The guys seem to take a step back from coming onto me. While I miss it, I definitely learn more this way.

My landlord is happy to get his rent and removes the eviction notice. He didn't actually file it before I paid the rent. I'm pinching pennies to make it to my first paycheck, but that's nothing new.

By Friday, I've found a rhythm to mornings and move through the beginning of the day effortlessly as I continue to learn more about the system and our company. Ours. I'm part of something bigger now and it makes me feel complete inside.

Noah is still the only one who has kissed me or touched me sexually. This is what I expected, but I feel a tightness in my chest and stomach like I've done something wrong. That I'm not what they want. That they appreciate my quick mind for administrative duties, but I'm not fuckable.

Lunch is on the schedule again. It's another meeting with William and Hunter Adams. I'm not looking forward to it, but I won't let him get me anywhere alone with him again. This one is in the main conference room, so it's on our turf.

Blake watches me from his doorway as I stride across the office to prepare the conference room for lunch. I'm setting up the smart board when the door closes behind me. I turn and hold my hand over my pounding heart.

Blake stands inside the door. "Are you anxious?"

I bite my lip and continue to fiddle with the smart board.

"I don't want to find myself alone with Hunter again," I mumble. It's best to get the truth out there.

"Why?" Blake steps closer to me, and my skin buzzes like an electric current runs between us.

"It's complicated." Blowing out a breath, I shake my head. I should tell him the truth, but how can I? I don't want Hunter to make sexual advances toward me. Even though I don't encourage him, he won't stop. If asked, Hunter will just say I'm a tease.

Blake nods thoughtfully and sits in the chair next to where I'm leaning over the table. His spicy cologne fills my lungs, making my insides soften at his closeness. Of everyone, he's been the most distant. Besides that day in Seth's office, he hasn't indicated he wants this to be more than what it is currently.

"You've had a week. What do you think about us?" Blake's hands are on the table, his long fingers splayed out.

I straighten and look down at him, concerned about the change in topic. He caught Hunter and me in what had to look like a compromising situation. But if he wants to let it drop, I'm more than happy to oblige.

"I'm learning more every day. The work is enjoyable and I'm getting to know you guys better." I'm spending my nights fantasizing about them all, but I'm not getting any play at work, which makes sense. I bend to connect the last cable to the ports in the center of the conference table.

His hand slips up the back of my thigh. I startle from his touch, but relax into the heat flowing from his fingertips into me. My flowing dress gives him all sorts of access. My pussy pulses. As he traces the edges of my panties, I get wetter.

He doesn't want me, right?

"Do you wish we would do more, like on Monday? Giving head to Noah. Getting naked for Seth. Fucking yourself for us." His deep voice sends shivers down my spine. His words make my pussy clench against the emptiness. My head drops to the table.

He stands behind me and lifts my skirt over my waist. "What did you think when you first met us?"

I press my hands against the table and whimper as his hand trails over my panties between my thighs. "I wanted you all to fuck me on this conference table."

"All of us, tiger?" he asks as he thrusts his hips against mine. His hard cock presses against my pussy, making me need more.

"All of you. I imagined me spread out over this table while each of you touched me and fucked me." I squeeze my eyes shut as his fingers slip under my panties and slide over my clit. I gasp at his touch.

He kicks his foot between my feet and makes me spread my legs wider. I lower my chest on the conference table, willing to let him do whatever he wants with me.

"So fucking wet for me, tiger."

"Yes." I'm not ashamed. I want him. I want them all. It would be humiliating to admit that and have them decide not to follow through, but this I have to be honest about.

He thrusts his long fingers into my core as he wraps his arm around my waist, holding me. Shivers race down my spine as heat licks through me. His thick fingers stretch me, but they don't go as deep as a cock would. His hips and the huge bulge in his pants nudge against me as his fingers fuck in and out of me, winding me up tight inside. I bite my lip to stop my moan.

"Do you want us all to fuck you today, tiger?"

My mind is a blur of desire as he winds me up. "Please."

I need release. I need what he can give me.

"Do you want our cocks to fill your body? Your pussy, your ass, your hands, and your mouth?"

The images his words conjure, along with his touch, make me come. I cry out as my body explodes. My pussy clutches at his fingers buried deep inside me. I want that. I need that.

He leans over me until his lips touch the back of my ear. He pinches my clit, sending a burst of aftershocks through my pussy. I gasp in precious air.

"Remember, tiger, you're ours. Don't let anyone else touch what's ours or I'll punish you."

He flicks my clit, and I spasm and moan, on the verge of coming all over again.

"I won't." It's a promise I intend to keep. I don't want anyone else touching me.

He withdraws his fingers from me and the sound of him sucking on them makes my pussy ache for more. I take a few deep breaths to return to normal. His hands fix my skirt. He tugs me upright, my back against his front.

"Maybe your fantasy will come true, tiger."

My fantasy can be my reward for making it through this meeting with Hunter.

Chapter 13

FML

Madison

William steps off the elevator and smiles at me. "You look so grown up, Madison."

I take his offered hand, and instead of shaking mine, he squeezes it between his own. "You let me know if these guys mistreat you. You always have a place at Taylor's."

"Thank you." I smile into his blue eyes. "You've always been so kind."

He releases my hand and steps to the side as Hunter approaches. I feel a quiver of fear race through me but brush it away. He can't get me alone here.

Hunter smiles wickedly, like he can read my mind and likes the fact I'm a little afraid of him. He reaches out his hand, and I can't refuse to shake it without starting something in front of William. So I force a smile and take his hand.

He lifts my hand to his lips and kisses it before I can snatch it away. "Lovely to see you, Maddy."

I've told him so many times my name is Madison that I don't even bother this time. I rub the back of my hand against my skirt while gesturing with the other to the conference room. "If you would follow me, the others will be out in a few minutes. I can get you some coffee while you wait."

The conference room is all set up for lunch and the presentation. I've sat in on a few meetings about this presentation to bring me up to speed on the products and services our company offers.

"Some coffee would be wonderful," William says as he and Hunter sit.

"I'll be right back." I inhale deeply when I leave the conference room. This is going to be a test of my willpower. I make sure Hunter hasn't followed me before disappearing down the hall to the break room.

When I return with the coffee, the guys have all joined William and Hunter. I pass out the cups and then take my seat beside Cooper to take notes on the tablet he showed me how to use this morning.

Seth glances my way to make sure I'm ready. When I nod, the meeting starts. Blake gives the presentation, discussing all the things they would need to do to make sure Taylor's network is secure and their data safe. Then he gives the breakdown of how we would go about implementing the system.

"These teams," Hunter interrupts, "they'd have to come out to our offices and do work, correct?"

Blake's face remains impassive as he studies Hunter for a moment before answering. "Yes."

Hunter smiles like the prick he is and almost puts his hands together like an evil villain when he says, "I hope Maddy will be on that team. It would be good to have her in our offices again."

My stomach clenches violently, and I almost feel ill at the clear amusement on Hunter's face.

"Yes, that's a great idea, Hunter." William practically beams at everyone. "Madison is an asset to any team. I'm sure in a few weeks she'll be all caught up to speed and able to at least shadow the team."

Blake clears his throat, and I wonder if he is going to say no.

"It's a possibility," Seth says before Blake can say anything.

My heart drops to my stomach, and I can feel the color drain from my face. There are too many opportunities to get me alone in that office, and Hunter would definitely be on me the entire time. I got lucky last time when someone interrupted him in the copy room. I'm sure he wouldn't allow that to happen if he got another chance.

"We'll see if she has the time," Blake says before continuing with the presentation.

After a few moments, my heart returns to normal and I can breathe a little easier. Cooper stands to take William and Hunter on a brief tour of the facility. Seth and Noah head into their offices while Blake hangs back with me.

I don't want to talk more about Hunter. So I gather up my things and take them to my desk. When I return, Blake comes over to me, so close my breasts brush his chest with my inhale.

"Rule one of being ours is that you are only ours." Blake takes ahold of my chin and tips my face toward his.

I don't fight him. I don't want to. His hands on me feel way too good. And I can't help but wonder how he'll taste. I don't want to be anyone else's.

"Do you understand?" He raises an eyebrow, and I focus on his impossibly green eyes.

I lick my suddenly dry lips. "Yes, sir."

His face softens, but he doesn't smile. His thumb rubs across my lower lip. "Do you want to be ours, tiger?"

A wave of desire floods my system. I touch the tip of his thumb with my tongue. His eyes darken. "Yes."

He nods and backs away, leaving me there alone with a fire raging through me. My panties are damp, and I want to beg him to finish what he started earlier. Bend me over the table again and this time, fuck me. Hard.

I try to shake the lust off as I grab the coffee mugs and head into the break room.

"So this is where you hide." Hunter's voice behind me makes me drop the coffee cup in my hand onto the tile. It shatters into a million pieces just like my nerves.

I spin and hold my hands out to ward him off. Hunter smiles at me like I'm prey and he has me cornered once again. Why does this keep happening? Where are Cooper and William?

He's blocking the escape route.

"You shouldn't be back here, Hunter." I keep my tone firm and loud, hoping someone is nearby. Praying for someone to save me.

"You shouldn't be working here, little bird." He reaches out, grabs my hand, and yanks me toward him.

I stumble but duck to get away from him. Hunter chuckles like this is a game. I can't call out for help. Blake would assume that I want this. That I want Hunter. Hunter would make it sound like I came on to him and then cried for help because I like to be caught. The fucker.

"Let go of my hand." I try to maintain a calm tone, but the edge of panic is there. Cooper can't be far, right?

Grinning maniacally, he tries to reel me in, but I keep my arm braced and pull to get away. "Come on, Maddy. This game is fun. I love a good chase, but you know you want me."

"No, I don't, Hunter. I never have. Please, just leave me alone." Fuck, I'm not stronger than he is. My heart is pounding in my chest so hard I'm afraid it will burst out. Sweat rolls down my back and my arm trembles. I'm losing this battle.

Hunter's smile isn't soothing. It's wicked and deceitful. "I'll let you go for now, little bird. If you give me something."

I feel the wall against my back before I realize he's trapped me once again. The arm that held him away collapses as he pushes into me. My other hand goes to his chest to stop him, but I'm not strong enough. I turn my head to the side and press against his chest in a futile attempt to keep him away.

"Kiss me, Maddy. If you hate me so much, kiss me so I know there's nothing here." His tone is coaxing. His other hand reaches out and fists in my hair. Tight.

I bite down on my lip to keep from crying out. He's close enough I could knee him in the junk, but that would only make him angrier next time. And the lies he would weave… a lover's quarrel, no doubt.

"I'm not kissing you," I hiss, low. "I'm not doing anything with you. We are not a thing. We will never be a thing. Leave me alone before you get me fired."

His eyes light up. "Maybe I want to get you fired."

Fuck, why did I say that? "I'll never come to work for Taylor's while you work there."

His smile drops and his fist tightens in my hair, making my lips part on a gasp of pain. "Now why do you have to be that way, Maddy? After everything I've done for you."

"You've done nothing for me except harass me from day one," I bite out.

Footsteps ring out behind Hunter, and his grin grows. I struggle to get away from him.

"Let me go," I grind out.

He leans in to my ear and whispers, "Never."

He releases me. I stumble away, cowering from him. Hunter walks across the room as Cooper appears.

"Sorry, got lost," Hunter says.

Cooper's blue eyes bounce between the two of us. Straightening, I can still feel the heat of anger in my cheeks. I resist the urge to reach up and rub at my abused scalp.

When Cooper's gaze narrows on me, I give him a weak smile to placate him. His eyes cut back to Hunter. The smile he gives Hunter doesn't reach his eyes.

"As you can see, there's only one way out." Cooper gestures.

Hunter pins me with a glare before he struts out into the hallway. Cooper's eyes soften as he looks at me. His gaze drops to the broken cup on the floor, and he frowns.

"Sorry, it fell." I take a deep breath and force a smile again. What am I supposed to do? I could tell him what Hunter tried to do. Would they believe me? I took their offer for sex with four guys with no misgivings. Would they ask Hunter and believe whatever bullshit he spewed? Or would they worry maybe I cave to any Neanderthal that tries to get into my pants?

That I have no backbone of my own?

I didn't cave to Hunter. I won't. Ever.

Cooper turns and follows Hunter back into the office. I sag against the counter, taking deep breaths. I can't be on that team for Taylor's. In Hunter's territory, he'd find a way to trap me where no one would be around to save me.

He wanted me to kiss him, but it wouldn't prove anything. Even if I remained passive while he kissed me, I don't think it would matter to him. He'd claim I want him, that I just won't give in. I shudder.

Tears prick at the back of my eyes, but I refuse to cry. Blowing out a breath, I clean up the broken cup, taking my time finishing the rest of the chores in the break room before returning to my desk.

By the time I reemerge, Hunter and William are gone. Thankfully.

I go back into the conference room to clean everything up. The door shuts and I jump. My heart in my throat, I turn to confront whoever it is.

Cooper stands there with his hands up. "It's just me."

The tension seeps out of me, and I collapse into a chair. He walks over to the chair beside me and sits with his elbows on his knees and his hands clasped between them.

"Are you okay?" His tone is gentle.

I take a deep breath and exhale. "Yes, you just startled me."

His lips press together as his eyes meet mine. "That's not what I'm talking about."

I cross my legs and hold my hands in my lap. Fucking hell.

"What happened in the break room, Madison?"

"Nothing," I blurt. While I don't want them to think I'm a slut, I don't want to be a victim in their eyes, either.

He sits up and puts a hand on the table. "This whole situation between us is about trust. It goes both ways, sweetheart."

I take a breath and meet his eyes. "I don't want Hunter Adams. But he's persistent."

Cooper nods. "Is this the first time he's tried to get you alone?"

I shake my head, feeling the prick of tears again, but I choke them down.

Standing, he reaches down to take my hands. When he draws me up, he pulls me into his arms and hugs me. My cheek rests on his heart as his clean, crisp scent envelops me.

"It's been a long week," Cooper murmurs in my hair. "If you need me to step in—"

"No." I shake my head, not releasing my arms from around him, taking solace in his hug. "I can handle it."

I hope. But Hunter is a client, and this is my new job. He caught me unaware twice. I'm going to make sure it doesn't happen again, even if I end up on his turf.

Cooper releases me and steps back. Reluctantly, I let him go. He brushes my hair out of my face and smiles. "This afternoon should be easy. We have our weekly meeting. Then it's the weekend. You can unwind from this crazy place."

I smile, but I can't help feeling a little sad. A weekend where I won't see them for two days. I've gotten used to them being around and touching me in small ways.

He brushes his finger over my lower lip and leaves me standing alone in the conference room. Does he believe me about not wanting Hunter?

They don't know me. But I've given them carte blanche over me without knowing them. What kind of woman do they think I am? My hand touches the conference table where Blake held me down and finger fucked me.

My eyes dart to the door Cooper left through. I don't know if *I* would believe me.

Chapter 14

Weekly Meeting

Cooper

She's hiding something. I can tell she doesn't want to talk about it.

I've seen the way Hunter watches Madison. A lot like we watch her. But his gaze feels more predatory. I don't want to alarm the others, but I'm not sure if some of those advances from Hunter might be wanted. She didn't call out for help, but she seemed frightened.

Was that because of Hunter or the fear of discovery?

Madison said they weren't wanted. For now, I have to trust her, but Andrea made us all a little warier. She used us to get what she wanted and started to try to work us against each other. She dug her red claws deep into Blake and the others, but I always saw that calculating look in her eyes.

You don't grow up wealthy without learning that look. The one that says, *How much can I make you give me?* Madison doesn't have that look. She has a heated look that she gives all of us. I can almost believe she really does just want us and not our money. But the two go hand in hand, so I can never be one hundred percent certain. We're young, attractive, and very wealthy men.

Many women have looked at us like a payday waiting to happen. I hope that's not Madison.

I'm early to the weekly meeting. I sit at one end of the long conference table. Will we actually go through with the "initiation" we planned for today? My dick twitches. Fuck, I hope so. We've all been good boys and kept our hands to ourselves after Monday.

Madison needed to focus on training. As much fun as it was to turn her on, we need a properly trained assistant too. She put her all into learning everything, and it seems like she's getting up to speed quickly.

Speaking of the devil, she strolls in. Her blue eyes immediately find me and she smiles. Not that weak smile from before. I wanted to deck Hunter Adams when I found him with Madison cornered. But our deal with her isn't complete until we have our signed agreement. Until then, Madison is free to do what she wants with who she wants.

I tip back in my chair as she approaches. "You ready for us, sweetheart?"

Her eyes widen, and she bites down on her lip. Fuck if I've ever seen anything sexier. She's like this naughty package wrapped up in an innocent wrapping. I know what she did with Noah, and on Seth's desk for him and Blake.

I've barely gotten any *quality* time with her. But right now, I have her all to myself. I glance at the open door and hold my hand out to her. When she takes it, I pull her in front of my chair.

I meet her eyes. "Take off your panties."

She glances toward the door as she steps out of her heels, but then lifts her skirt to shimmy out of her lacy panties. She didn't wear stockings today, so it's all smooth, bare skin from the waist down.

When I hold out my hand, she hands her panties to me without me needing to say anything. I shove them into my front pocket. Leaning forward, I catch the hem of her skirt and lift it slowly, watching every beautiful inch of skin revealed.

Her breath hitches, and I can feel her thighs tremble beneath my touch.

"Who's kissed you this week, sweetheart?" I pause midway up her thighs to watch her expressive face.

"Just Noah." Her blue eyes darken with desire. She doesn't drop her gaze from mine. Her voice is a little breathless, and her breasts rise and fall with each breath. Her tight nipples press against the fabric of her dress, begging for my touch and my mouth.

I want to savor every inch of her.

"Who's fucked you?" I inch her hem up again.

"No one."

I tsk. "That's a shame."

She lets out a little whimper that makes my dick even harder.

"Who's gotten you off?" I meet her eyes again, tracing my finger over the inside of her thigh.

"Noah, Blake, and Seth, though Seth had me do it myself for him." She bites her lip as I ease her skirt up so I can see her perfect pussy.

I smile. That makes sense. Seth likes to watch as much as he likes to participate. She'll find out soon enough that all of us will like to watch her get fucked. And fuck her while being watched.

"But I haven't?" I arch an eyebrow at her.

She shakes her head.

"Has anyone sucked your pretty clit yet?"

Biting her lip, she shakes her head again. That look in her eyes is hunger, want, desire, all rolled into one.

"Turn around, sweetheart."

When she obeys me, my dick weeps a little. I could stand and fuck her right now, and she'd let me in. She'd cry out my name and milk me fucking dry. Such an obedient pupil.

"Bend over and spread your legs." I stay seated behind her.

She leans over the conference table and rests her chest down on it. She spreads her legs and I get a full view. I drape her skirt over her waist and just look at her wet pussy.

Begging me to touch it. To feed it every inch of my hard length. To make it pulse around me in blissful orgasms.

Her breathing is heavy, and her fingers clutch at the table.

"Do you want me to get you off, sweetheart?" I lightly touch the backs of her thighs and she jerks a little. So fucking sensitive.

"Yes, please." Her words are almost a whisper, but I hear them.

"What do you want me to use?" I stroke my fingers down her thigh. "My fingers? My tongue? Or my cock?"

She whimpers. "Your tongue."

I smirk and breathe her in. The musk of arousal blends with her floral scent into a heady mixture I don't think I'll ever forget. At the first touch of my tongue against her pussy, she sighs.

She's spread wide before me like a veritable buffet, and I want to taste everything being offered. I slide my tongue through her folds and flick it over her clit. When she makes a needy little noise in the back of her throat, I smile.

I focus on the task at hand and suck her clit hard.

"Cooper," she cries out.

If the others weren't already on their way to the meeting, they'll be here shortly. As much as I want to get her off at least once before everyone else gets here, I take my time to explore her folds before thrusting my tongue as deep as I can into her core.

With a whimper of need, she pushes back against my mouth as I suck and thrust and lick. Her breathing ramps up, and her noises get progressively louder until she moans deep and her pussy gushes her release, bathing my mouth in her essence.

Her body sags on the table as I lean back in my chair.

Swiping my shirt sleeve across my mouth, I grin at Seth, Blake, and Noah standing in the doorway. I thrust my finger into her waiting pussy, and she groans low.

"Ready to start the meeting?" I ask.

Seth

Walking into the conference room and seeing Madison come is

my new favorite way to start a meeting. Her heated blue eyes open and see us, but she doesn't move from where Cooper has her splayed open on the conference table.

His fingers move in and out of her pussy while her lips part and her hips rock to follow his motion. I shift my cock to ease the ache. We talked about this, but I wasn't sure we would go through with it. I want to just say fuck it and move on to more pleasurable pursuits, but we're still a business.

"We have some things to discuss, Cooper," I remind him.

He flashes a grin at me as he leans forward and licks Madison's clit. Her eyes capture mine and hold. Her hunger and lust shine in them. As he quickens his pace, she bites down on her lip.

My gaze slips to her exposed pussy and his fingers thrusting in and out where my cock should be. He sucks her clit into his mouth noisily. The moan she releases when she explodes makes my cock throb.

He pulls away from her and smacks her ass lightly. She clenches and gasps but says nothing. Coop fixes her skirt and tugs her down onto his lap.

"Ready when you are, boss." Coop smirks at me.

Madison's face is flushed, and she leans against Cooper as he pulls his chair under the table with her still on his lap. Her pupils are blown, her cheeks flushed from coming twice already. The others go to their seats with raging hard-ons while I take my seat opposite Coop.

Her gaze meets mine and stays there. Coop's hand shifts beneath the table, and her eyes widen again.

"Madison, would you like to sit in your own seat?" I ask, giving her the option but not demanding it.

"She's fine where she is." Coop smirks once again. His arm moves and she groans. He kisses the side of her neck. "Aren't you, sweetheart?"

I raise an eyebrow. "She won't be able to concentrate if you don't take your fingers out of her pussy."

He removes his hand and licks his fingers clean. I can't help but lick my lips, remembering the taste of her on my tongue. Her gaze drops to the motion and her lips part.

Fuck, it's been a long week of watching Madison grow more confident in her actual duties. Each outfit she wore this week was another kick in the balls and made me want to lift my abstinence ruling. But once we can get our hands on her, that's all we'll be able to think about.

"We have a few things on the agenda." I nod to Madison. She pulls up the agenda on the tablet and casts it to the smart board. I take the lead of the meeting. We discuss the things that came up during the week that everyone needs to know about.

Having everyone on the same page is important in this business. It's how we work so well together. I get to the last item on the agenda.

"Madison?" I turn to her. She's still on Cooper's lap, but he isn't touching her. "Tell us about your week."

She straightens and glances at everyone before focusing on me. "There was a lot to learn, but I've got a much better handle on both the computer systems and the schedules."

She discusses where she is on the projects we've assigned her and what she still feels she needs more information about. Overall, she's brilliant. She has a quick mind, and even things we haven't discussed with her, she's picked up on.

As an assistant, she's an asset that will grow with the company.

I lean back in my chair and study her. She's beautiful and young. Blake worried about her being young and inexperienced, but I think that's what makes her so attractive as an assistant and as a lover.

No bad habits to break.

Her curiosity and need for knowledge drives her in both. That's fucking sexy.

"We have a week before we discuss whether we go forward with our arrangement." I lean forward with my forearms pressed against the table and my hands together. "But is that still something you're considering a possibility?"

"Yes, sir." A little smile quirks her lips.

My balls tighten when she calls me *sir*. It's definitely intentional.

"Do you want to wait to be fucked until after the agreement is completed?"

Her lips part and her eyes darken. Her tongue flicks out to wet her lips as she looks at each of us. She stops on me. "No, I don't want to wait."

My cock weeps, but there's more. "All of us have been tested, and with the way we play, we'd prefer not to use condoms. Is that an option?"

Her legs press together. "I haven't been with anyone in about a year. I've been tested and am on birth control."

"That's not an answer, kitten," Noah says. Her gaze swings to his. "We'll wear them if you want, but we'd prefer to fill you with our cum."

"Yes." The word comes out breathy, and she squirms on Coop's lap. "That's what I want."

Fuck if I don't want to fuck her right now, but there's still more we have to address.

"Today we want to fuck you. Are you okay with fucking us in front of each other and having us all touching you at the same time?"

Her lips part. "All?"

"We'll start slow, princess." I try to ignore my aching cock. "But we'd like to fuck your mouth and pussy at the same time. And all four of us want to fuck you."

Her eyes are wide, but she leans back against Coop. "I want that too."

I lean forward on the table. "If we do this, you are committing to us for at least this week, meaning only us."

"And only me for you, right?" She cocks her eyebrow at me when she asks.

"Yes, princess. We will only fuck you and you'll only fuck us." I lean back in my chair and look around the table. "Everyone is in agreement?"

Coop lifts Madison to stand in front of him. When she nods, Coop unzips her dress, and it flutters to the ground around her feet. Her eyes never leave mine. He stands behind her and undoes her bra. A shiver ripples through her.

She leans back against Coop, completely naked. Her skin is glowing. Her breasts are the perfect size for a man's mouth. Perky and tight. The curve of her stomach just above her pussy makes my mouth water.

"Meeting adjourned?" Coop asks me with a cocky smile.

"Meeting adjourned."

Chapter 15

Conference Room

Madison

I'm naked in the conference room. One of my fantasies brought to life. I drop to pick up my dress and lay it across the back of the chair. There's a damp spot from where I sat on Cooper's hard cock the entire meeting, imagining it inside me while trying to focus on what everyone else was saying.

And then Seth brought up sex. The thought of them all coming inside me got me so hot and wet. I don't want any barriers between us for however long this lasts. Standing naked in front of these four men, I smile. When the others stand, I take them in. I'm a very lucky girl.

The conference table isn't a huge one, but it's large. With his hands on my hips, Cooper draws me back against him. His fingers trail up my sides to cup my breasts. I lean my head back onto his shoulder as he toys with my body, adding gasoline to the already rampant fire within me.

My gaze flits over the other men in the room.

Seth removes his tie and slowly unbuttons his shirt. Blake and Noah follow his lead. I want to ask them how they got into this, fucking one woman together, but right now, I'm just glad they are. And that all this is for me.

"What do you think, sweetheart?" One of Cooper's hands glides down my trembling stomach. Every touch lights a fire beneath my skin until I'm filled with such heat I'm afraid I'll combust.

Desire flows hot and heavy through my veins as my thoughts spin around one thing. These men are going to touch me. And fuck me. All of them. Right now.

Cooper's fingers part my folds and slide over my clit. I open my legs to give him more access. His other fingers trace light circles around my nipple. His soft touch is a tease, a torment, and a temptation. Not hard enough to push me to the edge, but enough to key me up.

When Seth's belt clangs, my attention jerks to him as he unzips his pants. They drop to the floor with his boxers, revealing his thick, hard cock. Holy shit, it's big.

Cooper's finger slips inside my slick channel, and he murmurs in my ear, "Does that look good, sweetheart? Do you want his cock to split you in two while mine thrusts into your ass?"

I whimper and my wetness soaks his hand.

He chuckles darkly against my ear as his fingers move farther back to my asshole. He slides his finger inside my ass all the way to his knuckles. I've had guys tease me there, but not thrust knuckle deep before. My hands clutch at the arm around me, holding me up.

All my nerve endings stand at attention. My eyes close as my focus goes to his finger inside me.

"Have you had a cock in your ass before, sweetheart?"

I shake my head no. I can't speak. All I can do is feel.

His teeth capture my earlobe and tug as his finger starts to work in and out of my asshole.

Oh, fuck, it feels good.

Blake moves closer and pulls something out of his pocket. The squirt of a lube bottle and additional wetness dripping down my ass crack makes Coop's finger glide in easier.

Blake smirks as he steps away to finish undressing. He tosses the bottle of lube on the chair with my dress.

Coop's finger makes me want more and deeper as he teases the delicate nerves. "I want to be the first, sweetheart. When you're ready."

I want to say I'm ready now, but I know I'm not. When he adds a second slick finger, he presses past the ring of muscles, stretching me. If he wasn't holding me up, I would be a puddle at his feet. My hips follow his lead like he's a wicked pied piper.

I'm climbing higher and higher. Sensation buzzes through me. A warm body closes in on me from the front, and someone else's fingers press between my legs.

When I open my eyes, Noah's dark ones are there to greet me. He's completely naked. His clothes hid those sleek muscles. Every inch of him is toned. I want to touch his warm skin and firm muscles.

His hard cock rests against his belly. I lick my lips, remembering the feel of him inside my mouth. His fingers slide over my pussy, teasing my clit. I've never had two men touch me at the same time. It's overwhelming and so fucking hot.

Noah leans in and kisses me as his fingers ease inside my pussy. When I gasp at the feel of both of their fingers inside me, he thrusts his tongue into my mouth. He follows Cooper's pace. Their fingers slide in and out of my holes together, filling me the way their cocks will someday. It's too much, and I can't hold back any longer.

As my orgasm rips through me, I tighten around their fingers, crying out and grabbing Noah's shoulders for balance as my body falls apart. When I finally come down, I rest against Cooper's shoulder, feeling the brush of his clothes against my back. He moves my hair and kisses down my nape.

Shivers race through me as he removes his fingers and pushes me to Noah's chest before he walks away. Before I can react to the cold left behind, Seth slides behind me, warming me with his naked body.

I buzz with anticipation, still sensitive to their every touch. Seth's fingers trail down my back and grip my hips to pull me back against his hard length.

The guys are all built with lean muscles, rock-hard biceps, defined abs, and that V that leads to their magnificent cocks. Gorgeous. I catch Blake walking toward me. Completely naked. He's more buff than the others. Even his cock is larger.

My pussy clenches around Noah's fingers, and he chuckles in my ear. "See something you like, kitten?"

I lick my lips and nod, my heated eyes taking in every glorious inch of Blake. "Yes."

Seth's hands rub over my ass and settle on my hips. "Are you ready for us to play with you?"

I lean back against him. His warm skin brushes against mine. "Yes, sir."

His cock throbs against my ass. Noah removes his fingers from me and backs up a step.

"On the conference table," Seth says.

Noah offers me a hand and helps me up onto the table. My body trembles in anticipation.

"Lie back."

Every command from Seth's lips turns me on more. I lie down on the table. Spread out, I don't reach the sides, but the table is oval shaped. Cooper returns, drying his hands on a towel that he tosses on a chair.

My naked bosses stare down at my exposed body as I take in every inch of them. Two of them on either side of me. I'm so ready for these men to have their way with me. To let them lead me into the darker sides of desire.

The time for me to feel shy is long past. My skin tingles, waiting for their touch. Blake puts his hand on the inside of my thigh at the same time Seth does on the other side, and they part my legs.

My pussy is dripping and ready for them.

Cooper leans down and takes my nipple into his mouth, sucking on it before Noah sucks on my other nipple. My back arches at the unfamiliar feeling of two mouths, but then two hands are between my legs. Parting me, exploring me, teasing me.

My lips part as I close my eyes, trying to memorize every moment. Fingers penetrate me, stretching me, then one strays lower to my asshole and slips inside. When a mouth closes over my clit, I cry out, so close to exploding.

Cooper's mouth finds mine, and I kiss him for the first time as his fingers tease my wet nipple. A mouth brushes over my hipbone before sucking and nibbling at the flesh. I'm a mass of sensation as desire swirls hotter and hotter through my veins. It feels like I'm going to explode.

I arch against the hands on my body as I'm thrust into an orgasm so fucking hot I cry out a guttural sound. Cooper catches my noises in his mouth. So intense, my release takes my breath away and holds me locked in this moment.

They each lift their hands and mouths off me. My body sags on the table, limp and fulfilled. I'm theirs to do with what they like. I'm repositioned at the end of the table, where it's narrow enough for my head to fall off one side while my ass hangs onto the edge on the other side.

"Such a good girl." Blake holds my head in his large hand while Seth grabs my hips.

Butterflies jostle for space in my stomach at his words. Noah and Cooper spread my legs wide as Cooper latches onto my breast again, while Noah plucks my other nipple with his fingers. I whimper at their touch on my sensitive body.

"Open wide, tiger." The head of Blake's cock touches my lips. I stare up at him. My head is upside down, and I do as he commands. I'm ready for this. Holding my head steady, he feeds his cock into my mouth. I slide my tongue along him and meet his darkened green eyes. When he stops pressing in, I close my lips around his impressive width and suck. His lips part and they almost turn up into a smile.

Fingers part my pussy before I feel the press of Seth's cock against my entrance. When I moan around Blake's cock, he curses.

Ever so slowly, Seth presses inside me, filling me with his cock. Moaning at the delicious feel of Seth filling me, I take Blake deeper into my mouth, almost into my throat.

He's fucking huge, but I want him as far inside me as possible. Seth seats himself fully, and I whimper. It feels so fucking good. A cock in my mouth and one in my pussy at the same time while a hand and mouth play with my nipples. Yes, please.

"So fucking tight and perfect," Seth says as he squeezes my hips.

"If you keep making noises, tiger, I'm going to come in your mouth," Blake says. His finger traces over my stretched lips.

I suck a little harder on him, hollowing out my cheeks.

"Shit." He groans, low and dark. His hand grips my hair, tugging slightly. "Careful, tiger. You don't want me to punish you."

My pussy clenches at the thought of him spanking me. Noah pinches my nipple, sending a bolt down to my pussy. As one, Blake and Seth pull their cocks back before thrusting in deep. Fuck, sparks light like fireworks inside me. Cooper sucks harder on my nipple, teasing with his tongue as the guys build up a rhythm.

I let Blake control my head, and the guys still hold my thighs wide for Seth. I reach my hands out and trace one over Noah's arm while my other slides over the back of Cooper's neck.

The fullness of my pussy and mouth, along with the hands teasing over my body, is almost too much. And they want to put a cock in my ass too? Fuck. I can't even imagine how full I'll be. My body starts to tighten into another orgasm.

"Not yet, princess," Seth grunts as he thrusts a little harder into my pussy.

Fingers rub over my clit at the same time someone's wet fingers slide into my ass. My brain is melting as I become a mass of sensation, filled so fucking full. Blake thrusts in deep and I moan around him. Cursing, he comes. As I'm swallowing the cum filling my throat, I shatter on Seth's cock. Waves of pleasure crash over me, filling me with euphoria.

I've never felt anything quite like it before.

When Blake steps back, leaving my mouth empty, he holds my head and caresses my face while Seth thrusts into me hard a few more times before he stills. He comes with a deep, guttural groan.

I can feel the pulsing of his cock unloading his warm cum inside me. Another wave takes me under. Everything stills in me for a second before reality crashes back. My breath and my pulse are so quick. I don't think I'll ever come down.

Seth lifts me against him, still hard inside me. I wrap my arms around his warm body. His naked chest presses against my breasts. With my legs finally free, I wrap them around his waist, clinging to him like a life raft. His dark blue eyes hold mine before his mouth crashes down on my lips. Little aftershocks ripple through me as he claims every inch of my mouth as his.

I feel it down to the marrow in my bones. The thrill of their ownership. His tongue tangles with mine before he raises his head to look down into my eyes.

"Ready for more, princess?" He lifts me down from him. I nod, still captivated by his gorgeous blue eyes. "Hands and knees."

I drop to my knees and press my hands into the carpet. Cooper kneels before me, and I glance over my shoulder as Noah comes up behind me. Noah's fingers sink inside my pussy and I groan at the tenderness.

He withdraws his fingers, soaked with my fluids mixed with Seth's, and slides them over my clit. I widen my stance for him as my head drops between my arms. My hips rock with his every touch. I don't know how much more I can take, but I want it all. When Cooper lifts my chin, I meet his light blue eyes, darkened with desire.

I want to finish both of them. I want them all to have been inside me. To be filled with their cum.

His hand tightens in my hair. "Don't worry, sweetheart. We'll do all the work."

Swallowing, I lick my lips, ready and eager to be used for their pleasure. Knowing I won't be denied my own.

"Open up," Cooper says as he presses his cock against my lips. I lick his tip before opening wide.

Cooper slams deep into my mouth at the same time Noah thrusts into my pussy. I gasp around his cock, but then remember Cooper's words to let them do the work. Let them take me. I want this so fucking much.

"She's so fucking tight," Noah bites out. "I'm not going to last."

My body tightens around him at his words, and he groans. I relax as Cooper fucks my face, making me choke and gag around his thick cock while Noah holds my hips, dragging my pussy back and forth over his hard cock, stretching me. I want to rock back against him, but I let them use me.

My eyes tear from Cooper deep in my throat. I get a little dizzy before he draws out, and I gasp in a breath.

I've never done anything with multiple partners before, but it doesn't take my body long to want more. To crave more touch. To have all of them. To satisfy all my men. The heat stokes higher with each thrust, and my eyes lock on Cooper's wicked grin.

"Imagine how it will feel when my hard cock rides your ass while Noah's thrusting into your tight pussy. Blake's cock driving into your mouth while you stroke Seth's cock with his hand wrapped around yours." Cooper's words make me even wetter. "Pinch her clit."

Noah's fingers pinch my clit, and I explode. Cooper pulls out enough for me to moan, loud and long, before thrusting back into my throat and coming. My orgasm still pulses through me while Noah thrusts harder until he shatters inside me, filling me with his cum.

I swallow Coop's cum as Noah's slides down my leg. Everything in me wants to crash. To curl up and go to sleep.

Noah lifts me to sit back on his cock, still hard inside me, as Cooper moves in to press my body between the two of them. I'm like a rag doll. My bones have lost all substance.

Cooper claims my mouth while Noah bites down on my shoulder. An aftershock flutters through my weakened muscles around Noah's cock, and I gasp into Cooper's mouth.

When Cooper breaks off the kiss, he strokes his hand down my cheek and throat. "Thank you, sweetheart."

Smiling crookedly, I lean back against Noah, exhausted.

Blake holds out his arms and I don't hesitate to turn to him. When he lifts me, Noah's cock slips out and I miss the fullness of someone inside me.

I wrap my arms and legs around Blake. His hands cradle my ass. I rest my head on his shoulder and let out a shuddering sigh.

All my energy is gone.

Blake's cock is hard between my legs and rubs against me lightly, but he just carries me through his office and into the bathroom. He keeps ahold of me while he turns the shower on. I'm curious what they'll do. I figured we'd be done when they finished.

Once it's warm, he steps under the spray with me. I lower my legs and lean against him as he gently washes my body, his touch soft and thorough. So different from his indifference before.

Seth joins us after a minute and helps hold me up while Blake washes my hair with surprisingly gentle fingers. I've never had anyone wash me before. The water is so warm and so are their bodies. I touch their chests, marveling at the hard muscles beneath my fingertips. They don't make it into more.

After rinsing me off, they pass me into the towel Noah holds. He wraps the towel and his arms around me. For a second, we just stand there. Me in his arms, never wanting to leave. My head presses against his chest.

He takes his time as he dries off every inch of me. A fully clothed Cooper helps me dress, though he keeps my panties. I feel like I'm in a daze, but I also feel warm and cared for by these men.

"Ready to go home?" Cooper asks.

I bite my lip. I kind of hoped to just stay here, but I don't say that. This is all new and maybe space is what we need. For me, that was epic, but for them, it could have been the same thing they did with all of their assistants.

Shaking that thought out of my head, I nod. I can't keep

comparing myself to those women or I'll drive myself crazy. They aren't here. I am.

Cooper leads me to the garage. I'm still in a sex haze as we get into the black car with Tim. The divider comes up and Cooper tips my face up to his.

"You feel good, sweetheart?"

"Yes." So fucking good.

He steals kisses from me until the car stops. Then he opens the door and walks me to my apartment. "See you on Monday."

Fuck, two days without them. His fingers linger in my hand as I pull away to unlock the building door. I let myself in and watch Cooper ride off.

Robert doesn't bother me in the hallway tonight. After the sex I just had, I consider it a blessing as I start to unlock my door. I just want to put on pajamas and snuggle into a blanket and remember everything that just happened.

The door swings open and Valerie grins. "Hello, roomie."

Chapter 16

Cuts Deep

Madison

I almost step back from surprise, but I'm exhausted and walk into the apartment. "Hey, I just paid your half of the rent."

The door shuts, and I hear the lock snick into place. I turn to see Valerie leaning against the door, a sneer on her face.

"Color me surprised when I found that out." Valerie is taller than me by a few inches. Maybe five-eight? Her dark hair flows down her back, and her dark eyes pin me in place. "Where'd you get the sudden influx of wealth to afford my rent?"

She takes in my clothes when I don't answer. I don't owe her any explanation. I just want to crawl into my bed and dream of my bosses. Relive each moment when they caressed and fucked me.

"You take up turning tricks to make a living?" She laughs. "I highly doubt you have the balls to do that. So come on. Where's the money coming from?"

"It's called a job." I walk farther into the apartment and pick up a few things I left out last night to take into my room with me. I installed a lock on my door after the first time I met Valerie's boyfriend. He looked at me in a way I didn't like. Not like Hunter does, but in a considering way. Like he could get something from me. Use me for something.

"Whoa, there, roomie." Valerie's voice makes me turn back to her before I can disappear into my room. "You and I need to have a little chat."

"I don't think—"

The door to my bedroom opens behind me, and her boyfriend Jeff steps out. What the fuck!

I back away from him, suddenly aware that I'm not wearing any panties. "What were you doing in my bedroom?"

"Checking things out." Jeff scratches the scruff on his chin. "Lots of interesting new things in there. Expensive shit."

Icy hands grip my heart as I try to figure a way out of this. I have no idea what these two will do to me, and I really don't want to find out. They aren't exactly being friendly. Not that they ever were. But they always left me alone. Ignored me.

"Seems like someone has been on a shopping spree." Valerie closes in.

I go to walk around her to the door, but rough hands grab my upper arms, squeezing painfully and holding me in place. My heart clenches alarmingly. My breath catches in my throat along with the scream I can feel welling inside me.

"So tell us, little Madison, where'd you get all the dough so fast? Last week you were barely surviving on ramen noodles. Now you look like some rich bitch." Valerie sneers as she grabs the sleeve of my dress.

I'm all alone with them. They have full control of this situation. Maybe I can get to the door. Maybe I can escape. But more likely, I'll just end up another casualty of this city. Another no-name person murdered and not even mentioned on the news.

I swallow down the fear lodged in my throat. I need to be reasonable, not panicked. "Like I said, I have a job."

"As a hooker?" Valerie chuckles and flicks my hair. "Because if so, we'd like to try out the goods. Wouldn't we, baby?"

Her eyes meet Jeff's over my shoulder. I cringe as he hauls me back against his erection. "We like to play with hookers."

Fuck, no. I can't even think about that. Just keep talking and get them to let me go.

"I'm not a hooker. I work at Morrigan Technology Group." Lifting my badge from around my neck, I show her. I don't want to get involved in any kinky games they like to play. The minute I get free, I'm going to run for it. Twenty steps to the door. My purse is still across my body.

But where can I go? My mind flashes to the guys, but it's too soon for that. I could get Robert to let me stay with him, but again, the creep factor. I might be in trouble here, but somehow that might be running from one danger to the next. Maybe Hope...

Valerie steps into me, pressing me against her boyfriend. She reaches up and squeezes my breast hard. I whimper as my mind flails. They aren't going to take no for an answer. Ice races down my spine and pools low in my belly.

"Where's the rest of the money, slut?" Valerie steps back and slaps me across my face.

Pain flashes through my head as a million stars light behind my eyes. I can't think.

"I used the last of it to pay your half of the rent," I finally manage to get out. My head still rings from the slap. I can't even lift my hand to press against the ache.

"If you can't pay up, then we'll have to take it from you." Valerie leers at me while she steps back and sits on the couch. She crosses her leg and smiles at me like I'm about to be her entertainment.

If I stay reasonable, maybe it will de-escalate things. My breath shudders out of me. My nails dig into my hands until I feel wetness on my fingers.

"You don't have to do this. I can get you more money."

"Shut up and take it like a good slut." Valerie leans back with her arms spread along the back of the couch. "Don't worry, Jeff likes to fuck hard. Nothing you aren't probably used to."

My whole body shakes. My heart is going to explode. This can't be happening. This isn't supposed to be happening. I was safe with the guys just minutes ago.

Jeff releases my arms, and for a second, I think about lurching forward, but then his arm bands around my waist and lifts my feet from the ground. I kick my feet back toward him.

"Nooo," I cry out. "Let me go." It's useless. I can't demand anything in my current position. Valerie's laugh rings in my ears.

Jeff grabs my other breast and squeezes harder than Valerie. "Nice tits."

"She has that going for her," Valerie scoffs. "You want to pound her first or watch me take her?"

"What the fuck!" I struggle in earnest now, scratching any flesh I can reach. "They'll know it was you. You live here. You won't get away with this."

Jeff laughs and his hand wraps around my throat. Both my hands go to his hand as he squeezes. "Fucking bitch scratched me."

Valerie shakes her head. "Shouldn't have done that. Now, Madison, where's the rest of the money?"

A knock sounds at the door.

"Help!" I cry out before Jeff's hand squeezes so tight I can't scream anymore. I can still get in a little air, but if his grip tightens any more, I'm as good as dead.

"Shut the fuck up, slut," Valerie whispers.

I nod.

"Madison?" Blake's voice comes through the door. My head spins and tears well in my eyes. He's here.

Valerie turns to the door.

I kick over a chair, and it clatters on the floor. White splotches dance along my vision as the amount of air getting to my lungs decreases. Scratching and kicking as much as I can, I can't draw in a full breath. I have to keep fighting.

Blake needs to know I'm still here.

Blake

That was definitely Madison's voice. Fuck. I kick the door as something falls over in the apartment. It bounces under the force of my boot. I kick harder, and it gives way. When I burst in, a guy is choking Madison and a dark-haired woman hisses at me.

My pulse pounds, but my mind goes clear as I only have one objective: save Madison.

I shove the woman out of the way. She falls on the couch with a little shriek. I deck the guy holding Madison. She drops. But before she hits the floor, I grab her arm and ease her down, then go after the intruders. The guy looks like he's jacked up on something while the girl seems strung out.

What the fuck is happening here? I pull out my Taser and arm it.

"Fuck that shit, Val." The guy backs away with his hands up. "I ain't getting tased again. I pissed myself last time."

The girl—Val—glares before she flees out the door with the guy behind her. I follow for a step before Madison groans on the ground. My insides twist. Fuck. I still have to remain calm. The emergency isn't over yet.

I call Seth as I kneel beside Madison and check her pulse. She's breathing. Thankfully. The tightness in my chest eases slightly. I hope she just passed out, that he didn't choke her out. The damage that could do... My hands shake as I brush her hair out of her face. Fuck.

"Yeah," Seth says.

"I'm at Madison's—"

"We agreed—"

"Fuck what we agreed." My voice bursts out of me. "She's hurt. People were in her apartment and this dude choked her. They took off, but she's unconscious."

"Take her to St. Mary's. We'll meet you there." Seth sounds like he's walking.

"Need someone to watch her place. I had to bust in the door."

"Got it." He hangs up.

I slide my phone back into my pocket as I pull Madison up to a sitting position.

"Hey!"

I look up at a guy standing in the doorway.

"What are you doing with Madison?" he asks, taking a step inside. He's not a huge guy. If I have to take him out, I will. But I'm hoping this one is at least friendly.

I lift Madison into my arms and search my memory for the name of the neighbor she talked about. "You Robert?"

"Who are you?" His eyes linger on Madison with concern.

"I'm her..." Fuck. "I'm her boss. When I came to check on her, there were people holding her."

Robert looks around the apartment. The tipped over chair is the only sign of our struggle. "Who?"

"Someone named Val. Look, I need to get her to the hospital. Can you babysit her apartment until my men get here?"

Robert's eyes widen. "Your men?"

"I work at a security company. Some of my employees will be here to secure her apartment. I had to break in the door. The guy was choking her, and I need to make sure she's okay. We're going to St. Mary's." I walk past Robert and head down the stairs with her in my arms.

He doesn't need to know that it's a corporate cybersecurity company. We have security guards that Seth will have come watch her place.

This was not how I saw this going. I didn't even intend to come upstairs, but the outside door was open, and that made me nervous. Cooper made sure she was inside before leaving, but I needed to check for myself. I took the Taser from the glovebox just in case. I can hold my own in a fight, but sometimes just flashing the Taser is enough to make someone back down.

In the shower, she felt fragile in my arms. I'd been against leaving her alone for the weekend so she'd have space. I'd prefer her to stay in my bed, curled up all soft against me.

This week, I stayed away from her. My attraction is too strong, and I worried it would color how I saw her, hide who she really was just so I could justify having her. I studied her to see if she was going to hurt us. If the real reason she wanted us was for a payday bigger than the one we offered her.

But she worked. She listened and learned. I didn't miss her hurt looks at me. They didn't seem fake. In the boardroom, the way she took each of us. It was unlike anyone before her. There was no special person in her mind. She wanted all of us.

I lay her in the back of my car, trying to ignore the redness around her neck and arms. My hands shake as I take them off her. Hopefully, I got there before anything worse happened.

I head to the driver's side, keeping an eye out in case those two hung around. Anything they might think about stealing in the apartment can be replaced. Madison can't.

Right now, I ignore the tightness in my chest and my clammy hands. I need to focus on getting her safely to the hospital.

The hospital is only five minutes away at this time of night. I park in the ambulance loop, not giving a shit if they tow me. She groans as I lift her into my arms. Needing to reassure her, and me, that she's safe, I press a kiss to her lips. Fuck. I think this is our first kiss. I'm such a fucker.

So caught up in trying to make sure she didn't destroy us, but more than willing to take what she offered so generously.

I carry her inside. "We need help."

The nurses behind the desk come around and lead me back to a room, since she's still unconscious.

The nurse starts an IV and asks for information when the doctor walks in.

"What happened?" the doctor asks. She's early thirties, pretty, with brown hair and brown eyes. She frowns at me, though.

I'm not wearing my usual suit. Instead, I have on a black t-shirt and jeans. My black hair must stick up every which way from running my fingers through it on the way to the hospital. I doubt I look like a respectable businessman at this moment.

"I went to check on her, and two people were holding her in her apartment. A big guy had his hands around her throat." Anger flares through me again at the memory. "The girl and guy ran, but Madison collapsed. She hasn't woken up since."

The doctor nods and lifts Madison's eyelids to shine a light in her eyes. "We'll want to monitor her until she wakes. Do you know if anything else happened?"

I shake my head as my insides burn. "She was fully clothed. I'm not sure if they hit her."

There's a little redness on her cheek. The doctor checks her over and palpates her stomach. When she lifts Madison's skirt, her gaze comes up to mine.

Fuck, Cooper took her panties. "We had sex earlier. Consensual. And she left without her panties."

She nods and makes some notes. "We'll check when she wakes up if she'd like us to do a rape kit."

The doctor leaves.

I scrub my hand over my hair. If that guy... Fuck. I grab a sheet of paper and start writing everything I remember about the couple. I'm going to find that guy and fuck up his life for touching my woman.

"Blake?" Madison's voice is little more than a croak. She reaches up and touches her throat and then looks at the IV taped to her arm. "What?"

"Don't talk. You were attacked." I take her hand in mine and squeeze it. "When you're ready, we'll need to talk to the police about it."

Tears form in the corners of her eyes, but she doesn't collapse and fall apart. They just slip out, sliding down to the pillow.

"Did they do anything else?" I stroke a hand over her hair. It's still a little damp from the shower we took. I should have never let her go. I should have told Seth to fuck his stupid rules and carried her down to my bed, where she would have been safe.

She takes a breath and releases it. "Valerie is my roommate, and Jeff is her boyfriend. They threatened me. Jeff bruised my arms. Valerie slapped me. They both squeezed my breasts, but that's all. Jeff choked me."

That's all? My pulse rages, and the need to beat the guy to a pulp fills me. They scared her and touched her. I want to break every one of their fingers.

She squeezes my hand. "It's okay."

"No, it's not." I can't pretend it is. I shouldn't have let her go. "You were attacked. I knew you lived in a dangerous area, but I never thought... I should have done more."

She smiles softly. "I'm here. You saved me."

The doctor comes in, and she asks Madison what happened. She tells the doctor the story, and the whole time I hold her hand. Madison declines the rape kit. She didn't pass out until I showed up. The doctor eyes me like she's going to ask me to leave to make sure I'm not intimidating Madison. Fuck that noise.

Madison looks between the two of us. "He saved me. He's never hurt me."

She squeezes my hand. Her bright blue eyes meet mine. She believes in me. Not that I've given her reason not to, but I definitely haven't been as warm to her as the others.

The doctor nods and makes some notes. The nurse comes around the curtain.

"There are three guys out there claiming to be family." Her eyes bounce between me and Madison.

Madison nods, and a smile lights her face. "They are."

Something inside me falls into place. The doctor finishes, and the nurse comes back with Seth, Noah, and Cooper.

Noah brushes her hair away from her forehead and presses a kiss to it. "I've never been so scared in my life. How are you?"

Cooper takes her other hand. Seth stands at her feet and stares into her eyes.

"You're coming home with us," Seth says in his *no one argues with me* voice.

Nodding, Madison rests her head back against the pillow and closes her eyes. We all exchange looks. This one is already embedded in us. If she fucks us over, it could tear us apart.

Chapter 17

Home?

Seth

The police station is still busy at this time of night. A female detective led Madison back to a room to discuss the incident.

We sit in a waiting area with old coffee. Blake has connections at this station, so we're not in the normal area with everyone else.

Blake presses his hands against his eyes.

"The apartment is secure," Coop reads from his phone. "We called in one of our security guards who's been wanting overtime, and I arranged for a company to take over in the morning."

"This shouldn't have happened." Noah rubs his hand over his blond hair, and his gaze strays to the door Madison is behind.

"No, it shouldn't have." Blake stands and paces like a caged tiger.

I glance at my phone and pull up the report on Valerie Davis and Jeff Moore. It's not a lot yet. I'll have more by the morning. I need them to pay.

"How are we going to work this when we get home?" Noah's dark eyes meet mine.

Coop looks up from his phone and Blake stops pacing. I'm not taking back what I told Madison. She's not leaving our sight. But it won't be easy.

"It's early." I blow out my breath. "The optics aren't going to be good."

"Fuck the optics." Coop runs his hands over his jeans.

I shake my head. Out of everyone, he knows best that we can't ignore what might get out.

"She's hurt." I decide to focus on Madison. "Tonight she comes to our apartment. She's moving in. That means someone needs to arrange for her stuff to be packed and brought over, because she's not going back."

"I'm on it." Blake crosses his arms and waits for more.

"We need extra security on the building. We don't know what kind of people we're dealing with yet." I run a hand through my hair.

"He was high. They both probably were." Blake narrows his gaze.

People on drugs are more unpredictable. "If that's the case, they probably have a record, which means it might be easier to find them."

"You want me to hire the usual people?" Coop asks.

I nod. There are people in our world who cross the lines and know how to find people, even when they want to disappear.

"We need to take it slow with her." Noah's gaze lingers on the interrogation room. "This might take her time to get over."

That's the thing. She might need time and space after this. She was fucking attacked.

"We can let her make that decision." Coop stands and stretches his muscles. He glances at his phone. "I'm ordering in some real coffee. This shit isn't great."

"You can't have someone bring you coffee to a police station," Blake says.

"I'm a Graham." Coop smirks. "We make the world go round."

"Cocky bastard," Blake mutters.

Noah just shakes his head. When the interrogation door opens, he springs to his feet. The detective leads Madison over to us. I step forward, and Madison takes my offered hand as I pull her into my arms. The tension eases out of her as she rests her head on my chest.

She doesn't pull away or flinch. That's good.

"We'll let you know if we have any more questions." The detective turns and walks away.

I rub my hand down Madison's spine, and she presses in close to me with a little shiver. We shouldn't have let her go. My gaze meets those of my friends, my brothers. It's reflected in their eyes as they look at her.

"Are you ready to go home, Madison?"

Her wide blue eyes lift to mine and my gut twists. It's been a long night. She smiles and nods.

Madison

When the elevator opens to the apartment floor, Blake rushes forward to open the door.

"I can walk," I mention once again. Not that anyone is listening to me. My throat hurts with every word.

Noah shifts me in his arms and gives me a look before carrying me into the apartment.

It's late. Like the sun is peeking over the horizon late. The guys kept ahold of me while I was in the hospital. Grasping my hand, touching my leg. The doctor said I was fine and that my throat may be sore for a while, but to just take it easy. I'll have a few bruises courtesy of Val and her psycho boyfriend, but overall, no worse for wear.

The police station took forever, but the guys stayed with me throughout it. I don't know what to feel, except extremely grateful. I haven't had someone to look out for me in a really long time.

Cooper opens the door to what will be my apartment. Noah carries me through to the bedroom and sets me on the ridiculously enormous bed.

When I try to rise, Noah pushes me back down. I grab his hand.

"I have to go to the bathroom." I blush as he starts to pick me up. "Alone."

His eyes narrow on me, but I reach up and cup his jaw. "Thank you for taking such good care of me."

Each word is like glass shards in my throat.

He sits on the bed and gestures to the bathroom door. "Yell if you need anything."

I most definitely will not. There are some boundaries that I don't think I can cross. Peeing in front of someone I had sex with is one of them.

When I come out, the guys are all sitting on the edge of the bed. I pause in the doorway as they chat in low voices.

"They weren't able to locate them," Seth says, shaking his head as he looks at his phone.

"I clocked the guy." Blake flexes his fist. "I would have done more, but Madison..."

His face when he stormed into my apartment. He'd been like a wrathful angel. His green eyes blazed with fury, but his hands were soft when they lowered me down before I passed out.

"How are you?" Cooper's eyes meet mine.

"Tired." My voice is a little hoarse. I press my hand against my throat and wince.

Noah pulls down the sheets while Seth sets a stack of clothes beside him and gestures for me to come.

I stand between his legs, and he meets my eyes. "May I help you get ready for bed?"

Those stupid tears well in my eyes at his soft tone. I nod, not trusting my voice. Asking for my permission isn't necessary, but after what happened... A tear slips down my cheek.

Cooper rises and stands behind me. "May I?"

I nod again, knowing this isn't their usual, but also liking that they respect me enough to realize someone assaulted me tonight and took away my choice. They're giving it back to me. One piece at a time.

Cooper unzips my dress and kisses my shoulder as he lowers it. Seth holds out a pair of lacy panties.

I raise my eyebrow at Seth. Leftovers from someone else? Because those definitely aren't mine. I'm not wearing someone else's panties, and he must see it on my face.

"All new." His face flushes, but it's tempered by his concern. "I ordered some after Monday for you. I liked the way you looked in your underwear and figured it was a treat for you and not your usual."

My shoulders and face relax. I step into the panties, and he pulls them up before kissing my belly. Cooper releases my bra and I drop it with the other clothes. Seth rises before me. I look up and he drags a man's t-shirt over my head. It smells like him, sandalwood and sin, and hangs down to my midthigh.

"Is this new?" I gesture to the bed and hold my hand to my throat.

"You shouldn't talk, kitten." Noah walks in with a glass of water and hands it to me. I smile and wait for Seth's answer.

"We bought it after our last failed attempt. No one else has slept in it." Seth rubs the back of his neck as he eyes me with worry. "We knew next time we had to be upfront about our expectations, but we're still okay if you say you want to stay strictly professional."

I step into him and hug him around his waist, resting my head against his chest. He wraps his arms around me. He feels safe, like nothing can get to me as long as I'm in his arms.

I'm not sure what the rules are yet for what we are doing as a group, or what may or may not be allowed in the future, but right now is no-man's-land.

If I want to hug them, I can do that. Whatever I want and whatever they want, within reason, are all fair game.

Maybe hugging should be off-limits since it isn't really sexual, but neither is sleeping together, and with a bed this vast, sleeping together is definitely an option.

Seth helps me into the huge bed, and I notice the guys stripping down to their boxers. I should maybe draw the line, but as Cooper slides in next to me and drags me into his arms, I lose all desire to push them away. I snuggle into him, letting his warmth and his arms make me feel whole again.

Maybe I'll fall for them and they'll rip my heart to shreds. Tonight, I don't care. I want whatever security they can give me. Even if it's not real. Seth climbs in behind me and wraps an arm around my waist to spoon me. Noah and Blake also get into the bed and someone turns the light off.

Seth kisses the top of my head. "We'll work everything out in the morning. For now, sleep."

I wake to a pounding headache and the feeling of burning alive between the heat of two bodies. When I groan, the arm banded around my waist tightens.

Opening my eyes, I find Noah and glance over my shoulder to see Blake spooning me. Seth comes in. He's wearing athletic pants low on his hips and nothing else. I lick my dry lips. My body is definitely awake this morning. I probably shouldn't be feeling tingles all over, but I remember what they did to me yesterday, and I still want more.

He carries a prescription bottle and a glass of water. My heart thumps. That's so thoughtful.

"Figured you'd want pain meds." He holds out the water and drops a couple of pills into my hand when I sit up.

My throat feels full and like I swallowed broken glass. So I smile, not wanting to make it worse by talking, and down the pills.

"The doctor believes you passed out, but not because of oxygen deprivation." Seth sits on the end of the bed. "Too much stress. We need you to take it easy this weekend. Your throat may be sore and feel swollen. I can get you an ice pack."

I nod, and he goes into the other room, then comes back with one.

"I put a few in your freezer. There are more in the main freezer if you're in the living room." He hands me the ice pack.

I never imagined these guys would take care of me like this. I smile and try to thank him with my eyes.

"You should get more rest." His gaze goes over Noah and Blake, who are still sleeping next to me. He shakes his head. "We'll talk later. Rest now."

I lie back down, and Blake's arm goes around my waist, pulling me into his warmth. I put the ice pack on my neck and fall asleep again.

The next time I wake up, I think I'm alone in the bed at first. The ice pack is gone.

"You up for some soup?" Cooper asks from behind me.

I roll over, and he's sitting on the bed next to me, fully dressed, with his tablet. I rub my eyes and stretch. First things first, bathroom.

"Soup, sweetheart?"

Nodding, I shuffle out of bed to the bathroom. After using the toilet, I go to the sink and find a new toothbrush, toothpaste, deodorant, facial soap, and a hairbrush. I smile at their thoughtfulness. My parents need to know what's going on. I'll text them later though.

When I take a few moments to clean up, I notice the bruises forming on my neck and upper arms. I trace them with my fingertip. Tears swell in my throat. What would've happened if Blake hadn't shown up?

Shivers course down my back. They wanted money, and to play their twisted game with me. Tears well in my eyes, threatening to spill. They choke the back of my throat until I can't breathe.

Helpless. That's how I felt.

Completely and utterly helpless. They could have done anything to me, and I wouldn't have been able to fight back. I could have died.

A soft knock comes on the door. I try to reel the emotion back in.

"Madison?" Cooper opens the door slowly. His eyes capture mine in the mirror and his face softens. He steps close and wraps his arms around me. "You're here and you're safe. We won't let anything happen to you."

When a tear slips down my cheek, he catches it with his thumb. The night started amazing. Having all four of the guys with me, giving me pleasure and receiving it in return. And then it turned into a nightmare. They had to step up and protect me because I couldn't protect myself.

"Hey." Cooper turns me in his arms and lifts my chin so I look at him.

This wasn't supposed to be this way. They shouldn't need to protect me. He lowers his mouth to mine and kisses me softly, sweetly. Tingles work their way through me. I'm not up for more than this, but he's comforting me, not trying to get into my pants. It's confusing because that's what this contract is about. Sex. Drawing back, he rests his forehead on mine as his hand softly cups my bruised cheek. "We've got you."

I breathe in his breath and let it out before leaning my head against his chest and letting him hold me. This isn't the way this is supposed to go. He shouldn't have to comfort me. I'm supposed to be strong and independent.

But I can't be and I should have known that. I've struggled all my life to fit in and be who everyone thought I should be. My parents. My teachers. The other kids in school. They all thought I should be perfect. But I always fail. I always let them down.

Now I'm messing this all up. My perfect opportunity. My perfect job with the perfect guys.

I'm the thing that's not perfect, and at some point, they'll realize that no matter how hard I try, I'll always be less.

Noah

Madison is on our couch, watching some show on renovating old houses. She's cuddled under a blanket. Bruises mar her perfect skin, and my chest squeezes tight every time I see them.

We shouldn't have let her go.

It's only been a week. I'm stupid and reckless for falling so quickly for someone who is still a maybe. Theoretically, we aren't supposed to fall at all. The point of the whole *let's live with our assistant and fuck her* thing is the convenience.

But Madison isn't just convenient. The other women I could have taken or left, but Madison... Fuck, every moment I'm in her presence, she just fills me up. Makes me feel like I've found home. Of course, I can't tell the guys that. Or Madison.

But she's not someone you use and move on from. At least not for me.

The other guys seem to feel something more too. Fucking her together yesterday was amazing. She responded so beautifully to all of us, and she took everything we dished out. I crave more of her, so much more.

"Stop staring," Blake says gruffly. "You're going to make her feel self-conscious."

"Like she doesn't already." I'm working on my computer at the table, close enough to get her something if she needs it but far enough away so she doesn't feel crowded.

"We were supposed to give her space." Blake shuts his computer and leans back in his chair. His eyes lock on her.

"Which is why you went over to her place?" I would have gone, but I'm glad it was Blake. He looks like someone you don't want to tangle with, while I look like an accountant. I can hold my own when push comes to shove, but the guy probably pissed himself when Blake came crashing through the door.

Blake grunts and rubs his eyes. I don't think he slept until Madison was in his arms. I can't imagine what went through his mind. That had to be a fucked-up situation to walk in on. A guy choking our girl while she tried to yell for help. Fuck.

I close my laptop with a little too much force.

Madison looks over her shoulder at both of us. She hasn't spoken much today. Her throat looks bad, and it probably feels worse. But she smiles at us a lot. Like she does now.

I don't realize I'm up and walking toward her until I get close enough to draw in her floral scent. She pats the seat next to her and lifts the blanket in invitation.

I slide onto the seat beside her and draw her to lean against me. My heart fills my chest.

Yup, I'm a goner.

Chapter 18

Rest and Recovery

Madison

Noah draws me into his arms, and I let out a breath as I relax into him. Blake gets up and walks into what I assume is his room. If I could, I would have called out to him to join us, but resting my vocal cords is important.

I'm only half paying attention to the show. It's an old one that I've seen before. Noah's fingers brush up and down my arm, leaving a trail of sparks in their wake as I listen to the steady beat of his heart.

I pick up the remote and offer it to him. This show doesn't grab my attention. Not sure I can focus on anything today, but it keeps my mind from drifting back to the terror from last night.

"I don't normally watch TV," he says, not taking the remote.

I shrug and flip channels. If I could talk, I'd tell him I don't either.

One of the *Harry Potter* movies is on. Setting the remote down, I snuggle into Noah. His scent calms me with its outdoor smell, like a walk in a forest. I take his other hand between both of mine and hold it.

Not sure when we fell asleep, but the sounds of pots and pans rattling in the kitchen wake me. I press up from Noah, whose face is peaceful in his sleep. His blond hair falls over his eyes. He looks so young. I reach out and move his hair back. My heart stutters a little.

He was the first to kiss me. The first to give me an orgasm. The first I went down on. I snuggle back into him. When I'm in his arms, I feel safe and wanted. Fuck, I need that so much right now.

A hand touches my shoulder, and I turn to see Seth, holding pills and water. I sit up as he comes around the couch and sits on the ottoman in front of me.

I hold out my hand, and he puts two tablets in it and hands me the glass.

"How are you?" His fingers reach out to ghost over my cheek and throat. A shiver of awareness races through me.

I give him a thumbs up. I gave my statement last night about my roommate and her boyfriend. The police will be on the lookout for them, but they're still out there. Up here, behind these castle walls, I'm safe.

Seth brushes his finger over my bottom lip. "We need to talk about your living situation."

My lips part at the sparks from his touch. His words penetrate.

Living situation. I need to go back to the apartment for another week. My heart clatters.

I don't want to go back, but I will. I can get the locks changed. Talk to the landlord since I paid the rent myself this month. Maybe set up some booby traps since I don't have any money for an alarm system.

"We talked about it, and we want you to move in now. Not in a week."

I open my lips, but he covers them with his fingertips.

"I know it's not what we agreed to. We can still wait to discuss the arrangement. We can all keep our hands to ourselves and sleep in our own beds." Seth's dark blue eyes hold me still as his voice weaves its spell around me. "If that's what you want and need right now. You've been through a lot."

I shake my head.

"You aren't safe in your apartment—" He's not understanding.

I take his hand and place it over my heart. His eyes focus on his hand on my breasts.

"You're okay living with us?" Seth lifts his gaze and raises his eyebrow.

I nod and smile. Yes, so much. It's a weight lifted off me, and when I can talk again, I'll tell him.

"You want us to keep our hands to ourselves?"

I shake my head. Not at all. I want them to touch me all the time. It's frustrating not being able to talk.

"You want us to sleep in our own beds?"

I shake my head and shrug. Either way, I don't mind. I enjoy sleeping with them and waking up surrounded by their heat. But I don't want to force them to sleep with me if they'd prefer to sleep on their own.

His lips tip into an almost smile and I'll take it. I lean forward, pressing my lips to his, intending it to be a definitive answer to his questions.

His hand gently wraps around the back of my neck as he deepens the kiss. Everything in me wants me to straddle him.

Not breaking the kiss, I slide across to kneel on the ottoman over his lap before lowering onto him. Sparks light under my skin. His cock is hard between my legs. Desire swirls heavy and thick, making everything come to life inside me.

I want him, right now. I make a needy noise in my throat, but that hurts. When I whimper a little, pained, he pulls away. I touch my neck to show him it's not him.

"You'll be better soon." He grinds my hips down on his.

My lips part as desire floods my body. *Please don't stop.*

"Don't worry. We'll take care of you while you heal." The mischievous gleam in his eyes makes me smile. When he lifts me, I'm surprised that Noah catches me and lowers me down onto his lap. I don't know when he woke up.

"Lean back, kitten. Let us make you feel better."

I wrap my arm around Noah's neck behind me as Seth slides off my panties. I'm still only wearing panties and his t-shirt. Well, I was wearing panties.

Seth guides my legs to either side of Noah's, and Noah spreads his knees, opening mine obscenely wide. Seth leans back on his hands while he stares at my pussy. Just his eyes locked between my thighs are enough to make me dripping wet.

"Feel how wet she is, Noah." Seth's gaze goes to him.

When Noah slides his hand down my belly to slip between my legs, I catch my lip in my teeth. He parts my folds and strokes his fingers over my pussy. I gasp at the electric feel of his touch.

Noah's voice is rough in my ear when he says, "So fucking wet."

"Slide your finger inside her."

I whimper. My body heats up to the exquisite torture of hearing Seth's commands before they happen. I press back into Noah.

He follows Seth's instructions, and I suck in a breath at the bite of soreness. I'm still a little tender from them last night. It had almost been a year since I last had sex, and never with guys this big.

"Sore, princess?"

Nodding, I raise my fingers close together to indicate *a little*. But I don't want to stop.

Noah slides his finger in and out of my slick channel, teasing my clit before thrusting back in. My lips part, and I arch against him at the buzzing sensation flowing through my veins. I want them so much.

"Want to stop?" Seth's voice curls around my insides.

I shake my head. Definitely not. My eyes close as my arousal swells inside me.

"Good girl."

Hunger licks at my nerve endings.

"Think you can handle a cock, princess?"

Fuck, yeah. My eyes open to Seth's. I nod enthusiastically. His hand rubs over his erection. He's in those athletic pants that don't really hide anything. Noah is still stroking me, and I clench around his fingers. His hard length presses into my ass through his pants.

Seth chuckles and gestures for someone behind us. Knowing someone else has been watching stirs the flames hotter. I thought the person to fuck me would be Noah. Or maybe even Seth.

Seth pushes the ottoman back. "Kneel, Blake."

Blake lowers himself in front of me. My breath comes out in pants as Noah keeps winding me higher and higher. His thumb brushes my clit as he strokes inside me. Gasping, I burn from the inside out.

"Give her your cock, Blake."

My pulse races at Seth ordering this brute of a man around. Blake lowers his pants to reveal his thick, hard cock. I remember his thickness in my mouth, how it barely fit. The taste of him on my tongue.

Arching, I bite my lip and hum. My toes curl as I come in a burst of liquid heat all over Noah's fingers.

"Good girl," Noah whispers in my ear before pressing a kiss to my neck.

Noah removes his fingers from me, and Blake comes forward between Noah's and my legs. Noah's hands steady my hips as Blake presses the tip of his cock against my clit before sliding it up and down my slit, gathering my wetness on his shaft.

When he brushes over my clit again, sending an aftershock through me, I gasp. Noah drops kisses down my neck, leaving trails of sparks in his wake.

"Easy," he says.

My gaze lowers to where Blake teases me with the head of his cock. He dips his tip inside me and I whimper. Not in pain, but in aching need to be filled by him. My hips rock as much as they can in this position. I want him inside me already.

Blake eases forward, impaling me with more of his cock. "Fuck, you're perfect."

His voice makes my insides spasm as he fully thrusts inside me. He's so thick and long. I feel stretched and full with a small bite of soreness. His mouth captures mine in a hot tangle of lips as he begins a slow and steady pace. The soreness eases with every thrust. His tongue enters my mouth with the same insidious rhythm as his cock thrusts into my wet heat until I can't distinguish between the two.

My body is in flames, and the pressure bears down on me. I can feel the explosion waiting to happen. It's going to rip me apart and shatter me.

Noah's hands slide up my rib cage and gently stroke over my nipples. Shock waves roll through me. Blake reaches between us to circle my clit with his finger, and the explosion rocks me.

It's as devastating as I imagined. I arch into Blake and moan into his mouth as the waves crash over me. His pace increases until he strains and spills deep inside me.

He lifts his mouth and presses his forehead against mine. We breathe together, still connected. I close my eyes, feeling so close to this man who saved me, who cared enough to come to see if I was okay after being overwhelmed. I stroke my hand along his jaw as I stare into his green eyes.

"I'm sorry I didn't get to you sooner." His voice is barely a whisper. He doesn't have any reason to feel that way. He shouldn't have even been there. I'm just glad he was.

I cup his cheeks and stare into his beautiful green eyes. I squeak out, "I'm glad you came."

He claims my mouth again before backing away, leaving me empty but fulfilled.

"Think you can take more?" Seth's voice draws me to him.

When I nod, Noah lifts me, his cock sliding into me from behind. I lean forward, putting my hands on his knees to brace myself. Blake's cock stretched me out, so I don't feel that bite of soreness. Only the overwhelming feeling of being filled again. Noah's cock is buried so deep inside me. I groan. Fuck, that feels good, and the angle is amazing. Electricity flows through me like a buzz beneath my skin, bringing back the aching need to be filled.

Noah's hands lift my hips and lower me slowly onto his cock. I bite my lip at the intoxicating thought of his cock driving Blake's cum deeper inside me. When I lock eyes with Seth, he leans back to appreciate the view, taking in all of me. My pussy clenches around Noah.

Seth's intense gaze sends desire careening through me as Noah's cock slides along my already sensitive flesh. Both of them stir the flames higher again.

"The view could be so much better." Cooper slides to his knees before me and grins. I meet his blue eyes and groan when Noah fucks me onto his cock again.

Cooper lifts my hands from Noah's knees and places them on his shoulders. My skin feels tight and hot as Cooper grabs the hem of the t-shirt I'm wearing and lifts it off over my head.

His fingers ghost over my neck, sending shivers through me as Noah continues to gently guide me over his cock. Each stroke coaxing the fire higher and brighter.

"How are you feeling, sweetheart?" Cooper cups my cheek and stares into my eyes.

I can barely focus as I wind tighter. I feel reckless and needy. My mouth opens, but nothing comes out.

Noah rotates his hips beneath me, causing me to moan, and my head hangs. My hands dig into Cooper's shoulders as I bite my lip. The pressure is almost unbearable. I'm so fucking close.

"Need some help?"

My head rises at his words. Cooper smirks before his head lowers.

When he sucks my nipple into his mouth, my breath catches. So hot and wet, pulling at my nipple. Noah lifts me a little, and Cooper's hands take over holding my hips up. His mouth takes in as much of my breast as possible while Noah thrusts up into me. Harder, faster.

I raise my gaze to Seth's darkened eyes. He has his cock out of his pants, stroking it slowly while he watches us. I can't hold on any longer and fall over the edge. Tumbling into euphoria as my pussy convulses around Noah's cock, milking him. The swelling in my throat strangles my cry. Spasms rack my pussy, clenching around Noah's cock.

Cooper's mouth finds mine as Noah's hands grab onto my hips with Cooper's. Each thrust against my sensitive pussy makes me moan. Noah loses his finesse and pounds up into me until he pulls me down over him one final time. Groaning, he comes and bites down on my shoulder. My body trembles with aftershocks as I try to steady my breathing.

"More, princess?"

Cooper sits back on his heels, and I meet Seth's eyes. I want them all. I need to feel them all inside me, washing away the horrors of last night. The lingering potential for violence in that apartment as they tried to take whatever they could from me.

But these men aren't here to just take from me. They want to give me pleasure and I want it all.

I nod. Noah lifts me off his cock and returns me to his lap. Cooper licks his lips as his fingers dip inside me, pushing the cum that tries to slip out back in. Smiling, he rises on his knees and lowers his shorts, revealing his hard cock.

His fingers thrust in and out of me while he strokes his cock. A small orgasm ripples through me, making me shiver. He smirks as he withdraws his wet fingers and trails them back to my asshole, circling it. I've never had anyone play with my ass as much as he does.

My eyes widen as he shifts onto his knees again. His cock presses against my entrance as his finger presses against my asshole. Fuck. He thrusts both inside me at the same time, and a strangled cry bursts out of me at the sensation of being filled in both places. I wrap my arms around his neck and press my mouth against his shoulder, biting down at the overwhelming feeling of being so full.

He moves both his cock and finger at the same pace. The fire raging within me is so hot, I'm sure I'm going to combust. Noah keeps my legs spread wide when I feel the urge to close them. His fingers stroke down my back and then hold my ass cheeks apart.

Is he watching Cooper's finger penetrating my ass? That thought makes my skin buzz, and wetness drenches my pussy. The fullness is amazing, and I imagine taking two of them at once will feel even better. I bite down on the corded muscle in Cooper's neck when my orgasm shatters through me.

Groaning, he thrusts once more, filling me so fucking full of him, and explodes inside me. After he draws his finger out of my ass, he pulls back enough to kiss me. "Feel good?"

I meet his eyes and nod. Feels amazing. I want to feel his cock in my ass.

"We'll start prepping soon." Cooper leans in and kisses me again as he pulls out. When he moves out of the way, Seth is there.

I lean back against Noah, my legs wide, my pussy dripping. I stare greedily at Seth's long, hard cock. My nipples are tight and I'm a mass of need. I want them all. Crave them all.

"One more, princess. You ready?"

I grab his neck and pull him in for a kiss. His bare chest rubs against my breasts, and his cock nudges my entrance. I'm so fucking wet for him. He deepens the kiss as he thrusts into me.

I moan into his mouth. I'm a little more sore now, but that won't stop me. I want him. I want them all. He doesn't take his time, but pistons his cock into my pussy like a man on a mission. His mouth is ravenous against mine. His hands stroke over my nipples and down to rub my clit, fast and furious.

The waves of my orgasm hit me hard and fast as my pussy clamps down on him. I come so hard I see stars. My mouth opens in a silent scream as my orgasm drags him into his. He plows into me one last time and holds himself still as his cum rushes into me.

My chest heaves against his. My pussy aches around his cock, still thick and hard inside me.

"Fuck, princess, you're perfect," he says against my lips.

But I'm not perfect, and eventually they'll find that out. Then where will I be?

Alone.

Chapter 19

Movie Night

Seth

By the time I finish washing Madison in the shower, dinner is ready and on the table. Blake went by her apartment earlier and packed everything in her room. We put the boxes in the living room of her suite and figure she can put things away at her leisure.

I left her alone to get dressed. When she emerges, she stands in the doorway to her apartment looking so uncertain. She found a pair of jeans and a t-shirt to wear for dinner. Her feet are bare, toenails painted a light blue.

Her blond hair hangs loose past her shoulders. It has a soft wave in it. Her blue eyes look like she doesn't know how she fits in here.

I feel bad about fucking her. Not the actual act, but she's still healing. Her neck and arms are still bruised deeply. We *should* have waited longer. We *could* have waited longer. But damn if I don't want her again already.

Noah walks up to her, and she tips her face up to his as he says something only she can hear. Her smile lights up her face, and I can almost see the invisible threads weaving between them, curling around the two of them and forming a connection I'm not sure will be broken.

He isn't like the rest of us. Even with the other women, he participated occasionally but never sought them out. He kept to himself. But Madison draws him. He kisses her softly before taking her hand and leading her to the dining room table.

"He's smitten," Cooper says next to me with a smirk.

I shake my head and look at him. "And you're not?"

Cooper smiles and shrugs his shoulders. He's mostly unreadable, but I've seen him looking at her when no one else is watching. We're all in over our heads with this girl. I wouldn't call it love just yet, but it's definitely something more than simply lust.

Blake sets a bowl of pasta on the table. "Dinner's ready."

I claim the chair next to Madison and take her hand under the table. She turns and offers me a smile. Her bruises are more noticeable, and I fight off the urge to trace the edges of them. I want to erase them and take away her pain. The one on her cheek is a little swollen today.

She's so young and fragile.

If I'd been the one to walk in on the roommate and her boyfriend hurting Madison, I would have killed them. Painted the walls with their blood for daring to touch her. It's not rational, but they tried to take someone who's mine. Who's ours. They hurt her and meant to do a lot more harm.

When she told the police what happened and what they'd said, I had to clench my fist to stop myself from doing everything within my power to find and end them. But that wouldn't have helped Madison.

She needs us here with her. She squeezes my hand and turns to look over the food.

Blake can cook when needed. One of his go-to dishes is pasta with garlic and butter, with vegetables and chicken mixed in, paired with garlic toast and a good salad. Cooper brings out a bottle of white wine.

"None for Madison."

She turns to me with a frown.

"Not until you're off the meds," I explain.

She nods. Noah goes to the fridge. He brings back a root beer and pours it into her glass. She grins at him, and I furrow my brow.

"She told me she always loved root beer growing up, so I figured she'd like one." Noah shrugs like he didn't just say something I didn't know about her. Her hand comes up and touches his arm as he pours. He smiles down at her.

Unfortunately, her throat doesn't allow her to talk with us, so I won't learn more of her secrets tonight. I want them all. I want to know everything about her. Even the things she hides from herself.

We pass around the wine and the food until everyone has a full plate. We dig in.

Madison moans and grins with her first bite. I swear Blake's cheeks grow pink. He held back from her before, wanting to protect us, but I can't help but wonder if he's all in now.

"We don't do much work on the weekends anymore," Cooper says, putting his wineglass down. "When we first started the company, it seemed like all we did was work. Morning, noon, and night. It was hectic but worth it."

"Some of us still work on the weekend," Blake replies with a glare. "Not as much, but there's more to do than fits into the hours of the day."

"Now that you're up to speed, we'll have more projects for you to work on." Noah flashes her a smile. "You'll have to tell us if we give you too much. When you can talk again."

She eats and listens as we discuss this week more. Giving each other information that wasn't necessarily business important when it happened. She leans back but still has food left on her plate. When I raise an eyebrow, she frowns and pats her stomach.

The others keep talking while they eat. As we finish, we each get up and take our dish to the kitchen to put in the dishwasher. When she grabs her plate to follow, Cooper beats her to it. Putting his hand on her shoulder to keep her from getting up, he kisses the top of her head and takes her plate.

"We have nothing planned for tonight." I rise and pull her chair away from the table. When I hold out my hand, she slips hers in mine and stands next to me. "We can watch TV or a movie. Read a book. If you're tired, you can go lie down."

She turns and looks at the guys cleaning up the kitchen. From the look on her face, she wants to help.

"You need to rest and heal," I say softly to her, drawing her into my arms because I can. She rests her head against my heart, and it beats harder for her. "You can help when you're better."

She glances up at me with her eyebrows raised.

"We should really get you a whiteboard." I stop as my mind races ahead. "Wait right here."

I go into my room and grab my tablet, bringing up the writing app. I hand her the tablet and the stylus. She takes it and writes on it.

Thank you.

"You're welcome." I take her hand and lead her to the sectional in front of the TV. "What do you want to do tonight?"

Movie? She shrugs as she holds it up.

I nod and pull up Netflix. She sits next to me and curls her feet up on the couch beside her. Her head rests on my shoulder, and she lets out a yawn.

We all might be in trouble with this one.

Madison

The room is dark when I wake with my head in Seth's lap. The flashing glow from the TV is the only light. His fingers stroke through my hair. My feet are on Cooper's lap, and he's gently massaging them.

I have no idea what movie they're watching. I stretch and Seth's gaze drops to mine.

"Good nap?" he asks. Something explodes on the screen, but all I can focus on are his dark blue eyes. They're beautiful, captivating. Will they always be that way to me?

I nod. Today was exhausting. Maybe it's my body healing from being abused last night, or maybe it's all the sex and orgasms putting me into a coma, but all I want to do now is curl up and go back to sleep.

"I've got her." Blake's voice rolls over me.

I open my eyes, not knowing when I closed them. The TV is off and Blake's arms lift me against his chest. My head rolls on his firm pecs, and I lose track of everything again until I'm being put into my bed.

They tug my jeans off and remove my t-shirt. My bra goes next. I'm barely aware of the hands on me, undressing me. Nothing's sexual about it. They're just taking care of me, which feels nice. Then a nightgown is dropped over my head, and I'm allowed to cuddle back under the sheets.

"She's out of it," a voice says.

"She's had a long day."

A warm body draws me close and I slip away again.

I jerk awake to a darkened room. Arms hold me down and I cry out in fear. My nightmare has followed me into waking. I never got away from Jeff. His arm was steel around me, and his hand squeezed my breast, then Hunter was there leering at me while Valerie laughed in the background.

"Shh, you're okay. I've got you." Noah's voice filters through my terror, and the arm that had been gripping me eases. Seth's hands lightly caress my sides.

Sobbing, I curl into Noah. He holds me against him while his hand strokes down my back soothingly.

"I've got you," he whispers into my hair over and over.

I can't stop the tears or control the sobs coming from deep inside. He holds me tight against him as if someone would come and snatch me away if he let go.

The sobs tear at my throat, but even the pain doesn't make me stop. Helpless. Alone. Overpowered. It was my apartment. The place I'd called home for two years. I should have been safe there. I never imagined it would all go so wrong.

"Is she okay?" Cooper's voice is rough with sleep.

"She will be." Seth's hand rubs down my back as he closes in from behind me. Both he and Noah wrap around me like a cocoon as my tears flow freely.

"I should have been there sooner." Blake's voice is harsh as he berates himself once again. But it's not his fault.

"I'm the one who left her there." Cooper's tone is miserable. "I should have walked her to her door."

They couldn't have known any more than I could have. It was a trap set for me, and if I hadn't gone home then, it would have sprung on me later. And who knows if someone would have saved me that time.

I inhale, breathing in the combined scent of these men, and something settles deep inside me. I'm warm and safe and protected.

Needing to touch and reassure the others, I reach my hand toward Blake's voice, and he takes it, squeezing it gently. When he releases it, I reach out to Cooper. He takes my hand and kisses my knuckles.

When he releases it, I press gently on Noah's and Seth's chests to let them know they can give me space now. I hear water running. When I sit up, Blake sits at my feet and smooths a warm washcloth over my face.

"You've been through something unthinkable," he says as he cups my cheek. "We know we aren't to blame and they are, but it doesn't stop our guilt or your pain."

I crawl into his lap and wrap my arms around his shoulders. I wish I could take his guilt away. His arms close around me, and I breathe in the faint trace of his spicy cologne. His lips press against the top of my head.

When Cooper sits next to us, I open my eyes to meet his light blue ones. He has a glass of water and a couple of pills for me. I straighten in Blake's lap and take the pills with a drink before climbing into Cooper's lap.

I straddle his hips and rest my head on his shoulder as I hug him. He's warm and solid beneath me. His hands rub my back.

"Not your fault," I whisper in his ear.

He sighs. "I know, but I don't like that this happened to you."

It could have been worse. Much worse. The nightmare still creeps over me with hands to grip at my heart and tear it apart. Absorbing his warmth, I draw in Cooper's clean scent and let it wash over me.

I kiss his neck and just rest in his arms. The world is still dark, so it's probably the middle of the night. I should go back to sleep, but I'm afraid of what waits for me when I close my eyes.

I sit back on Cooper's lap, and he brushes my hair away from my face.

"Want some ice cream?" He cocks his eyebrow.

I don't remember ice cream from when I put away the groceries, but I shrug.

"Come on." Cooper wraps his arms around me and stands. I clasp him with my arms and legs to prevent falling on the ground. Hands holding my ass, he carries me into the kitchen and sets me on the island with my legs dangling off the edge.

"I had my tonsils out as a kid." He opens the freezer and pulls out a tub of chocolate ice cream. "Ice cream was the best thing ever for a sore throat, so I thought you'd like some." He shrugs his bare shoulder, and I smile.

After he grabs a spoon, he repositions me to sit in front of a stool. He sits before me and sets the ice cream container between my legs. When I try to scoot away from the cold, he gives me a wicked grin. "Don't worry. I'll warm you back up."

A shiver races down my spine. He opens the container and digs the spoon in to get a bite. He holds the spoon up to my lips. Holding his gaze, I part my lips to let him feed me. The ice cream melts on my tongue, and the soothing coolness of it runs down my sore throat.

"We all grew up together. Mostly." Cooper takes a bite and gestures toward the bedroom. The others didn't follow us out here, leaving us alone. "I'm technically the oldest. Blake and Seth were in the year below me. When Noah skipped a grade to theirs, the other kids didn't like it. So, we protected him."

He feeds me another bite and takes one for himself. "I always had a head for anything tech related, but I was a little out of sync with the guys. I graduated first and left for college alone. But these guys are my ride or dies. If they needed me, I would be there in a heartbeat. They followed me to college, and we rented a house together."

He keeps feeding me ice cream until I finally hold up a hand and shake my head. My throat does feel a little better.

He takes a few more bites. "We spend a lot of time together and know each other's rhythms and patterns. It's actually rare that we all find the same woman attractive."

He glances at my bedroom door as if checking to see if anyone else is listening. "Noah's had the most trouble fitting in. Especially with the women."

That surprises me. Though Noah seemed as nervous as me on my first day.

"The women try to baby him or ignore him because he isn't as aggressive as the rest of us."

I raise my eyebrow. Noah is not passive at all. Cooper laughs.

"Aggressive is the wrong word. Socially aggressive. He's not afraid to take what he wants, but he doesn't always feel comfortable around some of the women we've hired or dated in the past."

My gaze goes to my open apartment door. Noah was my first connection and still is. Whatever is growing between us is strong. I don't like that those other women underestimated him or dismissed him.

"He likes you. A lot." The statement is matter of fact.

I return my gaze to Cooper's pale blue eyes. The single light he turned on over the sink barely illuminates the area. He puts the lid on the ice cream and moves it to the side. He gives me a wicked grin.

"Lie back."

I lower myself onto the island and take a breath as the coolness of the stone meets my heated skin.

"I promised to warm you up." He drags my panties down and off. I have nothing to hold on to when he pulls my hips closer to him. His breath against my pussy is the only warning I have before he closes his cold mouth on me.

I gasp at the sudden chill, but his tongue warms me up quickly as he explores my folds. He goes slow, like he has all night to go down on me. My desire grows steadily with each touch. As he slides a finger inside me, he sucks on my clit. My back arches off the island as all my focus goes to what he's doing between my legs.

The nightmare has long faded from my mind, melting away as he told me about them growing up. Now all I have is the fire they always stoke in me. The fire Cooper stokes in me. He's gentle but insistent, always building toward the peak.

He adds another finger inside me as he strokes his tongue around my clit. I'm almost there when he draws his fingers out of my pussy and presses one into my asshole. I explode with the sensation. My eyes squeeze shut as he keeps me on the edge and then drags me over into free fall when his tongue presses inside my pussy. I can't breathe as my climax ripples through me.

Removing his hands, he drags me down onto his lap and captures my lips. I can taste myself on his tongue as he explores my mouth as thoroughly as he licked my pussy. His cock is hard and ready between my legs beneath his boxers. I reach for him, but he captures my hand.

"No, sweetheart. Not tonight." He kisses me and lifts me back into his arms as he carries me back to the bedroom. My panties and the ice cream stay forgotten on the island.

I start to protest about leaving them, but he kisses me, making me forget everything else until he lowers me onto the bed.

"Time to sleep." He leaves me to go into the bathroom. Seth draws me back into his arms. Noah takes my hand and presses it against his warm heart. My breath catches and releases. I'm safe.

Chapter 20

Noah

Madison

I wake up nestled against Noah again. The morning light comes in through the window. My thigh rests over his hip, and my nightgown bunches around my waist. His hard cock presses against my pelvic bone.

I turn and don't see anyone else in the bed or the room.

"You okay, kitten?" Noah's usually rough voice is deeper this morning.

I nod. No more nightmares.

He rolls me onto my back and rubs his hard cock against my pussy. I gasp. Only his boxers are between us. I left my panties on the kitchen island, or maybe Cooper retrieved them after he put me back to bed.

"You've had me hard all morning, kitten, lying next to me with no panties." He strokes up my thigh to tease my clit with his fingers. Circling it. Stroking it. Making me wet and achy. Needy noises come from the back of my throat. When he finally thrusts his fingers inside my pussy, I arch against his hand. "You up to helping me with this?"

I moan as he angles his finger to hit a spot that makes my toes curl. Eagerly, I reach for his boxers. Fuck, yeah, I want to help him with it. I push his underwear over his hips and spread my legs for him. He shoves his boxers out of the way before he thrusts his cock into me. I gasp at the delicious sensation.

He holds steady for a moment, our bodies pressed as close as possible. Our breaths in each other's ears.

"Do you want it slow and easy, or hard and rough?" His voice in my ear sends sparks winding down my spine.

No contest.

I put my lips next to his ear. "Hard."

His low, dark chuckle tugs at something carnal in me. He grabs my hands and pins them to the mattress beside me as he rears back and slams into me. I bend my knees and spread my legs wider as he thrusts into me. It's hard and fast and rough and beautiful.

Our bodies slide against each other, and he shifts slightly so he hits a spot inside me that makes me burst into flames. Unable to hold back, I come in a gush of fluid around him, my pussy clenching around his cock.

"That's a good kitten." He bites down on my shoulder, and I arch up against him as he slams into me a final time. My mouth opens, but nothing comes out as I'm still coming. His warm cum fills me.

Our breathing is erratic as he lies half on top of me while we come back down. He releases my hands and tenderly traces his fingers along my sides.

He pushes himself up to hover over me. His cock still mostly hard inside me. "Are you okay, Madison?"

I'm not sure what he's asking about. Is it the nightmare or the sex we just had?

I release a breath and smile. "I'm good."

My voice is hoarse, like I've smoked a pack a day for the past twenty years, but it's not as painful to talk today.

His hard cock stirs within me. My channel tightens on him. When he smirks down at me, his dirty blond hair falls over his eyes.

He slides almost all the way out before pushing slowly back in, keeping his weight off me.

Tingles fill my stomach as he keeps up the slow pace. I rise to meet him until we are moving together in sync, crashing together over and over. I bite my lip at the sweet swell of the wave inside me.

His dark eyes pin me in place. "Next time you and I fuck alone, I'm going to tie your wrists and legs to my bed and fuck you until you've taken every last drop from me. Until you've come so many times it's almost painful to come again."

His words drive me higher. I thrust my hips into his as my orgasm rips through me.

"You like that idea, kitten?" He groans as my pussy tightens around him and milks him, pulling him into another orgasm. He comes inside me, his cock pulsing. This time, he wraps his arms around me and rolls onto his back so I'm draped over him.

My ear to his chest, I listen to his heartbeat return to normal. He strokes his hand down my back, and I can't help the swirl of emotions within me.

"I like you," I say as I snuggle down on his chest.

"I like you too."

Warmth spreads through me at his words.

We stay like that for a few moments before Noah picks me up to take me into the bathroom. He sets me on the counter and starts the shower. I slip into the water closet. When I come out, he ushers me into the shower. We wash each other, our hands tangling as we get all the spots.

His hands flow with the water over my aching nipples. He leans down to take one into his mouth, sucking like he has all the time in the world. Arousal flows through me, hot and needy. His fingers slip between my thighs and part my lips to rub my clit. He trails kisses across to my other nipple and sucks on it.

Right when I'm about to come, he stops and steps back. That's not happening. I step forward, putting soap in my hands.

I take my time rubbing the soap up and down his cock while

watching his eyes darken. With a growl, he takes hold of my hands and presses me up against the shower wall.

"Noah," I whisper as his lips trail down my neck. He switches my hands to be in one of his, and his other slides between my legs, sinking his fingers into my aching pussy.

"Madison, I need to fuck you so badly," he whispers against my throat before biting down where my shoulder meets my neck. "Tell me you can take it."

"Please." My voice is barely audible above the shower. "I want it."

He raises his head. His brown eyes hold me captive as he lifts one of my legs before his cock sinks inside my pussy again, going deeper.

I gasp at the fullness of his cock inside me. He slides out and thrusts hard back in. Tingles wind their way up my spine. "More."

His fathomless dark eyes hold me hostage as we climb together. His wet chest rubs on my hard nipples. It's building again. That fire that only they can put out.

"Noah," I bite out as I come, free-falling over the edge. My head tips back as I arch into him.

"Fuck, Madison." Noah leans in and kisses my shoulder where he marked me before and latches on as he thrusts hard and fast within me.

My orgasm doesn't stop. My core pulses around him, and I cry out as I tighten on him once again. He slams into me and moans as he erupts inside me.

He releases my hands and I lower them to wrap around his neck. His hand strokes my hip as he frees my leg. His other hand catches my jaw and tips my face up to his.

Leaning down, he claims my lips in a kiss that says I'm his. I can't argue with that. He draws me back into the water and gently washes between my legs again, slowly, almost worshipful. It tugs at my heart.

When he shuts the water off, he wraps me in a towel before he quickly dries himself. His blond hair sticks up on end when he's done. I like this version of him. He takes my towel and dries me while I stand perfectly still in front of him.

What is happening between us? Does he feel it too? Every touch is gentle and caring and almost too much to bear. I'm not supposed to be falling in love with these men. I'm supposed to be catering to the part of me I didn't have time to explore.

But Noah... Fuck, Noah calls to something deep inside me.

He stops in front of me and straightens. His fingers trace my jaw and gently cup my bruised cheek. "Stop overthinking things."

"I'm not—"

"You are." He reaches out and strokes down the side of my breast.

"I'll try." My throat doesn't hurt as much, but my voice sounds strange to my ears.

Noah's blond hair falls over his dark brown eyes as he smiles at me. He looks so young right now. Naked in front of me. His jaw has stubble on it, and I reach out to run my hand over it.

I want all of him.

He rubs his cheek into my hand like a cat would before turning and kissing my palm. "Let's get dressed and get some breakfast."

Blake

Noah leads Madison into the kitchen. She slides into the seat at the island next to me. She's got on pajama pants and an oversized t-shirt that hides her tight little figure.

Such a shame.

"Good morning," she says. Her voice sounds like she's fighting off a cold. It's husky and, combined with her floral scent, makes me hard.

"Morning."

Noah doesn't seem to understand the whole *we should give her space* thing. Even if she is living with us. I stood in the doorway earlier with a glass of water for Madison and watched him slowly drive her out of her mind. He's gotten more time alone with her. At least more time to fuck her on his own.

I could have joined them, but in that moment, I felt like an intruder on something intimate.

There may be no rules right now. No contract to dictate what we want, but Noah deserves to have his time with her. Too frequently the women we chose treated him like a sidekick. Madison looks at him like he's a hero, and that makes her worth ten of any of the others.

When her hand closes over my knee, my cock twitches and I turn to look at her. She doesn't seem to want that space Seth swears she needs.

"You okay?" she asks, one brow raised.

Fuck, this girl asking me if I'm okay, like I'm the one who took a beating. I take a drink from my coffee mug and turn to watch Noah making eggs and bacon for him and Madison.

When I meet her wide blue eyes, something catches in my chest. I could look into those eyes forever. "I'm good. You?"

Her cheeks flush. She smiles, and it rips through my soul. She's a survivor. That's what she is now. I'm not sure she could have survived what those assholes were talking about doing to her, though. They could have broken her, and we would have never been able to reach her.

As it was, they took some of that peace out of her. That feeling that nothing bad could happen. I wish I could have followed them and made them pay for what they did. But she's more important.

"I'm doing better." She touches her throat in the front. "Still a little sore."

I nod. "That's to be expected."

Noah puts a plate in front of Madison and takes the seat on her other side.

"Thank you," she says and leans in to kiss him like it's the most natural thing in the world. Domestic shit. Maybe it *is* easy between them. Maybe I'm a little jealous.

When she turns my way, she kisses my cheek before she eats.

I resist the urge to reach up and touch where her lips brushed me.

"What's the plan for today?" she asks, looking between me and Noah before biting down on some bacon.

"I have to go up to the office and work for a while," Noah says. He slips his hand over hers, and she turns it over so they are holding hands. Natural.

My chest tightens. But then she turns to me.

"What about you?" Her eyes are bright and alert this morning. She hasn't had any pain meds, and I can see the hint of pain lingering in her eyes.

I stand and go to the cabinet and pull out the Advil. Sitting, I hand her two pills.

"Thank you." She acts like I gave her a diamond necklace. She's so different from the ones that came before her. They all wanted something from us, and not just sex.

"I have time if you want to do something," I say before I can think better of it.

"I guess I'm supposed to relax still." She glances around as if looking for the others. Seth would probably say that she should relax, and in all honesty, she should. The physical and emotional toll on her probably hasn't hit that hard yet.

"We can figure something out." I shrug like it isn't a big deal.

She grabs my hand and squeezes it. Noah's eyes meet mine, but he's not jealous. Of course not, he just fucked her. He smiles indulgently at her before kissing her again.

"You two have fun." He puts his plate and hers into the dishwasher before claiming her mouth one last time. This time, kissing her until she can barely breathe. When he backs away, her hand goes to her chest. "I'll see you later, kitten."

I swear there's a bounce to his step as he leaves the apartment.

Chapter 21

Blake

Blake

Madison turns on her chair to face me. "What do you want to do?"

All I can think of is fucking her. Shit. I'm probably as bad as Noah. My cock is definitely on board.

"I have to review some reports." The words slip out before I can take them back. It's true, though. My mind couldn't focus on them yesterday with what happened.

"Need my help?" She arches her eyebrow.

"You can keep me company." I stand and offer her my hand. After she slips her hand into mine, I lead her to my bedroom door. I want her to rest, but I also want her in my bed. Not where she just had sex with Noah.

When we enter, she looks around. I watch where her gaze lands. First, the king-sized bed with its black satin sheets and red comforter. Then her eyes widen when she finds my display of paddles and whips. She walks over to the wall and strokes her finger down a paddle.

When she looks over her shoulder at me, her eyes have darkened. "Is this just a display?"

Shaking my head, I swallow. "I'm a dominant."

She lowers her arm and turns to face me. Her eyes are wide, with no judgment on her face. "Like spanking?"

"And other things. Mostly I like to control my submissive and punish her when she's out of line." I walk to the bed and sit on top of the covers against the headboard. I pat the spot beside me as I pick up my tablet.

She crawls onto the bed and sits next to me, her warmth against my side. Her gaze strays to the display again. "Do you want to do that with me?"

Her gaze flicks up to mine.

"Yes, if you want to. It's not about taking. It's about giving for both of us. If you don't want to do any of that, I won't force you to. It will only happen if it's something you want to do or try. But we would both have safe words to break out of the scene."

She licks her full lips, drawing my attention to them. "I'd like to try sometime."

My cock throbs in my pants. I lift my tablet. "Right now, I need to go over these reports."

She frowns, probably wondering what she can do.

I hold up another tablet and hand it to her. "I thought you might like to read."

She grins and takes the tablet. Resting her head against my shoulder, she scrolls through the apps to find what she wants. I try to control the overwhelming need to fuck her.

Instead, I open my reports and focus on the task at hand.

After a while, she sighs next to me. I glance over at her from my tablet. Her pupils are dilated. Her lips part as she plucks at her lower lip while she reads. I glance at what she's reading, but my eyes only focus on a few words: cock, pussy, thrust.

I set my tablet aside, and she glances up at me.

"What are you reading?"

She swallows and her eyebrow lifts. "A book."

"What book?"

She closes it and sets it aside. She gives me a slightly wicked smile. "One that involves BDSM."

My balls tighten as my cock hardens. "You were enjoying it?"

She nods.

"Do you want to play, tiger?"

Her eyes widen eagerly and she nods again.

"You'll need a safe word. Something you can say that will stop everything." My fingers tighten as I think of all the things I want to do to her. The things we can try together. But for now, I'll keep it tame.

"Gold."

"So if I'm doing something you don't like or is too far, you say..."

"Gold." She squirms next to me.

I nod to the floor next to the bed. "Undress."

She scrambles to her feet and takes off her shirt and pajama pants. She's wearing red lacy panties and a matching bra. When she reaches to take them off, I shake my head.

"Leave it on for now." I stand in front of her. She meets my eyes. "Lower your eyes to the floor. Hands clasped behind your back."

She does as she's told. I sit on the edge of the bed to take her in. Her neck is bruised, the skin mottled with purple and almost black in spots. Her golden hair hangs in waves around her shoulders. The bra and panty set she wears is perfect against her pale skin. The tops of her arms are also bruised, but not quite as badly. I tip her chin to the side to see her cheek.

"Does it still hurt?" I ask.

"Yes." She hesitates for a moment before adding, "sir."

I slide my hand over her shoulder and knock her strap off it to hang on her arm. Her nipples harden. When I do the same on the other side, she doesn't move, but her breath quickens.

"Have you ever been spanked before?"

A shiver races over her as she shakes her head.

"Do you want me to spank you?"

Her breath comes out in a rush as she lifts her eyes to mine.

"Yes." Her answer is breathy.

"Head down," I say.

She drops her gaze to the floor.

"Turn around." I stand in front of her, and she turns her back to me. All that beautiful pale skin on display. I can't wait to watch it pinken. "Hands on the wall."

She takes a step forward and I grab her hips to stop her.

"Did I say move forward?" I put some annoyance in my voice just to see what she can take. I don't want to frighten her, but I do want to control her, to have her give in to me.

She glances over her shoulder and shakes her head. She leans over and presses her hands to the wall. Her arms stretch out above her head as she's bent over in front of me. My cock weeps. The scrap of red fabric that hides her from me is darker between her legs from her arousal.

"Spread your legs." I take off my sweats and toss them to the side. I didn't bother with boxers today.

Whimpering, she obeys. She's already soaked her panties. So fucking wet all the time for us.

"What's your safe word?" I drag my finger up the center of her.

"Gold," she says as she tries to remain still.

"Good girl." I caress her ass and feel her muscles flinch beneath my touch. "Normally I would give spankings as a punishment, but sometimes they can just be for pleasure or a need to blow off steam for either of us."

"Either?" She tips her head toward me but doesn't raise her gaze to mine.

"You giving up your control to me can be very centering for you." I slip my finger beneath the edge of her panties and trail it through her wetness. Her head hangs down again. "Do you want to give up control, tiger?"

"Yes, sir." She shudders beneath my touch as I lightly toy with her clit.

"I'll only use my hand on your ass this time. If something's too much, tell me." I take ahold of her panties and tug, ripping them.

She moans as I drop the shredded material onto the floor.

"What's your word?" I thrust my fingers into her cunt.

"Fuck. Gold." Her hips try to move on my fingers.

"Do you want to stop?" I ask.

"No, sir," she breathes out.

I slap her ass cheek with about medium force. She cries out, and her pussy clamps down on my fingers, soaking them. Perfection.

I rub at the redness forming on her pale skin. She moans and tries to rock her hips again. I smack her other ass cheek.

"Don't move, tiger."

"Yes, sir." She bites her lip. Her breasts hang down, the bra doing little to stop their swaying.

My cock twitches, and I pull my fingers from her to stroke her wetness over my dick a few times, staring at her red ass and pink pussy spread before me. I want to plow into her and make us both come, but I also don't want this to end so soon. Waiting will make it sweeter.

"More?" I ask.

"Yes, please."

When I thrust my fingers into her soaking cunt again, she lets out a little cry. I spank both cheeks, one after the other, before rubbing the ache away. "Do you like that?"

Her breath pants out of her as she nods. Her head hangs.

"Do you want me to fuck you?"

"Yes, please, sir."

I draw my fingers out and thrust them back in. She lets out a huff. Her fingers curl on the wall. I slap her ass cheeks again. The redness is even brighter now.

"Please, Blake," she moans, as I don't move. "Please fuck me."

I pull my fingers out and thrust my cock inside her in one motion.

"Yes," she cries out.

I grab her hips and set a steady pace of thrusting inside her. I can feel her tightening around me.

"Don't come or you'll be punished," I warn her.

She whimpers and I pick up speed. Her tits sway with the motion of my cock in her cunt. She keeps getting tighter and tighter as she holds off the orgasm trying to slam through her.

"Please, Blake," she pants. "I can't hold back."

"If you come, you'll get punished," I grit out again, close to coming myself. I don't let up, though, knowing it will drive her over the edge.

"Fuck," she yells in her hoarse voice as she clamps down on my cock, forcing me to come with her. Her cunt shudders and pulses around me as I fill her.

I pull out and stroke my cock to keep it hard. "On your knees facing me."

She turns and drops to her knees. My chest throbs. There's something so sweet in her complete surrender.

"Open your mouth and tip your head back. Show me your tongue."

She does it. The look on her face almost makes me come again. She's eager and willing. Fuck, this girl is fantastic.

I stroke my cock in front of her face. Her eyes watch my hand as she squirms on her knees. Her hands rest on her thighs.

"Don't swallow until I say so."

I jerk off to the sight of her kneeling before me. Her mouth wide. Her blue eyes locked on mine but hooded with desire. Every inch of her is beautiful, and all I want to do is throw her on the bed and fuck into her over and over again until we're both satiated.

With a groan, I spill into her mouth, coating her tongue. Fuck. When I'm spent, I look down at her mouth filled with my cum.

She holds it open for me, waiting. My cock twitches.

"Swallow it all."

She closes her mouth and swallows twice.

"Show me."

She opens her mouth for me to see it's all gone.

I stroke my hand over her hair. "Good girl."

She smiles, proud of herself. I lift her into my arms, carrying her into the bathroom and setting her on the counter. She sits quietly watching me while I draw a bath in the slipper tub. I add bubble bath.

This pull between us only grows with every moment I'm with her.

"The most important part is the aftercare," I explain.

I take off my clothes. Moving to her, I remove her bra, the only thing she has left on. My fingers trace her nipples and she sighs. I lean in and kiss her briefly before shutting off the tub.

When I lift her in my arms again, she wraps herself around me.

"Stay standing." I set her on her feet in the tub before climbing in. After I sit, I reach a hand up to her. The warm water engulfs her as she lowers down. Sighing, she settles her back against my chest.

"Did you like that, Madison?" I stroke my hands over her arms.

"Yes." Her head rests against my shoulder and she closes her eyes.

"Anything you didn't like?"

She shakes her head.

"Good."

She releases a breath and sinks into me. I grab a washcloth and drag it over her skin.

As I trail water down her shoulders and her breasts, my voice is low when I admit, "I wasn't supposed to be there."

She half turns to look at me, her blue eyes wide.

"We were supposed to give you time to adjust. To think about what happened in the conference room and decide whether you wanted to continue with us. We were afraid we were moving too fast."

She relaxes her back against my chest and takes my hands in hers, squeezing them lightly. She brings my knuckles to her lips and brushes a kiss over them.

"When I carried you to the shower that night and held you, you seemed so dazed and fragile."

She settles more into me and wraps my arms around her as she turns her cheek against my chest, over my stuttering heart.

"I didn't like leaving it like that. It didn't feel like enough after everything you gave us. Everything you gave me." My voice breaks a little and I clear my throat. "I wanted to make sure you were all right."

"You didn't do anything wrong." Her voice is a little more hoarse. She turns in the tub and straddles my lap. Her hands go to my cheeks, and she forces me to look at her. "Hey, you didn't do anything wrong."

"We sent you home. We forced you into that situation. If I'd kept you—"

"They would have gotten to me another time." Her smile is a little sad. "They were determined to take what was mine. Nothing would have stopped them from trying."

I curl my hands around her hips and draw her into me. My cock has already recovered. This woman makes me hard constantly, but this moment isn't about sex. I need that connection to her. To feel her all around me.

As if she senses what I need, she rises and lowers her pussy onto my hard cock.

"I should have gotten there sooner. I should have never let you leave. I should have kept you in my bed and away from harm." My hands brush her hair out of her face. "I never should have tried to shut you out. I was afraid you'd be like the others, but you are nothing like them."

She takes my mouth as she rides my cock, slowly rocking her hips over me while our tongues tangle.

This isn't about getting off. It's about the connection that began the moment we talked on the phone for the first time. Those little catches in her breath like she loved listening to me talk. The wide eyes filled with need when we met in the conference room for the first time, and the bolt that rocked me the first time we shook hands.

Every moment since then until this moment right here.

"I will always be grateful you showed up, Blake." Her words have a breathless quality to them as her body seeks release. "But I'm not in here because of gratitude. I'm in here because I want you. I need you. I crave you."

"I want you, tiger." I run my hands over her soapy breasts and down to her hips, guiding her to a motion that will get us both there. "I need you." Kissing the corner of her lips. "I crave you." Kissing the other corner of her lips. "I want you."

Her pussy tightens on my cock as she falls over the edge, taking me with her. Stars burst around the edges of my vision. I wrap her in my arms and hold her tight, knowing how close we got to losing her. How close they came to breaking her.

We stay still for a few minutes. I could stay like this forever. But when she shivers a little, I help her out of the tub and we dry ourselves off. She slips into the pajama pants without her ripped panties, then her bra and oversized t-shirt. I grab a pair of sweats and pull them on.

I take her hand as we go back into the bedroom, and I pull her down onto the bed. She scoots in close to me as I pick up my tablet and read my reports. After a few minutes, she's asleep, snuggled up against me.

I brush her golden hair off her cheek, and peace settles in my chest. I don't want this moment to end. That thought should disturb me. This isn't anything more than convenient.

But Madison makes it different. She makes it feel real.

Chapter 22

Cooper

Cooper

When I get back from my workout, it's a little after lunchtime and no one is in the main apartment. I head into my room and take a quick shower. When I come out of my room, I pause by Madison's door, wondering if I should knock or just go in.

We turned off the security lock for now. None of us wants to be locked out of her room, though if she needs to, she can reengage the lock.

Fuck it. I open the door, and no one is in her living room or her bedroom. I even check the bathroom. A little pinch of fear goes through me. What if she left?

When I come out of her bedroom, her suite door opens. Madison stands there rumpled with some serious bed head.

"Take a nap, sweetheart?" My voice startles her. Her gaze bounces up to mine.

She smiles when she realizes it's me. "Yeah, Blake was reading reports, and I fell asleep."

Her cheeks flush with color. I'm sure that's not all she did in

Blake's room. What all did he do with her? He has some pretty kinky shit in his room. I'm kind of sad I missed it.

"How are you feeling?"

"Still a little sore." She touches her throat. Her voice is huskier than usual.

"Do you have plans for this afternoon?" I raise an eyebrow. I know exactly what I want to do, but I'll let her choose.

She shakes her head with a shy smile and gestures toward her bedroom. "I need to freshen up, though. This place is rough on panties."

I close in on her and run my hands down into the back of her pajama pants, finding only bare skin. She hisses a little at the touch.

"Did Blake spank you?" I lift an eyebrow.

She nods warily. I spin her around and press her hands to the door. "I want to see."

"Go right ahead." I can almost hear the eye roll in her words.

Not that it would stop me. I tug her pajama pants all the way down. Her ass cheeks are a little pink. I trace over the faint outline of Blake's hand. "You like being spanked, sweetheart?"

"Yes." Her head drops as my touch trails lower. She sucks in a breath.

I lower my voice. "How much have you been fucked this morning?"

I slip my finger inside her wet pussy. She stops breathing.

"Three times with Noah. Twice with Blake."

"And yesterday with all of us." I close in on her back as I pump my finger in and out of her sweet pussy. I reach around her hip to stroke her clit. "You getting sore here, sweetheart?"

She leans back against me and shakes her head.

"You want more?" I kiss the tip of her ear and trail kisses down to right behind her ear.

"Yes." She exhales.

"Can I play with you?" I add another finger inside her and circle her clit.

"Yes, please." She wraps her arm around my neck as she shatters for me. So beautiful. I stroke her through her orgasm and then remove my hands. When she turns to face me, her eyes are warm ocean pools begging me to dive in.

"Clean up. I'll wait." I press a chaste kiss to her lips.

Her eyes narrow on me, but then she shrugs, grabs her pajama pants, and walks around me to her bathroom. I sit on the edge of her bed while I wait for her. With four of us to keep satisfied, she has her work cut out for her.

She comes back out with her t-shirt and pajama pants still on, but she drops her bra into the hamper.

"Going without?" I raise an eyebrow as I hold out my hand.

As she takes my hand, she shrugs and smiles. "They just get in the way."

A chuckle escapes me. She's not wrong. I'd applaud her efforts, but I don't want to share her right now.

"Come on." I take her into the apartment and unlock my door. When we walk in, her eyes go to the pale gold wall. "Looking for toys stuck on the walls like Blake's room? I'm a little more discreet."

She blushes. I lead her to the bed. My cotton sheets and duvet cover are cream. A throw blanket in gold lies across the end of the bed. A dark leather chair sits in the corner.

I sit down next to the nightstand and tug her to sit beside me. Opening the drawer, I take out a vibrating bullet and a couple of butt plugs, one small and one medium. I also set some lube on the nightstand.

She picks up the vibrating bullet. Turning it on, she holds it against her other finger. She flips it off and picks up the butt plugs.

"Have you seen these before?"

She nods. "But I haven't ever used anything like it. I have a rabbit vibrator at home." She blushes and gestures to the door. "I mean, I guess, here now. In a box."

She ducks her head, and I lift her chin to look at me. "Never be ashamed to chase your pleasure, sweetheart."

Unable to resist her pink lips, I kiss her softly. Before either of us tries to deepen the kiss, I pull back. "I want to work on preparing you for anal."

Her eyes widen and she swallows.

"If you don't like something, or if anything hurts, you let me know right away. We'll get you off, but don't worry about trying to get off. We need to work those muscles a little before we get to the ultimate goal."

Her lips part, but she nods.

I lift her shirt off. Her breasts are the best size. Not too big, but not too small. A good handful. I take the bullet in one hand but softly caress her breast with my other. "Remember, tell me what feels good too."

She nods and watches my fingers tweak her nipple. She lets out a little gasp and squirms. If I reach between her legs, she'll be wet, which is the goal. I need her aroused for this to work.

Lifting the bullet, I show her before I turn it on. I run the bullet across her hardened nipple, and she moans.

"That feels good," she whispers.

Smiling, I take her other nipple into my mouth while I continue to tease her with the bullet. One hand braces herself while her other threads through my loosened, shoulder-length hair.

When her breathing becomes shallow, I back away to watch the bullet around her nipple before bringing it over to the other. She sucks in a breath and her eyes close. I take her other nipple into my mouth and tease it slowly with my tongue and teeth.

"Cooper." Her hips rock a little.

"You can call me Coop." I capture her lips and press her down onto the bed. We taste each other's mouths as the bullet teases her nipples, one then the other. I flatten it against her sternum and ease the bullet down her stomach.

I lift my mouth from hers and watch her expressions as I slide the bullet beneath her pajama pants and to the top of her pubic bone. Her darkened eyes watch mine as she bites on her lip.

"Does that feel good?"

She nods and her eyes widen when I turn up the vibration.

I slip the bullet down between her folds, and she arches up against me. When I finally press it against her clit, her hands grab my arms.

"Coop. I don't— I'm going to— Fuck." Her mouth opens wide as she gushes her release onto my hand. She shudders against me as her thighs tighten together.

"Don't fight it, Madison." I kiss her before drawing the bullet away and setting it aside. "If you need to come, come."

She nods and watches me greedily as I drag her pants down and off. I stand and take off my athletic pants. She wets her lips as she takes in my hard cock. Scooting her farther onto the bed, I lie down beside her. Every inch of her makes my mouth water and my cock harden.

I kiss both of her breasts, taking time to tease her nipples with my tongue before trailing kisses down her stomach. There's this delicate curve that women have that I just adore, and Madison's is no exception to that. My tongue dips into her navel.

She arches up beneath me, seeking more. I lift my mouth from her.

"If you don't like something..."

Her pupils are so blown I can barely see the thin ring of blue. "I'll tell you."

I kiss her stomach before sliding between her legs. My tongue flicks over her clit and I push her knees up. She tastes like heaven. I can't get enough of her. She rocks her hips against my mouth as I tease and taste every inch of her wet pussy, exploring the folds and peaks, listening for that hitch in her breath when I do something she loves. Learning her. I dip my tongue into her needy cunt and feel it squeeze around me.

Her breathing grows ragged as I drive her closer and closer to coming. I shift lower until my tongue brushes over her puckered hole.

"Coop?" She sounds unsure.

"Try it, sweetheart. If you don't like it, I'll stop. Relax." I lick her puckered hole and she whimpers. I push her knees out, spreading her open before me. She quivers beneath my tongue. My cock twitches, so hard it feels like it's going to burst if it's not allowed to play soon. She's so responsive and accepting of all we want to do to her. She's perfect.

I slip my fingers into her pussy and work them in and out while I lick at her asshole. Her hips follow my fingers. When I feel her relax, I dart my tongue into her ass.

She squeaks but doesn't say stop. I thrust my tongue inside in rhythm with my fingers in her cunt. She moans and makes little noises that drive me crazy. Her hips rock against my mouth until she comes again with a little shocked cry. Her cunt convulses, tightening around my fingers.

Needing to see her, I lift my head, keeping my fingers inside her, slowly stroking to keep the fire lit. Her golden hair spreads around her head as she pants. She looks like a fallen angel. Her darkened blue eyes meet mine. My fallen angel.

"Hands and knees." I draw my fingers out and help her flip over. I press on her upper back until her head is down and her ass is up.

I squirt some lube on my finger and show it to her. "One to begin with. I'm going to rub the muscles inside to get them to loosen up."

"Fuck, Coop." Her forehead drops to the mattress and her ass lowers a little. "I don't know how much more I can take."

"Take it all." I grin before I lick across her puckered hole again. She moans and turns her face so I can see every expression. I kiss her ass cheeks as I slide my lubed finger into her hole. She tenses and I wait for her to relax. Going slow, I push in and pull back out, getting a little farther each time until my finger is all the way inside.

"Good?" I ask. My cock is dripping with precum as I watch my finger move in and out of her asshole. She's so fucking tight. I want to feel this ass squeezing around my cock, but it will have to wait.

"Yes." She rocks with my motion. Her lips part.

"Feel good?"

She nods and meets my eyes over her shoulder. Fuck, she's hot. I wish I could just slam my cock into her ass and take her hard and fast, but I'm not an asshole.

I still my finger deep in her and press against the walls slightly, rubbing and feeling them loosen beneath my touch. She relaxes under me and the muscles ease with her. It's a slow process, but it will help.

She moans as I pull my finger out. I grab a wipe off the nightstand and clean my finger before grabbing the small plug. I wait until she looks at me to see what I'm doing.

"I'm going to see how you do with the small one, and we may work up to the medium one today, or later." I spread lube over the small anal plug and stroke my cock a few times.

She watches my hand and licks her lips. "Okay."

She widens her stance, putting that pink pussy on full display. Fuck if I don't want to just... I kneel behind her and slide the tip of my cock along her clit.

She exhales shakily. "Coop. Please."

I thrust my cock inside her pussy, and she makes little needy noises I can't resist. I thrust a few times before I still inside her, trying to find my control. She presses her ass against me, and I can feel her pussy quiver around my dick.

"Soon, Madison." I slide the butt plug along her crack and dip the tip into her asshole. Slowly, I push it in and then ease it all the way out repeatedly, while controlling my breathing. My cock pulses inside her, eager to come, but I want to make this good for her.

I'm more than my cock.

The plug slides in farther and she moans. I pick up the bullet in my other hand and turn it on. The plug slides all the way inside her. I let her relax and make sure it's good to keep going. I can feel it squeezing her cunt tighter around me. Through her thin walls, the plug is firm against my cock.

"What do you think, sweetheart?"

"Full. Please." She pants as her hips try to rock against mine. "More."

I press the bullet against her clit as I pull my cock a little way out before sliding deep again.

"Coop!" she cries out as I stroke my cock inside her. We move together as I hold the bullet on her clit. I tug a little on the plug. Crying out, she tumbles over the edge. Her pussy soaks my cock and my hand. I thrust a few more times and shift the plug in time with my thrusts. She clamps down on me again as she moans deep and long, dragging me into my orgasm.

Groaning, I let go and come inside her. Warmth and wetness consume me. Her pussy flutters, squeezing my cock as it twitches and empties. Her ass tightens around the plug and then I ease it out.

An aftershock ripples through her, and she tightens again on my dick. Fuck if I don't want to start all over again, but her head barely lifts off the bed. Her breathing is evening out.

I pull us both onto our sides with my cock still buried in her pussy. Normally, I'd be off the bed and in the shower before the condom hit the trash can, but with her, I want to stay and hold her. I stroke my hand over her side and kiss the back of her neck. "Thoughts?"

"Fuck," she whispers as a little aftershock pulses around me again.

"Just wait, sweetheart. It'll be even better when it's my cock."

Chapter 23

Seth

Madison

I wake with Coop's arms around me in the middle of his bed. His hard cock remains inside me. Given my year-long sex hiatus, the guys are sure making up for lost time. I rock my hips against him, pushing my need higher, and he hardens more inside me.

His hips take over the motion as his hand trails down. His fingers circle my pulsing clit in small, tight circles until I can barely breathe. I didn't think I had any more to give, but my body uncoils, and an orgasm screeches through me. Coop thrusts hard a few more times before he stills deep inside me and comes.

He holds me as our hearts and breaths slow down.

"Good nap?" He kisses my shoulder, teeth trailing over the mark Noah left.

I gasp at the small sting. "Yes."

When he pulls out, his fingers push his cum back inside. I should be all tapped out, but my body warms under his probing fingers.

I roll to look at him. "Why do you do that?"

He brings his cum-tipped fingers to my lips. I look him in the eye as I lick them clean, tasting him and me mixed. My pussy clenches as that need returns. His eyes darken.

"I want you filled all the time."

"With you guys, I will be." I press a kiss to his lips. When I pull away, he gently holds the back of my neck to keep me there and deepens the kiss, tasting his cum on my tongue.

"Good girl." Those words send the butterflies in my stomach into a whirlwind of flutters.

When he leads me into the shower, I put my hair up, and we wash each other's bodies. He takes special care between my legs and my ass until I'm keyed up all over again. His hot skin brushes against mine.

He chuckles when I lean in and kiss his wet chest, but he doesn't make me come. Is it even possible at this point? I probably met my quota. I'm not sure how much more I have left in me.

After we dress, we head into the living room. When Coop pulls me down on the couch and puts on a movie, I lean into him and sigh. This is comfortable and not a situation I'm used to dealing with. I've never really had a boyfriend. No one ever snuggled me the way these guys do. A girl could get used to this.

The movie goes on while I just absorb this feeling of contentment.

"Hungry?" Seth's voice cuts through the movie sounds.

I find him in the kitchen, fixing something. Kissing Coop on the cheek, I walk over to Seth and stand next to him in my bare feet. He's a lot taller than me without my heels.

He glances over at me as he chops vegetables. "You have a good day?"

"I have." I lean against the island.

"What did you do?"

My face heats as my mind says, *Noah, Blake, and Coop.*

He smirks at me, not quite a smile, but close. I'll get a full one at some point. He wipes his hands on a towel and grabs my waist to lift me onto the island next to where he's working. "Entertain me while I make a salad to go with dinner."

I notice a couple of pots on the stove and the oven on.

"What do you want me to do?"

"Tell me in detail about your day." He raises an eyebrow, as if daring me to recount what happened.

I lean back on my hands. These guys are not shy about sex, so there's no need for me to be. "I woke up to Noah alone in my bed. Hard. He asked me if I wanted to be fucked slow and easy or hard and fast. He took me hard and fast until I came and then went slow and easy."

Seth nods like I just told him about the price of beans. "What else?"

Okay, I can do this. "Then we showered, and he fucked me up against the shower wall."

"What position?"

My breath stutters, and I feel hot under the collar, remembering while I describe it. "My back against the wall. Hands trapped above in his with my leg hitched up so he could go deep."

Seth moves to the fridge and grabs a cucumber. Setting it on the cutting board, he slices it. "Go on."

"Then we came out and had breakfast with Blake. Noah had to go to work, and Blake needed to read some reports. I went with Blake to his bedroom, and while he read, I read some erotic romance."

"Did it turn you on?" Seth's dark blue eyes capture mine. His voice is so rich, coaxing me to tell him everything.

"Yes," I whisper and squirm on the cool island. My pussy is warm and getting warmer by the minute.

He holds up a slice of cucumber to my lips. I take it with my teeth and eat it. He nods for me to continue as he takes an apple from the basket on the island and sets it on his cutting board.

"Blake asked me to strip to my underwear and lean against the wall. He tore my panties off and spanked me before he fucked me.

Then we took a bath, and we fucked in the water." My breath shortens and my cheeks feel hot.

Seth slides a piece of apple on my lips. When I part my lips, he pushes it inside. I eat the tart, juicy apple, becoming more and more aroused.

"I napped for a little while. After that, Coop took me to his room to train me for anal." My chest rises and falls with every word. My nipples ache, they are so hard. My pussy pulses.

"How'd he do that?" Seth asked nonchalantly.

"He had a bullet vibrator and a butt plug." I squirm and whimper, hoping all this is going somewhere because I need to get off again. "He licked and tongue fucked my ass and used his finger to stretch me first. Then he thrust his cock into my pussy and worked the plug into my ass. When it was fully inside me, he used the vibrator on my clit while he fucked me."

Seth sets his knife down and steps between my legs, pushing them wider. "Did you come hard, princess?"

I nod, unable to say anything with his full attention on me. My focus goes to his lips and I lick mine.

"Did you sleep?"

I nod again, watching his lips move and wanting them on me.

"Did he fuck you when you woke?"

Fuck, I want his lips on me while he fucks me hard. I nod.

"How's your throat?"

My gaze shoots up to his eyes at the change in topic. "It's fine."

"No one fucked your mouth?"

I shake my head. "Blake came on my tongue, but I didn't suck him off."

"Good girl." He leans close. His shirt brushes against mine, such a tease of a sensation. When he breathes against my neck for a moment, I hold my breath, waiting for him to touch me. Pinpricks bathe my skin in anticipation. He steps away and puts all the ingredients in a bowl before setting it aside.

I want to scream in frustration and aching need, but I wait patiently.

"Take off your pants." His words are soft as he washes his hands in the sink.

I shimmy them down over my hips and let them drop to the floor. My hot pussy bare on the cool marble island makes me suck in my breath.

"No panties?" He arches an eyebrow.

"Blake tore them." I shrug. "They just get in the way."

Seth picks up a washcloth and wipes down the counter beside me. "Remove your top."

I do as he asks, and his gaze takes in my hardened nipples. He moves away from me and hangs up the rag before washing his hands again.

"Put your feet on the edge of the counter."

I go to scoot back, but Seth shakes his head.

"Right where you are, princess."

Wetness trickles out of me as I do as he asks, opening myself up to his gaze. He leans against the counter across from me and stares between my legs.

"Do you feel thoroughly fucked, princess?" Seth lifts his gaze to mine.

I'm not sure what answer he wants. Am I thoroughly satisfied? Yes. But do I want more? Also yes.

"Yes." The word comes out hesitant.

"You don't sound sure." He lowers his gaze to my pussy again, and I swear the heat inside me is radiating. "Are they not satisfactory lovers?"

"Yes, they are," I blurt.

"But you're missing something?" He raises an eyebrow when he lifts his eyes back to mine, pinning me in place.

I bite my lip and nod. "Yes."

"Do you want me to fuck you, princess?" Seth doesn't move from the counter. My gaze drops to the hard cock outlined in his athletic pants.

I lick my lips. "Yes, sir."

"Touch your pussy and get your fingers nice and wet."

I exhale and dip a finger inside myself, spreading the wetness over my pussy and my fingers at the same time. He watches me without moving. His eyes never leave my pussy.

"Rub your wetness on your nipples." His darkened gaze lifts to mine.

I groan at the feel of my wet fingers tracing over my hardened nipples. One of the chairs scrapes on the floor behind me. Seth's gaze goes over my shoulder for a moment, but then returns to focus on me.

"Fuck your pussy with your fingers, princess."

I slide my fingers inside my tight core and thrust them in and out, wishing it was Seth's cock instead. My breathing is erratic. I'm getting close. He steps forward and grabs my wrist.

"Relax." He waits until I release the tension in my arm. Holding my wrist, he slows down the thrusts of my fingers, controlling me. He leans in and licks my nipples clean while fucking me with my own fingers.

It's so fucking hot and winds me so tight. I'm almost there, right on the edge of something amazing all over again. I just hope he doesn't leave me wanting like Coop did in the shower.

"Lie back, princess."

I meet his eyes and do as he asks. My heated skin feels like it steams as it meets the cool counter. I tip my head up and look into Blake's and Noah's eyes. When I turn my head, I see Coop on the couch, watching me and not the movie.

All I need is Seth to flick my clit, and I'll come long and hard with all of them watching me. Fuck, I want that. To be the object of their desire.

"Look at me, princess. They've all had you already. It's my turn." Seth's rich voice is stern, and I return to his mesmerizing blue eyes.

His hand continues to move my fingers in and out, building me up to another climax. "Give me your other hand."

I hold it out to him. He positions my fingers so two fingers are extended while the others curl into my fist. He brings them to his lips and sucks them into his mouth. I gasp as my pussy tightens around my fingers. His eyes hold mine while he licks and sucks my fingers, while he thrusts my other fingers into me a little harder.

I whimper at the need for release. His eyes scorch me as he pulls my fingers free of his mouth and rubs them on my clit. Moaning, I shatter. He pulls my hands out of the way and flattens them on the counter beside my hips.

My release pulses through my pussy. His pants rustle before he slides his cock inside me, stretching me. I suck in a breath at the sudden fullness. It feels right, like I'm finally whole. I'm sore, but fuck do I want this.

His hands go to my knees and press them out while he pistons in and out of me. I can feel the others' hot gazes on my tits as they jiggle with each thrust, but I keep my eyes locked on Seth's.

He watches his cock disappear inside my pussy, and just knowing that's what he's doing makes my blood boil with need and want and lust until the dam bursts again. My back arches against the island as I cry out Seth's name. My pussy clutches at his cock, needing more, wanting more.

He thrusts hard in and out, until with a roar, he comes inside me, filling me with his hot cum. My pussy spasms around him, wanting it all.

He thrusts deep one last time and holds himself there for a moment. My chest rises and falls quickly, and I take a deep breath to try to steady myself.

Releasing my legs, he pulls out before shifting his pants back into place. He lifts me down from the counter and puts my shirt on before holding my pajama pants for me to slip my feet into and pulls them up.

Moving me over to the sink, he crowds behind me. His still-hard cock presses to my ass as he turns on the sink and washes our hands together. An aftershock ripples through me, and I let out a surprised gasp. He dries our hands and then smacks my bottom lightly.

"Dinner time."

Seth

Madison sits beside me at the table. She's dripping with my cum as I pass the salad to her. Nothing is hotter than her at this moment. She blushes at me as she takes the salad. We pass around the spaghetti and Italian sausage I made for dinner.

Carbs are good for energy, and our girl needs it to heal. And to keep up with us.

The marks on her neck are a more pronounced purple and black today, making me want to hunt down the asshole that did it on my own. I did a little digging earlier today. Seems Valerie Davis and Jeff Moore have been busy. They were picked up on possession of an illegal substance at least twice this month and made it out on bail both times.

Makes sense why they needed to get money from Madison. My fists clench under the table. If we hadn't given her that bonus, she would have been homeless. Her next-door neighbor enjoys talking and told me all about the eviction notice.

Robert seems a little too keen on Madison, but I've got a background check running on him too. So far nothing, but that doesn't mean he's harmless.

Madison leans into Noah as she laughs at something he says.

I'm not surprised the guys played with Madison all day. Her willingness to share the details with me makes me happy. It means she isn't trying to hide anything between us. Not from each other.

That's a good start, and fucking her before dinner so she would sit with my cum inside her, well, that was a little territorial. I don't begrudge the others their fun or refuse to share, but that doesn't mean I won't mark our girl as mine too.

Maybe it's because she's vulnerable right now, but the other women weren't like this. They definitely didn't get fucked from the time they got up until they went to sleep. And if they had, they would have complained about it.

But not Madison.

Work starts again tomorrow, and that means back to the real world.

"How do you feel about work tomorrow?" I ask Madison.

She puts her fork on the edge of her plate. "I should be fine. It's mostly desk work, and if I get worn out—"

"You'll come down here and nap," I insist.

She nods as she picks up her fork and spears a piece of sausage.

"You won't leave the top floor except to get groceries." I meet the others' eyes in turn, and they each nod subtly in agreement.

She shrugs. "I don't have any reason to go downstairs unless one of you tells me to."

"You need to heal, and we don't need to start rumors about one of us choking you." I arch my eyebrow.

She touches her neck. "But you didn't—"

"We moved you in a week early. There will be talk. It's best if you lie low until your bruising fades."

The rumors after Rachel left were awful. Some said we drove her out. Others thought we got rough with her. There were more rumors than truth flying around downstairs.

"That's fine." She chews a bite thoughtfully. "Can I have Hope up sometime this week?"

I check with the others. "It shouldn't be a problem. You can entertain her in your suite."

She smiles at me. "You guys intimidate her, so yeah, we'll hide in my living room."

I nod curtly. Hope Williams has been with us for a while. She'd make an excellent assistant if we didn't have the qualifier on it. It's not like we couldn't find a woman to sleep with and have an assistant too.

It just seems more convenient to do it this way. To have an all-in-one solution. We can discuss anything with our assistant present, but not always with a lover or lovers present. Not to mention having multiple women in our space hasn't always worked out well. Coop had a girlfriend that almost tore us all apart. Girlfriends don't like the time we spend together.

Besides, Madison is perfect for us. She's curious and submissive but intelligent and warm.

"I think we should sleep in our own beds tonight," I announce when we've almost finished our dinner, ending a conversation about zombie movies and shows.

Madison's eyes dart to me and then to each of the guys. "Did I do something wrong?"

I take her hand. "You need rest and recovery. Not someone jabbing you with their cock during the night."

She glances down at our joined hands. She straightens and smiles. "Of course. Whatever you need."

My brow furrows at that, but that's exactly the way she should act if this goes forward. This is what we want: a compliant assistant to help organize and work for us, plus someone to satisfy our carnal needs. Both of which Madison embodies beautifully.

"We should watch a movie tonight." Coop glances at everyone around the table.

We'll never all agree on a movie. But it's worth a shot.

Chapter 24

Nightmares

Blake

I glance at my clock. One o'clock in the morning and I'm wide awake. Fucking Seth and his rules. I kick off the sheets and tug on some boxers before heading out to the kitchen.

A muffled scream hits my ears. Shit.

I run to Madison's door and barrel through her living room to her bedroom. The lights are all off, but she's thrashing on the bed. My heart pounds in my ears as I search for the threat. Another strangled cry fills the room.

I stare down at her slight form on the huge bed. She's curled into a tight ball and jerks every now and then.

Nightmares. It's to be expected, given her recent trauma. She's been cheerful during the day, but the four of us occupy a lot of space. I sit on the edge of the bed and touch her foot.

She bolts upright. Her eyes lock on mine, and her mouth opens in a scream, but nothing comes out. I crawl up next to her on the bed and pull her onto my lap, wrapping my arms around her.

"Hey, now," I whisper against her hair. "I've got you. We've got you, tiger."

It takes her a moment for recognition to set in, but her body relaxes against me. "Blake?"

I brush her hair out of her face and tip her chin up so her eyes can find mine in the moonlight. "Yeah. I'm here."

She shudders in my arms but rests her head against my chest. "I was back there, but you didn't come." A warm drop of water touches my chest as she rests her head against me.

Tears. Fuck, I'm not the right one to handle tears, but I'm the only one here.

"Maybe it will help if you talk it out," I suggest as my hands stroke over her back.

"They were in my apartment. Talking about using me. Wanting money from me I didn't have. I couldn't move. I couldn't breathe. I couldn't run. And then Hunter came in, and Valerie laughed as he pushed me up against the wall. I couldn't fight back." More tears flow and she sniffles.

"That's not what happened." I keep my tone rational, trying to ease her out of it. I still had my doubts on her and Hunter's past, but the fact he was in this nightmare speaks volumes. "I got there before they could do more than bruise you. I got there and brought you to safety. No one can get to you here. You're safe with us."

She clings to me and tips her head up. Her eyes are dark and watery in the dim light the moon casts. "Will you stay with me?"

"Of course." Fuck Seth. I wasn't sleeping, anyway.

I arrange us under the covers. When I lie on my back, she drapes herself over me. She lets out an exhausted sigh. How long was she fighting that nightmare before I came in?

The doors are still open, but that's fine. Her breathing evens out quickly, and I'm sure she's asleep. I'm not hiding the fact I'm in here from the others. Though I wish I'd brought my phone to tell them. It's my last thought before I fall asleep.

An alarm plays softly somewhere in the room. It isn't my alarm. It isn't my room. Madison lifts her head from my chest and doesn't even open her eyes.

"Morning." Her face crashes down on my chest and she falls back asleep. The alarm keeps playing, but a dark shadow moves through the room. My arm tightens over Madison.

"Fuck off, Blake," Coop says as he stops her alarm. "I'm not here to run off with the girl."

I relax into the bed. "She had a nightmare last night. I heard her screaming."

Coop sits on the edge of the bed and runs a hand through his loose, dark hair. "That's fucked up."

His eyes flow over Madison. Her cheek presses against my chest. Her arm and a leg are around me. She has on her top and bottom, and I'm wearing boxers. If we'd had sex, we would be naked.

"Is she okay?" When he brushes her hair off her cheek, she blows out a breath.

"She will be." They didn't break her. I got to her before they completely broke her. "I don't think the sleeping alone thing is going to work for a while."

Coop nods thoughtfully. "Maybe we can trade off. Each take a night."

"That makes sense." It would keep things equal without anyone's panties getting in a twist. Seth is all about equality, after all. All or nothing. "I'll talk to Seth about it."

Coop strokes his hand down Madison's back, his gaze thoughtful. He shakes his head. "I know what we're asking isn't normal, but she doesn't feel normal, either. Like I'm not usually someone to dwell on a chick after I fuck her, but Madison..."

Yeah, I know all too well what Madison is like. She's warm and kind and soft and submissive and curious and intelligent. If someone had to handcraft a woman to suit us, Madison would be the result.

I nod and tighten my arm around her. Coop sighs as he gets up and leaves the room, still leaving the doors open.

I must have fallen asleep again, because the next thing I know Madison jolts away from me. The sun is much higher in the sky.

"Blake?" Her voice is still hoarse, but it's starting to heal. She sits up and looks around for something. "Did my alarm go off?"

"Coop turned it off. You needed more sleep." Sitting up, I rub my eyes.

"I need to get to work." She shoves off the bed and heads into the bathroom. I look at the closed door and shake my head. Can't fault her work ethic.

I climb out of the bed and close her doors behind me as I leave. Seth steps in front of me as I close the last door.

"Not now." I press past him. "She had a nightmare. Should I have left her to scream herself to sleep?"

Seth sighs behind me. I turn to see him contemplating her door. Concern etches his face.

"Coop came in this morning to shut off her alarm. She's stressed about being late as it is. No one had sex last night. We should discuss a better solution. Maybe rotate who sleeps with her, or she sleeps with one of us each night." I open my bedroom door but pause before I go in. "She's been fucking traumatized, Seth. If we can get her through the nightmares by sleeping with her, I'm all for it. She slept like a fucking log on me last night."

Seth turns, and he nods once at me. "We'll discuss it at lunch."

We don't have a client lunch today, so guess we're all going to eat together. Fun.

Madison

I'm fucking late. I tap my toe as the elevator goes up one floor. I rush into the break room, and there's already a pot of coffee and the dishes are put away.

Fuck. That's my job and I'm already failing today.

I grab a cup of coffee and sit at my desk to run the reports. Just as I finish running them, I feel someone come up behind me.

"How are you?" Coop asks.

Tired. Cranky. Stressed out beyond belief. "Fine."

He squats beside my chair. His long hair is back in his bun and his face freshly shaven, begging me to reach out and trail my hand over his jaw. "You could take the day off, Madison. You're still healing. We know you work hard and understand our business. You aren't really on trial anymore or we wouldn't have fucked you Friday."

I close my eyes and pinch the bridge of my nose. "I work. That's what I do, Coop. I can't just stop working. It keeps me sane."

He reaches out and covers my hand. "Okay. Then if it gets to be too much, let me know. I have some things you can do while you rest in bed."

I glance at him sharply.

He brushes his knuckle over my cheek and gives me a sly grin. "Work related. Honest. Just some files you can catch up on."

I release the breath I was holding. I don't want them to see me just as a fuck toy. As much as I want them to touch me and fuck me, I also need to be useful. I need to keep learning and advancing. Not stagnate.

"You'll let me know if you need to lie down?"

I meet his light blue eyes. "I will. Thank you, Coop."

He straightens to his full height and grabs my empty cup. "I'm heading to the break room. Want another cup?"

I give him a soft, appreciative smile. "Yes, please."

He gives me a wicked grin before he rounds the corner. I take in a breath and blow it out slowly. First thing is to create a to-do list which includes the grocery order today. Other than that, no one has anything major on their schedule. It should be a light day.

I glance up as Seth walks off the elevator. He heads straight for me. I meet his eyes and notice a package in his hands.

"For you." He sets the package on my desk.

I lick my lips nervously and open the box. Three beautiful silk scarves lie under the tissue paper. "Thank you."

"It will allow you to leave our floor more readily. But I still don't want you going anywhere alone in the building today or this week." Seth's blue eyes hold me captive. "Those people are still out there. I'm sure they won't come at you again. Not while you're here. But we can't be certain. I just want to keep you safe."

"Okay." I pull out a cream scarf with a pink floral pattern and wrap it around my neck. The material is soft, smooth, and cool against my skin. The bruises on my neck look worse today, and no amount of makeup could help hide them.

"We'll have lunch in the apartment today." Seth clears his throat. "We have things to discuss."

Fuck, I hope it's not about being late this morning.

His face softens. "Take it easy today, please. I'd rather you rest and be at full strength than have you limp along for a week because you overdid it."

When he reaches out and fixes my scarf, my breath catches at the simpleness of his action.

I nod, and he goes around my desk and into his office. All their doors are open except for Blake's. The elevator doors chime, and Blake steps out, dressed for the day.

He gives me a curt nod before hurrying into his office, leaving his door open. I worried the sexual tension that hovered in the air all last week would still be here, but it seems as if the only tension is whether I'm okay.

We definitely eased that sexual tension this weekend. My cheeks burn as I look over my to-do list and try not to think about what each of them can do to me.

Coop drops off my coffee and flicks my scarf before heading back into his office. For an hour, everyone just works.

"Madison," Noah calls for me.

When I stand in his doorway, his dark eyes take me in.

He gestures to the stacks on his coffee table. "Those need to be refiled, please."

"Of course." As I sit on the couch and quickly order them, I can feel his gaze on me. I meet his eyes before taking the first stack to the filing room. He gives me a brief smile. After two more trips, I'm finished and return to my desk to work on some other projects.

"Lunch time." Coop reaches out his hand for mine. I finish typing the email I'm working on and press send. When I take his hand, he helps me up and leads me to the elevator.

"Should we wait for the others?" I glance over my shoulder, but the elevator arrives, and Coop tugs me along with him.

"They know the way." He hits the button and backs me against the elevator wall.

My toes curl as he dips his head to my ear and kisses me right behind it.

"This is our time off for today, sweetheart," he whispers in my ear. "Let's take advantage of it."

Chapter 25

Lunch

Cooper

Right now, I have about ten minutes to make Madison come before the others arrive. When the elevator stops, instead of heading for the main apartment door, I take her to mine.

"I thought we were all having lunch together." She glances toward the elevator as it closes.

"We are." I open my door and lead her inside. "But I want to eat first."

My gaze drops to her skirt. Her cheeks flare hot.

"Take off your panties and your skirt." I go to my drawer of goodies and pull out the medium butt plug and lube.

Half-naked, she moans at the sight and presses her thighs together.

"Are you wet, sweetheart?"

Her blue eyes meet mine. "Yes."

My cock throbs. Soon. I nod to the bed as I stroke lube on the toy.

"Lie on your back. Knees up."

She follows my orders so readily. I have to adjust my erection in my pants to be more comfortable.

Fuck.

I drag her to the edge of the bed and kneel on the floor. Her legs go over my shoulders before I close my mouth over her pussy. She jolts upright on a gasp, but then settles back as I lick and bite and suck on her clit until she moans and thrashes with need.

Starting slowly, I press the tip of the butt plug against her asshole while my tongue thrusts into her cunt. She arches off the bed, and her hips press into my mouth, seeking more. I slide the butt plug a little deeper every time I pull it back out, until she's rocking her hips to get more inside her.

"Coop. Fuck." Her head thrashes from side to side as I feel the pulsing of her pussy against my tongue. She's so fucking close. So fucking responsive. I'm surprised no one played with her ass before us. I can't wait to be the first to give her the pleasure of my cock buried deep inside her.

She pushes back to meet the last thrust. When the plug is fully seated inside her ass, she releases a guttural moan, then breathes deep.

"You're doing so well." I flick my tongue on her clit, and she jolts like a bolt of electricity hit her.

Sliding my tongue down, I thrust my tongue into her pussy over and over until she cries out. I keep thrusting as she gushes her release. Fuck, she's amazing. Rising, I pull my aching cock out of my pants.

"How does it feel?" Stroking my cock, I take in the beautiful view of her spread before me. The plug fills her ass, opening her puckered hole. Her pretty pussy throbs, needing to be fucked.

"More." Her eyes are dark pits of desire as I meet them. "Please. Fuck me, please, Coop."

I hook her knees with my arms and thrust into her tight pussy in one smooth motion. She groans as her core ripples over me in an aftershock. But we can do better than that.

"How does it feel to be stuffed full in both holes?" I pull back and thrust forward again. She's so tight around my cock as I rub up against the solid toy.

"So fucking good." Arching up into me, she bites her lower lip as she closes her eyes.

"It'll be better when it's me in your ass and Blake's fat cock in your tight pussy. You won't be able to do anything but scream as we make you come over and over again." I quicken my pace as she pants. I reach lower and thrust the plug into her ass at the same pace.

This time when she comes, she screams. Her pussy clamps down on my cock, and it's impossible to move the plug. I'm unable to hold back my orgasm, and it rips through me. Shuddering with release, I thrust deep inside her and fill her with my cum.

Her face slowly sinks into a peaceful grin. I step back and ease out the plug. She trembles with an aftershock, but she's a limp mess on my bed. Using my fingers, I press my cum that leaks out back into her cunt. It pulses around my fingers in tiny aftershocks.

"So fucking perfect," I murmur. When I bring my fingers to her lips, she holds my eyes boldly as she licks and sucks them clean. My cock hardens already. I can't wait to take her mouth again.

"Wait there." I go into my bathroom and wet a washcloth.

When I return, I spread her legs and wash her gently. I could spend all day taking her over and over again. Even though my cock is up to the task, I press a final kiss to her pussy. "Get dressed, sweetheart. We need to join the others."

Madison

My pussy still throbs from the quick fuck Coop gave me as we leave his room and join the others at the island. Seth watches me as I gingerly sit in the chair. I can feel the heat in my cheeks like I've done something wrong, but technically, we weren't on company time.

Not that being on the clock stopped any of them before.

The guys have lunch ready in a few minutes. Noah helps me down from the island stool and leads me to the table. I almost protest that I can help, but Blake sets my plate in front of me. Coop brings me a glass of water.

Clearing his throat, Seth sits at the head of the table. My heart drops into my stomach. I almost forgot he wanted to talk with me. Am I going to be punished for being late to work this morning?

"We need to discuss the sleeping arrangements."

I pause with my sandwich halfway to my mouth. When Seth ordered me to sleep alone last night, I couldn't help feeling a little rejected. Is he going to be mad that Blake slept with me? I still don't know what's acceptable and what isn't.

That's what the agreement is supposed to outline.

Setting my sandwich down, I pick up my water for my suddenly dry throat. The pills rattle in a bottle, and Blake hands me a couple of Advil. I smile and take them.

When Seth turns his dark blue eyes to me, I can't help getting caught in them. "You've been through hell this weekend. I imagine you don't want to be left alone any more than we want to leave you alone."

I press my lips together against the sudden fullness in my throat. Having them with me definitely helps.

"We can do this one of two ways. You can rotate between our beds or we can rotate in yours." Seth gives me a questioning look.

I swallow the lump in my throat. Always giving me choices. I look around at the others. Each of them looks eager for my answer.

"I'd prefer to go to your beds, if that's okay." My bed is fine, but it's giant, and without all of them, it feels empty.

Seth nods. "You sleep with me tonight."

My core clenches at the thought of being alone with each of them. To explore their individual desires like I did with Blake and Coop yesterday.

"I've sent you a comprehensive list to look over." Seth takes a bite of his sandwich, and my attention returns to him. "It's what we'll build our arrangement on. We need to know what hard limits you have, as well as things you might be curious about."

I swallow my bite as my body hums with awareness. I fight the urge to pull up the list and read through it right now. Instead, I take another bite.

"We'll discuss the arrangement, if you are still agreeable to it, at the Friday meeting."

Like a Pavlovian response, my panties dampen at the mention of the Friday meeting. Two of them taking me at once. I want more of that.

"Yes, sir." I glance at him to see his smirk at the *sir*.

"It might make sense to sleep in our beds during the week, but Friday through Sunday, we'll all sleep with you in your bed." Seth's words keep keying me up.

I cross my legs at the ache there. "I'd like that."

The guys stare at me with hungry eyes. I'd like that a lot.

"Good." Seth pauses until I raise my gaze to him. "About this morning and being late—"

"It won't happen again," I insert quickly.

He reaches across the table and takes my hand. When I look into his eyes, they've softened. "You're still recovering. Sleep is vital to that."

His piercing gaze meets each guy's in turn. "That means making sure you get plenty of sleep. If that means sleeping in, then that's what you should do."

My heart lightens, and I squeeze Seth's hand.

"After the groceries arrive, stay up here and take a nap."

I want to protest, but I know my energy is still low. I finish my sandwich while the others talk about business, listening for anything that might be important to make a note of.

No one protests when I help clean the kitchen. I mean, my hands and legs still work. It's just my throat that's irritated, and my head still aches.

As we finish, Blake draws me into a kiss that is everything but brief. When he lifts his head, I want more. He smiles as he spins me to Noah.

Noah catches me and captures my lips. Desire weaves its spell on me as he thrusts his tongue into my mouth the way he fucks me. My insides ache with want. When he lifts his mouth, he presses his forehead against mine.

"If you need to rest, use my couch, kitten." His deep voice makes shivers race down my spine.

I definitely wouldn't want to just *rest* on his couch. As Noah backs away, Cooper steals a kiss. His fingers dig into my ass cheeks and I gasp against his mouth. When he deepens the kiss, my pussy aches with the need for release.

When he finishes, I'm a mess, and that's when Seth moves in.

"See you upstairs, kitten." Noah's words come from a distance.

Locked in Seth's gaze, I barely register the others getting on the elevator. My lips part as he grabs my hips. He backs me up until my ass hits the back of the couch.

"Feeling needy, princess?"

"Yes." My hands are on his chest, waiting for him to kiss me.

"Coop didn't satisfy you?" He lifts a golden eyebrow.

"He did," I acknowledge. "But I want more."

I've always had a healthy sexual appetite, but with these men, it feels like it's on overdrive. I can't get enough of them.

His thumb traces my lower lip, and he tugs down on it before slamming his mouth on mine. I can taste his need and desire. His hard cock presses against my stomach. Fuck, the craving is intense. I want him right now.

When he lifts his head, my lips feel bruised.

I try to draw his lips back to mine, but he spins me to face the couch and presses down on my back until my hands brace on the cushion. He flips my skirt up and grabs my ass cheeks, spreading them, massaging them.

"Has he taken your ass yet, princess?"

Unable to speak, I shake my head. Longing courses through my veins.

Seth slides my panties over my hips, and they flutter to my

ankles. When I try to lift my feet, he slaps my ass. I cry out from the suddenness, but it didn't really hurt. Fuck, that feels good.

"Those stay right there." He rubs the sting out and then parts my cheeks. I can't see him, but I imagine him eyeing my asshole and pussy. It makes me even wetter. "Do you want him to take this ass?"

"Yes."

His fingers thrust into my aching core, and I groan, wanting more. Rocking my hips, I try to widen my legs, but my panties keep me from going farther.

When he pulls his fingers out, my core pulses, empty.

"Seth, please."

"Don't worry. I'll make you come, but not yet." His wet finger slides into my asshole, and my mouth opens at the sensations flooding me. He presses around like Coop did yesterday, rubbing the muscles and the sensitive nerves until I squirm beneath his touch.

His zipper going down sounds over my harsh breaths. I try to widen my legs again, but they're stuck. He adds another finger to my asshole and scissors them inside me. Wetness trickles down my thigh.

"You like having your ass played with."

It's not a question. "Yes."

The tip of his cock brushes my clit, and I hiss at the overwhelming sensation. He slides up to my entrance and inches in. Every inch is a little punishment, as it's almost the friction I need but not enough at the same time.

His fingers are still in my ass when he finally presses his cock deep inside me. It throbs against my walls, and my pussy clamps around him.

"You might need to give us your hard limits tonight at dinner." He pulls almost the entire way out before slowly easing back in.

I bite my lip against how good it feels and how badly I need more. So much more. When he's fully inside me, he draws his fingers almost out of my ass before thrusting back in. I moan. My legs try to spread to take him deeper. My hips lift in an effort to move him, but I can't move in my current position.

I'm helpless to seek my own release. But being helpless to Seth isn't a bad thing.

He chuckles darkly as he keeps up his torturous pace, thrusting first his cock and then his fingers until I'm a writhing mess beneath him.

"Please, Seth," I get out between moans.

"What do you need, princess?" He pauses with his cock and fingers buried inside me. "Tell me exactly what you want."

I only hesitate for a moment. I need him more than I need to preserve any dignity I have. "Fuck my pussy hard with your cock. Make me come."

"What about your ass?"

My pussy pulses around him at those words.

"Fuck my ass with your fingers. Make me scream until I'm hoarse."

His dark chuckle lights me up inside. "As you wish."

He works his cock and fingers in tandem, first thrusting hard into me with his cock then his fingers, until I can't even think anymore as the pleasure rises inside me. Not being able to spread my legs makes my pussy feel even tighter as he works his huge cock inside me, and the angle rubs me just the right way.

"Scream for me, princess." He picks up the pace, and soon all I can do is feel the friction against my every nerve.

My pussy tightens, and pulses ripple through me as I explode with a scream. He keeps dragging his cock and fingers over my sensitive nerves. I can't come down and my orgasm seems to last forever.

He takes his fingers out of my ass, and his hands grip my hips as he pounds into my tender pussy. A second orgasm takes me. Bright stars light behind my eyes, and I can barely breathe as I feel him shatter. His cock throbs, spilling his warm cum into me.

I breathe heavily over the back of the couch. Everything tingles. My bones have no mass as he pulls out of me. His fingers rub over my clit, and I bite my lip as an aftershock rocks my already spent body. His dark chuckle weaves around me.

He moves away, but I can't stand yet. I don't think I'll ever be able to hold myself upright again. When he returns, he presses a warm, wet cloth between my legs. After drying me off, he drags my panties back on properly. He lifts me upright against his chest.

"Maybe a nap before groceries?" he asks.

I glance over my shoulder at him. But seriously, if he wasn't holding me up, I'd crumple to the ground. He kisses the top of my head, and I sigh.

He lifts me into his arms and walks to my bedroom. I should protest. I have a lot of work to do, but when he lowers me onto the soft bed, my eyes close. It's futile to fight the sleep waiting to drag me under.

Chapter 26

Hard Limits

Madison

I startle awake at a hand on my hip. Blake sits next to me on the edge of the bed. "Time to wake, tiger."

When I stretch, I feel good all over. Until I glance at the time. Fuck. I slept the afternoon away. "I didn't get the order in."

"I did." Blake caresses my hip. "Fox should be here soon. You need to get ready."

Crawling out of bed, I walk into the bathroom to quickly right myself. My dress doesn't look like I slept in it, fortunately. When I come out, Blake draws me between his legs. I tip my head down to meet his green eyes.

"You doing okay? Need any more pain meds?"

Taking a quick inventory, I shake my head. "I'm good."

He stands and pulls me into a hug. "You got this?"

Groceries. "Yeah, I've got this."

"Good." He tips my chin up and kisses me briefly. He tucks my hair behind my ear and leads me out of the bedroom.

The apartment is empty. Blake goes to the elevator and presses the button.

"Don't let Fox give you crap."

"I won't."

"He's a little flirt." Blake shakes his head, but his eyes stay on me, maybe to see how I respond.

"Not interested." I'm not. Fox is a good-looking guy, and probably somewhere between Noah's and my age, but he's not one of these guys. Four guys are plenty for me.

The attraction I have for them is intense, but there's these moments where it feels like more than just sex. Maybe it's the respect they have for me that not all my previous partners had. But I never wanted more than sex from those guys. My gaze raises to Blake. These guys aren't offering more either.

"Good," Blake says.

The elevator opens and we both step in. Blake presses the button for the top floor and backs me against the wall. My breath catches at the hungry look in his eyes, even as my panties dampen. Anticipation rages like a fire throughout me. He captures my lips and kisses me as we go up.

When I open beneath him, he takes full advantage, sweeping in to tangle our tongues together. My body heats. His hands on my hips scald me. When the elevator dings its arrival, I already feel like a mess from that kiss.

He smirks and brushes his thumb over the corner of my mouth before exiting the elevator. I take a deep breath and press the ground floor button. I skim my fingers over my bottom lip. It's crazy that I could still want more after both Coop and Seth gave me orgasms at lunch. All of them set me on fire, making me crave more of them.

I fan myself to cool down. It's time to get back to work.

As the elevator comes to a halt, I straighten my scarf and draw in a deep breath. I added a little more makeup over the bruise on my cheek to hide it and wore long enough sleeves to cover the bruises on my arms. But I still feel self-conscious. I'm not the same girl as last week. Now I'm a victim and more wary.

Stepping into the bustling lobby is like stepping into another world. Being isolated all weekend made me forget about the thriving metropolitan below us. It's almost overwhelming, and my fingers check my scarf again.

I search for Fox. He isn't in the lobby. The brunette hater stands next to the front desk, and her scornful gaze scans over me before she says something to the receptionist.

When she glances at me, she says something that makes the brunette woman cackle. Hope doesn't like these women, and I understand why. Even though they're talking about me, I just tip my chin up. I have nothing to be ashamed of.

Fox comes in through the front door and stops at the women. They both smile and touch their hair as he grins at them. I'm too far away to hear their conversation, but both women turn and watch him walk toward me.

"You made it through the week!" His brown eyes sparkle as he unloads his grocery bags off his cart into the elevator.

"I did."

His personality is big and fun. I can't help but return his smile as he says, "Be back in two shakes with the rest."

He walks out of the building and disappears. My gaze falls on the two women, and they arch their eyebrows at me before turning away. I wanted to make friends at work, but I'm not sure how much effort I want to put into making friends with those women.

Fox bursts through the doors carrying another full load of groceries. He winks at the women and heads toward me. "This is it."

He sets down the bags, and we both find a space in the elevator.

"You like working here?" Fox leans into the corner with his ankles crossed and his hands in his pockets. His hair falls into his eyes as he tips his head down and glances up at me.

I've known guys like him. Incorrigible flirts. But damn, do they make it easy to want them. Fortunately, I have four men who have my undivided attention. And don't need any more cock in my life right now.

"I love working here."

His eyes narrow at the hoarseness in my voice.

I clear my throat and cough a little. "I had a little cold over the weekend."

"Cup of tea will clear that right up." Fox goes back to checking me out. "I like the scarf thingy."

I touch it with my fingertips. "Thanks."

Mercifully, the elevator stops, and I rush forward to open the door. He carries the bags into the kitchen and sets them on the island.

"Want me to help put them away?" He gives me a searching look.

I smile. "No, thank you."

I move so he can come out and then close the door to the apartment. He leans into the same corner of the elevator and watches me hit the button for the lobby.

"Did you grow up around here?" he asks after a few seconds.

"No." I don't elaborate. I don't want to encourage him.

"You have this girl-next-door vibe that says you aren't from the big, scary city. Kind of vulnerable."

My gaze sharpens on him. I'm not weak. I've been helpless before, but I won't cave to anyone else.

He holds up his hands. "No offense. Really. It's sweet and refreshing. Those other dames scared me with their sharp edges."

The other women. I wonder if the guys will ever tell me about them. How they felt about each of them? Did they ever love any of them? My gut churns at the thought of the men looking softly at another woman.

Fuck, I shouldn't be getting attached. Yes, the arrangement will be for the foreseeable future, but it isn't permanent. I'm not permanent to any of them, which is fine. If I try to give them my heart, these guys could destroy me.

I need to keep myself in line.

"Hey, you checked out there for a moment." Fox smirks.

"Sorry, lots to do today and still not feeling entirely well." I give another little cough.

"I think I saw some soup in that order, so make yourself a bowl. You'll be right as rain before you know it."

When the elevator stops, he exits into the lobby. His gaze holds mine for a moment. "Stay sweet, Madison."

After I put away the groceries, I head up to the office and try to get as much done in the remaining hours as possible. The guys each swing by my desk offering me water, coffee, a sweet. It's nice, and I feel taken care of, but I need to focus, and they are huge distractions.

I barely notice the fading light. Then the guys head out for the day, except Seth. He remains in his office while I'm busy trying to figure out a financial problem Noah has me looking into.

"That's time, princess." Seth flips off the light in his office and comes out to my desk. "Shut it down. You need dinner and some downtime before bed."

I want to argue with him about the downtime. I barely had downtime during college. It's a luxury I'm not sure I can afford. I have so much to learn and do that I'm afraid I'll always be behind.

But instead of protesting, I turn off my computer and grab my purse out of my drawer. I know I don't technically need it, but if I want something from the vending machine, it's easier to have access to my money than to stop at the apartment first. Not that I'm allowed to go to the vending machines on the lower floor right now.

When I stand, Seth takes ahold of my elbow and leads me to the elevator. "Did you get a good nap?"

Was I fucked into a coma? "Yes."

"I'm sure the days will get easier as the week wears on." The elevator arrives and we step into it. "Did you look over the list?"

I shake my head. "I can look over it tonight."

He nods thoughtfully. "You don't need answers for everything, but we need to know what you definitely don't want so we don't cross any lines."

"I thought that's what the safe word was for?" I tip my face up to his as the elevator stops. We walk to the door, but he stops before we go in.

"There are things none of us will be into."

"Then why are they on the list?"

"It's a comprehensive list. We'll each fill one out for you for Friday to tell you what we want." His lip quirks up but not into a full smile. "But there are things, if they're a hard limit for either of us, we can avoid. That way, you don't have to say *stop* as someone is peeing on you."

"Ew." I didn't even consider golden showers. And I'm not going to. "That's definitely on the not-in-this-lifetime list."

His low chuckle fills me so full. "So look over the options and make your hard limits list. On Friday, we'll get into soft limits and enthusiastic yeses."

I have a feeling I'm going to have a lot of enthusiastic yeses with these guys.

Seth opens the door for me. Noah is in the kitchen making dinner while Blake and Coop sit in front of the TV watching some baseball game. Seth's hand brushes over my hip as he makes his way over to join the guys on the couch.

My insides tingle as I walk over to Noah. "Can I do anything to help?"

When he grins, his dark eyes dance with mischief. "You could do what you did while Seth made the salad last night."

I laugh. "I'm not masturbating before dinner every night."

Noah closes in on me and tips my chin up. "I could just fuck you against the kitchen island."

My laughter dies as his lips slowly lower to mine. He kisses me softly and all too briefly. His thumb traces my jaw before he backs away.

"Everything is almost done, but if you want to set out the plates—"

"On it." I grab a stack of plates from the cabinet and some silverware and make the table. The guys all cheer on the couch. I glance at the TV to see if I can figure out what happened.

"Dinner's ready," Noah announces as he walks to the table with a casserole dish.

I'm going to get fat with the way these guys feed me. It looks like baked chicken parmesan. My stomach rumbles and Noah chuckles.

The guys mute the game and come to the table. I'm not used to eating with others or being fed. The food is delicious, as always, and the conversation is entertaining. They talk a little about the game, but then, to include me, we discuss some new shows that are out.

This time they let me help with the dishes. Blake and Seth settle in front of the game, while Coop goes to work out. Noah slips into the library. I head to my room. After freshening up from the day, I change into a pair of sleep shorts and a tank top.

With my phone in hand and a notebook, I head into the library to review the consent list. Noah looks up from the book he's reading and nods at me as I head to the table.

I pull out my Bluetooth headphones and put on some music. My eyes widen as I look over the list. I make notes on the ones I most definitely do not want to do.

Some I have to do a search on to figure out what they are talking about. Some that I'm more interested in, I fall down a rabbit hole of information. I know some of the guys' kinks already. Noah has mentioned bondage. Blake is a Dom and is into impact play.

Coop wants anal, but I wonder if there is more to his kink. He said he likes to play games on my first day. Maybe role-play or scenes. Seth is a voyeur for sure and likes to be in control.

Maybe I'll learn more this week while sleeping in their beds. Tingles work their way through my veins. I find a few digital erotic romance novels that go along with the kinks I know and a few with some of the other things I found on the list that might interest me.

A shadow falls over me. I glance at Coop, who smiles wickedly. The others are making their way toward the table. I have my arms around my left knee with my foot on the chair. I turn off my music and set my AirPods on the table as they all take a seat.

"Meeting time?" I raise an eyebrow with a small smile.

Seth leans back in his chair. "Have you had time to go over the list, princess?"

Four sets of hungry eyes wait for my answer.

I set my phone down and lean back. "I think so."

"Hard limits, sweetheart." Coop leans forward with his hands together, elbows on the table.

I swallow and begin with the one that terrifies me the most. "No choking."

"Not something any of us are into, but understandable." Seth's eyes linger on my bruises.

Noah clears his throat. "What about holding you by your neck? No squeezing or choking."

I swallow. My fingers run over the skin of my throat, remembering my attacker's fingers tightening on me, taking away my breath. "It might be too much. Can we call that a soft limit?"

A soft limit is something I can decide on in the moment. I'm not opposed to the idea, but I think it may be something we need to discuss.

"If I want to incorporate it, we'll talk about it beforehand and go slow." Noah's brown eyes meet mine. He can tell this bothers me, but I want to try for him sometime.

"Not right away," I say softly.

He smiles. "Of course not, kitten."

My eyes linger on the paper with my notes. Seth mentioned this one, but it bears repeating. "No bodily fluids on me."

"Are you okay if we come on you?" Coop raises an eyebrow. "Like on your stomach or face?"

My initial thought is *maybe*. It depends on the scenario. "A soft limit?"

"Fair enough." Coop looks at my notebook like he's trying to see what else I wrote.

"No fisting or torture of any kind. No clamps or knife play." Not that I think any of them are into it, but Seth is right. I don't want to be in the moment and have to say my safe word. "I don't think I want to do anything that can cause actual damage."

When the guys nod, I release a breath. I wasn't sure if that was something one of them might like.

"Pinching or leaving marks that fade will be okay?" Blake asks.

Oof, yes please. "Yes, I liked when you spanked me. I just don't want to have scars from our play, if that makes sense."

Blake's green eyes smile. "We can find your limits together with our impact play, but I promise not to do anything that will leave a permanent mark."

I breathe out.

"Anything else?" Noah asks.

I put my hands on my notebook and shake my head. "There are some things I'm not sure of right now. I want to do more research."

"You're okay with all of us having sex with you at the same time?" Blake tilts his head to study my reaction.

I cross my legs against the hot ache lingering there. Biting my lip, I nod. "Definitely. I'm here to explore my sexuality and because I'm attracted to all of you. I liked Friday night and Saturday. But I also like being with you one-on-one."

Coop's wicked smile makes my cheeks flush.

"Do you guys prefer to play together?" I ask, lifting my gaze and meeting all of theirs.

"We enjoy sharing a woman's pleasure. The way it overwhelms you." Seth pauses, and my breath catches as he takes in my hardened nipples, pressing against my pajama shirt. He licks his lips, and my pussy pulses empty. "When you surrender to us, it's a power exchange that's heady. Besides, I like to watch."

I'm on fire with need, remembering him making me touch myself for him and Blake.

"I enjoy being with you all." My voice is a little breathless, but they do that to me.

"You have a safe word picked out?" Seth raises an eyebrow.

My eyes meet Blake's. When he asked for one, all I could think of is wanting to be first place, striving for. "Gold."

"You understand when to use it?" Seth asks.

"Yes. When I want everything to stop or pause to talk about something." My gaze moves to meet all of theirs. They're all trying to make sure I know what I'm getting into. I swallow before I ask, "What other kinks do you guys have?"

"I like to watch, be in control, and play with toys." Seth licks his lips and my panties dampen further.

"Bondage." Noah leans in. "We can explore your limits as we go on, but simple stuff to start. Tying you down, blindfolding you."

Fuck. I hope Seth plans to fuck me tonight. I'm soaking from reading about and imagining all these things. Then the guys around me discussing sex and what they want to do with me. To me.

"Anal." Coop draws my attention. He grins. "Toys. Role-play. Games."

"Dom, impact play."

"I don't know about whips and canes." My cheeks heat when I look at Blake. I don't want to take away from what he likes, but I can't find myself wanting him to actually hurt me.

"Not my style, but we'll go slow, like Noah said. We'll find your limit." Blake smirks.

My panties are drenched as I think about how he spanked me and then fucked me, bent over with my hands on the wall. His to do with whatever he pleased. My core clenches.

"I don't want a slave, but I do want your total submission when we are in a scene." Blake taps his finger on the table. "I want you to obey my every command like you did yesterday."

I swallow and nod again. Pressing my thighs against the aching need, I'm more than willing to be what these men desire. "That sounds good."

"Tonight, princess, you sleep with me, but first..." Rising, Seth reaches for my hand.

I take it. He draws me close against him and tips up my chin. "I want to see you take all three of their cocks, and after, take mine. What do you think?"

My heart races. My gaze stays on Seth, not the others who are all standing. Is all this sex my new normal, or is this just them playing with their new toy? I shove that thought to the back of my brain because I want whatever they'll give me.

I lick my lips in anticipation. "Yes, sir."

Chapter 27

Come Again

Madison

Seth brushes my hair off my cheek and claims my mouth. When he deepens the kiss, I feel it all the way to my toes. Hands reach for my sleep shorts and panties. I break away from the kiss as someone lifts my top off. My body is naked against Seth's. He still wears his dress shirt and slacks from work.

"How's your throat, princess?" He ghosts his hand over the bruised flesh. "Can you take a cock in your mouth?"

I shiver. "Yes, sir."

His hands skim down my sides, leaving sparks in their wake. My breath catches in anticipation.

"Hands and knees." His tone is more stern, making me want to obey him. Making me *need* to obey him.

I drop to my knees before him. I'm so wet and aching, ready for whatever he'll give me. He cradles my cheek and brushes over my hair.

"Good girl." Those words, that dark, rich voice of his. I'll do whatever he wants if he keeps talking to me like this. He steps back. His praise fills my insides as I put my hands on the floor.

Already stripped naked, Blake kneels behind me. Anticipation buzzes along my every nerve. Noah kneels before my head and Cooper kneels on my side. I can almost imagine the day I can take them together—one of them in my pussy and the other in my ass.

Cooper's hand runs over my nipple as Blake rubs the head of his cock over my wet pussy. I gasp at the sensations rippling through me. Noah edges forward to press the tip of his cock against my lips. My eyes lift to his brown ones. Cupping my cheek, he smiles down at me.

"Think you can take them all at once, princess?" Seth asks.

My pussy throbs. Yes, I want that. I need that. I turn my head to see Seth sitting in the chair with his cock in his hand, stroking up and down. "Yes, sir."

Cooper shifts to his back and scoots under me. His tongue flicks my nipple as both Blake and Noah sink inside me slowly. I moan around Noah's cock.

"Wait," Seth says, and we all pause, my pussy and mouth full. Except Coop. He keeps sucking on my breast. My pussy clenches around Blake's cock. "We can do better. Noah, stand. Blake, sit back, keep your cock in her pussy. Madison, sit up. Noah to one side. Coop on the other."

Everyone follows their orders. This is obviously not the first time Seth's ordered them around. When I'm situated, I turn my head toward Noah while my hand reaches for Coop's cock. I roll my hips on Blake as I suck on Noah's cock and stroke Coop's. Blake's hand slips between my thighs and teases my clit, lighting me up, while Noah and Coop cup and tweak my nipples. Desire rages through me, making me need to shatter for them.

As the others fuck me, I hold Seth's gaze. I can't move much in my current position, but I feel full and powerful, working on bringing three men to their knees for me. I add my other hand to Noah's cock to stroke what I can't fit in my mouth.

Power courses through me as they focus all their attention on getting me off. Every tug on my nipple shoots straight to my pussy, where Blake makes small circular moves with his hips. I suck on Noah's cock and glance up at him.

His lips are parted. His eyes glazed with need. He slides his hand into my hair with a smirk and pulls me almost all the way off.

I pop off him, taking a second to lick his tip. Then I turn my head to Coop's cock. His attention was on my breast. As I take him in my mouth, he lets out a muffled, "Fuck."

I continue to stroke both men and alternate, taking one, then the other into my mouth. Soon, Noah fists my hair when I have him in my mouth.

"Make me come, kitten."

I suck a little harder and cup his balls. He goes off down my throat, filling me with his cum. I swallow and stroke my tongue over his cock as it slips out. He sits in the chair behind him.

I turn to Coop and take him back into my mouth, sucking harder. Blake rotates his hips under me and arousal drips down my thighs.

"Back on your hands and knees, princess." Seth's voice is like a physical caress.

We change positions, and Coop kneels before me. I lower my mouth over him as Blake begins to pound into my pussy. Every stroke, I push back to meet him. As I suck and lick, my orgasm swells within me, getting closer and closer to tipping over the edge.

"Suck me, sweetheart." Coop thrusts deep into my mouth, and I suck, hollowing out my cheeks. He comes in my throat with a roar. Satisfaction floods me. I'm the one making them come, even if Seth is in control.

I swallow Coop's cum as Blake thrusts harder and faster. My thighs spread, and I brace my arms as I rock with him. My orgasm crashes over me in a wave, drawing Blake into his. We keep bucking against each other for a few seconds before we collapse.

Seth puts his still hard cock away and lifts me into his arms. "Good night, gentlemen."

The others all wish us good night as Seth carries me into his room. I barely take in the sky blue walls and light-colored bedspread on his king-sized bed before we are in his bathroom. The marble in here is Carrara in white and gray. The walls are a soft gray and everything else is white and crisp.

He sets me naked on his counter and turns on the shower. Searching a drawer, he pulls out a hair clip and hands it to me. All I can do is stare at it for a moment. Is it one of *theirs*? Those other women's? Left behind and forgotten? Would he even remember which one left it?

Seeing my hesitation, he cups my cheeks and meets my eyes. "It's new. I would never use something I used on someone else with you. Neither would the rest of us. We are as much yours as you are ours."

Relief pours through me. My heart spins drunkenly though at the thought of being theirs. It's hard to remember this isn't a relationship, but a contract. Especially when they look at me like this.

His dark blue eyes hold me as I pull my hair back and clip it out of the way. Relaxing against the mirror, I watch him as he strips down, still hard. I want to take him right now, feel his large cock inside my body. I want all of them, but he usually has other plans. He checks the temperature of the water. It must be perfect because he lifts me against his naked body.

Goosebumps burst out all over my skin from his touch. I don't think I'll ever get used to the way these guys make me feel.

"We just need to clean off." He lifts my chin so he can look into my eyes. "I'm not going to fuck you right now. I have some toys I want to try."

Pouting slightly, I press my lips together and nod. He hands me a new poof and a bottle of my body soap. That he thought to have it in his shower for me makes me smile. I wash quickly and step out to grab a towel to dry off.

When I glance at Seth, he's watching me while washing himself. I set the towel on the counter and sit on it. His eyes are curious as he rinses off the soap. I trail my hand down my chest to my nipple and circle it slowly with the pad of my finger, imagining it's his fingers on me.

My breath catches in my throat. Loving the look in his eyes, knowing he loves to watch.

He steps out of the shower and dries off. His steady gaze never leaves me. I slide my other hand between my legs, parting my pussy lips. He hangs up his towel and approaches me. I want him to take over, for him to be the one with his hands on me.

"Hand me your towel." He doesn't look away from my eyes. Sliding off the counter, I stand before him and give him my towel. He hangs it on the rack and starts for the bedroom. "Come."

A delicious shiver races through me at the command in that word.

I'd be happy to come, but that doesn't seem to be in the cards right now. At least we're both naked. That's a good start. He opens a drawer and pulls out a couple of different vibrators and a few other things I haven't seen before. My eyes widen as I sit on the edge of his bed.

"Move up to the headboard. Push the sheets down and spread your legs." His voice is commanding and hits something inside me that wants to cave to his every demand. He puts some toys away and some on the bed and grabs a bottle of lube.

Leaning back on the pillows, I follow his orders, curious about what will be next. I'm wet and ready for whatever he has in mind.

"Did you like being fucked like that?" Not looking at me, he raises an eyebrow as he decides on a toy. Picking one up, he strokes some lube on it, though I'm plenty wet. It's a rabbit vibrator with a clitoral stimulator like the one I have. I squirm with eagerness.

"Yes, I did." I'm owning my sexuality here.

"Have you ever felt something in your ass and cunt at the same time? Besides fingers." He moves to sit next to me on the center of the bed.

"Coop used a plug and his cock at lunch."

He turns on the vibrator and it buzzes. "Did you like that?"

I bite my lip, remembering the sensation. Fullness, and then when he moved... I get even wetter thinking about it. "Yes."

"I'm going to fuck your pussy with this vibrator."

I swallow, widening my thighs. "Okay."

He comes closer and spreads my lips apart. When he drags the tip of the vibrator over my clit, I let out a little gasp. When he slides it inside my pussy, he doesn't press it all the way in. The clitoral stimulator is just out of reach.

"Show me how you like it." He leans back on his hands.

I take ahold of the vibrator and look at his hard cock, imagining it's him inside of me. I thrust the toy a little deeper, seeing how deep it will go. One toy I owned bumped against my cervix. This one is a little smaller, but the stimulator lines up on my clit perfectly.

Heat courses through me as he watches me. The toy brings me close to another orgasm. I turn up the vibration and stroke it in and out of me. Seth's eyes are glued to my pussy gently sucking at the toy.

"Lie down," Seth commands.

I do as he says, with my knees bent and spread, while I work myself with the vibrator. My breathing is rapid as I wait for his touch or an orgasm. His hands part my ass cheeks and something solid and slick and round slides into my asshole. Beads?

"Let me know if it's too much."

He pushes the beads one by one up into my ass. Each bead is a little thicker than the last, spreading my asshole and filling me full. When he inserts the last one, he sits between my thighs with his legs crossed.

My breathing is heavy. With him sliding things into my ass and the vibrator working on my clit, it won't take much more to drive me over the edge. His darkened eyes watch me squirm before him.

"Take out the vibrator."

I do as he says, but that leaves me empty. When he holds out his hand, I pass him the vibrator. He shuts it off, setting it to the side. He holds his hand out to me. Not knowing what will happen, but needing relief, I take it. He pulls me onto his lap, straddling him.

"Take my cock inside you." He leans back on his hands.

Keeping my eyes locked with his, I rise, and holding his cock steady, slowly sink down on him, feeling more full with the beads in my ass. I whimper at the fullness and perfection of this moment. He feels so much better than the vibrator.

Warmth flows through me from where we're connected.

"Fuck me, princess." It's a command, not an expletive. My insides burst with heat.

Holding on to his shoulders, I roll my hips over his. With the beads filling my ass, my pussy feels tighter around his cock. The beads rub against his cock through my thin wall with every stroke. Each rise and fall shifts things inside me. My nipples graze his chest with every move, sending bursts of sparks through me. My lips part as I build back up to the orgasm that was just out of reach.

I can almost imagine how it would feel to have Coop behind me, his cock buried in my ass as I ride Seth. Seth slides his hand between my thighs, and something cool brushes my clit before it buzzes.

Oh, fuck! My nerve endings explode and I come. My pussy drenches his cock as I tighten all around him. Breathing becomes impossible as I ride him through my orgasm. He reaches around me and yanks out the beads all at once, and I shatter again. Everything tightens, and my vision goes white as I pulse around him.

He rolls me onto my back and starts thrusting hard inside me through my never-ending orgasm. He groans loudly, and his face twists in ecstasy as he comes, pulling me against his body. Sucking in breaths, I start to come down from the orgasmic high. Warmth fills me from head to toe.

His body presses mine into the bed. I could stay like this forever. His skin feels delicious against mine. He shifts and I know this part is over.

Turning us on our sides, his hand comes out to caress my face.

His fingers draw across my brow and cheeks and nose and lips. "Good?"

I laugh, causing my pussy muscles to tighten around him again. Maybe this is all normal to them, but to me... My insides are all soft and gooey. "Good? Yes, fuck yes. Very good. Amazing. Spectacular. Fucking awesome."

His smirk makes my heart skip and he kisses me. "Good."

Chapter 28

Client Meeting

Seth

Waking up with Madison is next-level shit. She's draped over me like a blanket, her pussy warm and wet against my cock. I slide my cock over her clit and press against her entrance. She groans a little, not quite awake.

I shouldn't. There's a lot we haven't discussed yet. We haven't presented her with our wants yet. But she didn't list this as a hard limit. Maybe she didn't think of it.

This is why we need the arrangement, but as open as she is to sex... Fuck it.

I roll with her and take her mouth as I thrust deep inside her. She arches into me with a little gasp. Her pussy is soaking wet and tight around my cock. For a moment, I hold myself there and just appreciate this gorgeous woman beneath me. Her soft curves cradle me as I hold myself above her.

When her mouth comes to life under mine, I deepen the kiss. Her tongue strokes inside my mouth, brushing my tongue, sending pleasure throughout me. She wraps herself around me, and I thrust, slow and easy, her hips lifting to follow mine.

"Seth," she breathes out.

"Open your eyes, Madison." I want that connection. So she sees me as well as feels me. It's not a pressing need to claim her, so I continue with the slow thrusts.

"Mmm." She blinks awake and meets my gaze. "Fuck me harder, sir."

I do as she asks, fucking her hard, each stroke burying deep and then dragging almost all the way out before thrusting back inside, grinding on her clit. All the while, I watch her eyes. Her lips part on a pant as I drive us both closer to oblivion.

"More, Seth," she whimpers. "I need more."

When I reach between us and rub her clit, she bursts into a deep throaty moan as her pussy clenches around me. I bite out a groan as I unload my cum, my cock deep inside her. Keeping myself from collapsing, I hold myself above her as we both slow our breathing and come down.

"Good morning." I capture her lips into another thorough kiss, not giving a damn about morning breath.

When I pull away, she whispers, "Good morning."

With a wide grin on her lips, she stretches beneath me. My cock hardens, but work waits.

I roll out of bed and grab a t-shirt to give her. "So you don't have to walk naked through the apartment."

"I'm not sure anyone would mind."

She's not wrong.

She drags on my t-shirt, and I'm tempted to fuck her again. She sits on the edge of the bed. Her hair is a mess. Her face is flushed. Those blue eyes are slightly dazed, and the smile tipping her lips up is naughty.

Fuck, she's a siren, luring me away from what's important. We have a full schedule today, and every day if we want to remain one of the top cybersecurity companies in the business. Madison is supposed to be convenient, not a distraction.

"Need to get ready for work," I say more to myself than to her.

Because part of me doesn't give a shit about work, knowing it will be there even if I'm an hour late.

She sighs and gets off my bed. "You're right, boss."

I grab her ass and pull her against me, claiming her mouth like we have all the time in the world. When I lift my head, she's a little breathless, and her eyes are darkened with desire.

"Try not to get fucked on the way to your room, princess." I tap her ass before going into my bathroom.

"Easier said than done," she calls out with a laugh before disappearing out my bedroom door.

I take my shower and get ready for the day. By the time I'm in the kitchen making breakfast, Madison reappears, ready for work with one of the new scarves I bought her around her neck. A burst of possessiveness floods me.

I need to lock that shit down. She isn't mine. She's ours.

But seeing her in my t-shirt and now in something I picked out and bought her? Fuck. I want to drape her in clothes I've selected for her. All the way down to her panties and bra.

"I need to start unpacking." She sits at the island and puts her head in her hands.

"Need meds?" I offer before sliding an omelet and some of the sausage I cooked in front of her.

"No meds. Thank you." She smiles at the omelet. "Maybe I should have gotten fucked on the way to my bedroom, then I would have burned enough calories to eat this all. You guys are too good to me."

"Eat it all anyway. We'll burn those calories later." I give her a wink before plating my food. "If you want, I can show you the company gym so you can get some exercise."

"Soon. Not this week, though. My head still hurts a little."

I set the Advil bottle next to her glass of orange juice. She glares at it but takes a pill.

"We have lunch out today. I would normally have you come with—"

She straightens and holds her fork out at me. "Then I'm coming with. This is part of my job."

"Fine, but if you're too tired—"

"Naps are for losers." She arches an eyebrow at me as she bites off the end of her sausage.

I shake my head, knowing this isn't an argument I'm going to win, or even need to win. "You let me know if you aren't feeling good."

She softens. "Of course."

We eat in silence until Noah joins us. He grabs a sausage link from the extras and eats it before leaning in to kiss Madison.

"Morning." Madison's smile is soft, and her eyes might as well throw hearts at Noah. My heart squeezes a little. We're all moving faster than planned, but it's so easy to be consumed by Madison. I just hope Noah doesn't end up hurt when this is over.

"Morning." He brushes his lips over hers once again before going to the stove and starting his own omelet.

"We ready for the lunch with Harper Associates?" Noah flips his omelet.

"They're sending a team of four to meet us at the restaurant." My gaze lingers on Madison. "The files should all be on your computer for your review."

Nodding, she finishes her omelet and her orange juice. She rinses her dishes before loading them into the dishwasher I unloaded this morning.

"I need to head up." She walks toward the door.

"Wait." I rinse and put away my dish before joining her. "Share an elevator?"

She gives me a coy smile. "Sure."

Madison

The morning went well. I had more energy, my throat doesn't hurt any more than it did yesterday, and except for my weird voice and the bruises taking on a greenish tinge, I'm doing better. I wrote out a to-do list for the afternoon right before we were supposed to leave for lunch.

I have my tablet ready to go to take notes on. I've read through the client files and have a good handle on what they need and what we are going to propose.

Noah walks out first and stops at my desk. "Doing okay today, kitten?"

"Of course." I smile to cover up my husky voice.

"We'll leave in ten." He leans back against a support column. His eyes are heated as they meet mine. "You're riding with us this time."

Heat creeps down my spine to pool in my gut. The others join us, discussing this and that until we are all gathered and ride the elevator down. My body grows even warmer with the men all around me in the tight space. Fuck, they're potent.

Though they occasionally brush against me, no one does anything overt.

When we hit the basement level, Noah puts his hand on the small of my back and leads me to the second car this time.

Seth gives him a look, but Noah ignores him. Maybe I was supposed to ride with Seth again. Coop climbs in on my other side, trapping me between them in the back. Before the driver arrives, Coop rolls up the privacy screen and gives me a wicked grin.

"Fifteen minutes to the restaurant, sweetheart."

I glance between Noah and Coop, not sure what they hope to accomplish. "Okay... ?"

My skirt is loose. Both Noah and Coop run a hand up my thighs, pulling my legs against them. Fire licks my skin beneath their touch. Oh. My breath comes out in a harsh exhale as they both tease the edges of my panties. My heart thumps against my chest.

I'm already wet with anticipation.

The car starts and so do they. Their fingers delve under my panties and stroke through my pussy lips against my clit. I tip my head back against the car seat and close my eyes. Their other hands hold my legs spread open. Coop's fingers slide inside my core, thrusting deep, as Noah keeps circling my clit. I bite my lip against the moan bearing down on my throat.

Noah leans into my ear. "On the way back, you're going to ride my cock and then Coop's. Quick and dirty until everyone comes."

I whimper. Coop's fingers thrust into me over and over. Hard and fast, winding me tighter and tighter. My legs strain against their hands to close around the sensation. When he slips one finger out, he slides it back to my asshole and eases inside. I bite harder on my lip as Noah's fingers wind up my clit. He presses his fingers into my pussy next to Coop's, stretching me, filling me.

Noah curls his fingers and brushes that spot that makes me see stars. Heat floods me quickly. I lift the back of my hand to my mouth and bite my thumb as I cry out. My orgasm shatters through my body almost violently as they stroke me through it. When I come down, they remove their hands from my body.

Coop takes out two wet wipes, hands one to Noah, and tears open his own. They both wipe their hands off. Coop reaches between my legs and straightens my panties. Their cocks are hard for me, tenting their pants, but the car comes to a stop.

Smiling, Coop opens the door and steps out.

Making sure my clothes are straightened, I step out into the daylight. We're outside of a fancy restaurant. Noah joins us on the curb. As one we walk in, the guys on either side of me. My insides still tingle.

While Cooper heads to the bathroom, Noah's hand settles on the small of my back as he leads us to a private room. We're the first inside and take seats on the far side of the table.

I clear my throat, hoping my face isn't as flushed as it feels. "Do you know any of the people who are joining us today?"

"They didn't give us names, but the owner will attend. Jason Harper is a young billionaire with his fingers in a lot of companies. This is his holding company." Noah leans back in his chair. His blond hair falls over his dark eyes. "Really, this meeting is for Seth and Blake to lay the groundwork. We're here in case they have questions only we can answer. It saves Seth from having to say, *We'll have to get back to you on that.*"

"So we're here to eat a good meal and pretend to listen." I raise an eyebrow.

"You're here to take notes and be eye candy." Noah rubs my thigh under the table.

"Eye candy?" I purse my lips like I'm upset, but I'm not, and he can see I'm not. He doesn't actually mean that. They all appreciate me for my mind too.

Coop walks in and sits on my other side. "Wonder what's taking everyone so long."

Seth and Blake walk in, giving us a strange look, before the client comes through the door. We stand and join them.

"Jason, you've met my team before," Seth starts, "but Madison is new to us."

Jason is a strikingly handsome man with hazel eyes and dark brown hair. He's got a little scruff on his jaw, and he smiles like he's just met his best friend as he holds out his hand to me. "I've always admired these men's taste in assistants, and you, my dear, don't disappoint."

I go to shake his hand, but he lifts it and kisses my knuckles with a wink. I pull my hand away but give him a polite smile. "A pleasure to meet you."

"Let's sit and I'll introduce you to my team."

We take our seats and the others from Harper file in. There's another man about the same age as Noah and two women, both stunningly attractive. One has blond hair and brown eyes, while the other has black hair and green eyes. The black-haired woman's gaze lingers on me.

My fingers touch my scarf to make sure my bruises are still covered. I can feel the tension in my guys as we all sit. I don't understand what's causing it.

Jason smiles. "This is Alex, Bethany, and Rachel. Your recommendation for Rachel was so glowing that I had to snap her up."

My breath stalls in my chest. Rachel? *The* Rachel who gave her two weeks' notice and then left after one? Did she have a relationship with my guys? Is that why she gave me that look? Did they used to be hers?

"I'm glad Rachel found a company better suited to her." Seth tugs at his collar and looks decidedly uncomfortable.

All the guys seem a little more twitchy, but as the server brings drinks and takes orders, I keep watching. None of them make eye contact with Rachel. They seem nervous and on edge. I figure something went wrong or she would have finished out her two weeks.

I haven't pried too much into their background. I'm not sure how much they'd be willing to tell me if I asked. That might be part of the arrangement discussion.

After the server leaves, Jason and Seth talk while Blake adds something in occasionally. I take notes when I feel something is important. Noah and Coop contribute facts when needed.

When the food arrives, conversation winds down to everyday things instead of company business. I excuse myself to the restroom and see Blake begin to stand to follow. He's been extra cautious with me.

And I'm grateful, but I don't need an escort to the bathroom in a fancy restaurant. Valerie and Jeff couldn't make it past the hostess of this place. I shake my head and he remains seated. I can find the bathroom on my own.

As I'm washing my hands, Rachel walks in. She nods at me before going into a stall.

"How long have you worked at Morrigan?" she calls out.

It surprises me. Breaking some sort of girl code about talking with a stranger in the bathroom while peeing. "A week."

"Fresh meat," she mutters, but I hear her.

"Sorry, I didn't catch that." I turn off the water and dry my hands.

"You should know there are catches to your work situation." She flushes and, after a moment, comes out. As her eyes drag over me, she washes her hands.

"Catches?" I play dumb.

"You seem young and naive enough that you might fall for their whole thing, but trust me, they're perverted men." She shakes her head and leans in conspiratorially. "I can't tell you any details, but you should find another job before they give you their secondary offer."

She gives a little shudder like it was horrifying. Maybe to her it was.

"You want me to give up a job you walked away from because they offered you something that made you think they're perverts?" I raise my eyebrows and put a lot of skepticism in my tone. "That sounds a lot like sour grapes."

She shrugs her shoulders. "I'm just a woman trying to warn another woman, but I can't fully disclose the situation."

Ah, the NDA. So that's what's keeping her mouth shut.

"I'm sure I'll be fine." When I try to walk past her, she grabs my wrist.

"You ever wonder why these men always hire pretty, *young* assistants?" Rachel's fingers clasp my wrist. I want to shake her off, but I don't.

Shrugging, I give her Noah's answer. "Eye candy?"

She snorts and releases me, as if she's giving up on me entirely. "Whatever. I tried to warn you. My job is done."

I meet her eyes and smile. "Just because you didn't like what they were offering doesn't mean I won't."

Chapter 29

Confession

Seth

Sitting across the table from Rachel is brutal. I was the one who wanted her. The one who fought for her. The one who fucked it all up and lost a perfectly good assistant by asking too much.

When Madison goes to the restroom, Jason draws my attention and leans in to say, for my ears only, "Your new assistant is just as hot as the last one."

"Smart as a whip too." Pride fills my chest.

"Surprised you let Rachel go."

My gaze darts to where Rachel sat, but she isn't there. "We didn't really have a choice. She put in her two weeks, and no amount of convincing could change her mind."

I waited too long to offer the sexual arrangement. She lived with us for six months and did a great job in the office. We even got to be friends somewhat, but she always held herself apart from us.

When I let her know I was attracted to her and wanted to pursue something, she seemed willing to be with me. But when I opened up about how being in relationships with different women made things difficult for us, so we found that sharing worked best... it all fell apart.

"Your loss of Rachel is our gain." Jason leans back and grins. "Such an amazing assistant, and good looking too."

Jason hires the best for his company. The best at the job and the best looking. He wants his office to be as conceited as him.

Madison slips back into the room and takes her seat. Her cheeks are flushed, and a smile graces her face, but tension lines her shoulders. Rachel comes in a minute later and sits at the table.

Fuck. There's nothing Rachel could tell Madison that she didn't already know, except for the fact she used to be our assistant. Though Jason brought up the recommendation, so maybe Madison already assumed.

"How are things going?" Rachel asks in a bright voice. Her green eyes lock on me. "Are you all dating anyone?"

Madison coughs lightly. Jason's brow furrows as he looks at Rachel. Not exactly an appropriate conversation for a business lunch.

"Not at the moment." I finish my drink and pay the bill. Time to go.

"I can't believe not one of you has a woman in your life." Rachel smiles. "You're all so handsome. You must have women falling all over you."

Jason glances at Rachel like she's grown an extra head. It's one thing for him and me to have a side conversation, but to bring up dating at a business lunch in front of everyone isn't exactly the best idea.

"We have very busy and very *private* lives." I lean back in my chair and consider her. She won't go so far that she breaks the NDA. She took a really hefty bonus to sign it and would owe us that plus interest if she broke the deal.

"It's just so unusual. Four guys in the prime of their lives, and not one of you has someone special." Rachel practically emphasizes every word.

"Maybe some of us have higher expectations from our partners," Noah says as he stands. He pulls out Madison's chair, and she stands with him. "Thank you for your time, Jason. It was a pleasure to meet all of you, but we need to return to work. We have important business to attend."

His hand guides Madison by the small of her back. Coop says a quick goodbye before following them out.

"I think our business partners have the right idea. It's getting late." Standing, I hold out my hand to Jason. "We've got notes to go over and should have a proposal to you by the end of the week."

He takes my hand. "A pleasure, as always. If you're looking for women, you should join me out sometime. I know this great bar—"

"Thank you, but business is brutal right now. Maybe later." I release his hand and nod to his associates. My gaze lands on Rachel. I give her a nod. "Rachel."

She glares. I don't care if she hates me. I don't actually think about her at all. But if she fucked with Madison's head, I'll make her life miserable.

Madison

The car door shuts behind Noah and me. The privacy window is still up.

Noah sighs and runs a hand through his already disheveled hair. "Rachel used to be our assistant before you. She was never party to this part of our arrangement. She was upset when Seth offered her the option. She'd been our assistant for six months and lived with us. Unless there was a project to work on, she didn't hang out with us outside the office."

I take Noah's hand in mine. "It's fine. Hope mentioned Rachel. I know she was your assistant, and that she gave her notice and didn't stay the whole time. But now I understand why." I shake my head and chuckle a little. "She thinks you guys are perverts."

Coop slides in next to me and laughs. "She wishes. I was against offering her the deal after Andrea. Rachel worked well as an assistant. If I wanted to get some, I could just go out and find it."

I purse my lips and narrow my eyes at Coop, but he just gives me a cocky grin and shrugs a shoulder.

Noah shakes his head. "Pretty sure she wanted to lock down Seth. Only Seth. When that didn't happen, especially after she declined the offer, she went nuclear and left."

"Then why offer the deal to me?" I arch my eyebrow at him. After all, they failed twice before. It seems like what they wanted probably wouldn't happen.

Coop rubs the back of his neck while he talks. "Because you want us. All of us. It's in your eyes and your body language. Even on that first day, I could tell. And we all want you."

"So if I'd been someone you weren't attracted to, you wouldn't have even offered me the job?" I'm trying to figure out where they draw the line here. Yes, I want this, but if I hadn't, would they have still hired me? Do they see my value as an employee or just as a sex object?

"You're bright and an asset to the company. So yes, we still would have offered you the job, but we would have blue balls from being around you without being able to fuck you." Cooper draws me onto his lap as the car starts. "Honestly, it's hard to find someone we're all attracted to, and someone who wants to play with us equally."

I smooth my hand down his tie, remembering their promise on the way here. "Is that what you want? To play with me equally?"

"Fuck, yes. If you have more questions, I'm willing to answer them, but we have limited time in this car, and both Noah and I have to fuck you at least once. Can we be done with the conversation for now?"

His hands slip under my skirt and pull my panties to the side to slide his fingers through my wetness.

I nod and whimper as sparks race through my veins. I take his face in my hands and lower my lips to his. We explore each other's mouths like it's been forever.

He's right. I want it all. Not just half measures.

He undoes his pants and teases my clit with his cock before I sink down over him. I press my forehead to his as I ride him, watching his light blue eyes. Resting my forehead against Coop's, I tip my head to the side to see Noah watching us, his cock in his hand, stroking it slowly.

Rachel is a fool. But I'll forever be grateful she turned them down. That she never got to experience this with them. That's the real reason she should be bitter. I wouldn't give this up for the world. The way these men make me feel...

Coop slides his hand between us and circles my clit with the pad of his finger. "Come for me, goddess."

Meeting his heated, light blue eyes and seeing the desire reflected in them, I tip over the edge, my pussy clutching his cock. I slam my hips down, taking his cock in deep, and moan as my pussy contracts around him. His moan joins mine as his cock jerks and his cum fills me. I barely catch my breath before he passes me to Noah. My knees go to either side of Noah's hips.

"Noah." My hands cup his face as I take his cock inside me. My lips part at the ecstasy of him filling me.

"Only you, kitten," he whispers.

I rest my forehead against his as I ride his thick, hard cock. His dark eyes are mesmerizing, holding mine without any effort. My core is so sensitive that my breath hitches with each stroke. I tangle my hands in his hair, not caring if I mess it up.

He guides my hips over him and thrusts hard, pressing against my clit until my toes curl. I come harder this time. My lips part, but no sound comes out as I ride the wave and draw him in after me.

"You're so fucking tight." He slams me down on his cock one last time. His moan mingles with mine as he fills me with his cum. My pussy clenches around him again. Our lips collide in a frantic kiss that is part need and part want and part fear.

I wrap my arms around him, wanting to relieve that part that's fear, but I'm not sure I can. Because I feel it too. This whole thing is amazing and uncertain at the same time. What we are building is fragile and new. They break me down every time I'm with them, and I know I won't be able to hold my heart away.

Noah's hands stroke down my back.

When I lift my head, Coop turns my face to his and kisses me just as hard and needy, thrusting his tongue into my mouth. A tiny aftershock ripples through me, tightening my pussy around Noah's cock. He groans.

"You're welcome, dude." Coop winks. I smile and turn to Noah.

"Fuck off, Coop." Noah grins. The car makes a turn, and the sunlight goes away. "I wish we could stay in this car all day and just keep fucking you."

I sigh. Me too.

Seth

Everyone is back at their desks working. The office is quiet. It's been a few hours since lunch. Madison slipped in ten minutes later than the rest. She must have stopped at the apartment first. I still don't know what I'll say to her about Rachel, but I have to say something.

She's working diligently when I pause in my doorway. Her blond hair is tied up in a knot. Her wearing the scarf I bought her makes my cock ache. This morning, I ordered more clothes for her. Panties, bras, garter belts. Dresses and skirts. Even some shoes.

We're all very wealthy men thanks to Noah's brilliant brain. I can afford to splurge, but I don't know how she'll like me spending money on her. While she takes everything we give her sexually, she also has this spark of pride.

None of us realized how dire her living arrangement was.

"Are you just going to watch me?" She doesn't even turn in her chair.

I smirk. "I do like to watch."

She laughs. The sound is a little hoarse from her injury still. She spins in her chair and crosses her legs. "Do you need me?"

Her blue eyes are darkened a little, and her lips part. Yes, I do, and that's beginning to frighten me. The other women were just as attractive and followed my orders. But Madison tugs at something inside me. I can't afford to be blinded by my attraction to her.

As much as I want to trust her, I've been deceived before. It almost cost me my relationship with Coop, Blake, and Noah. I can't let another woman try to come between us again.

"Come into my office, princess." I return to my desk and wait for her.

Her skirt dances around her knees as she walks in carrying a notepad. She closes the door and pauses beside the chairs, waiting for me. For permission. Perfection.

I nod to the chair, and she takes a seat.

"Rachel was our assistant." I'll just lay this all out.

"I know," she says softly. Her eyes aren't accusatory or jealous, just full of gentle understanding.

I take a breath and lean back. "After Andrea claimed we sexually harassed her, we decided not to try again. We hired Rachel purely for her work experience and references."

Madison nods and sets her notepad on the other chair. "I understand your reluctance."

I rub the back of my neck. "She worked great with all of us. When she moved into the apartment, she kept to herself. Occasionally she'd join us for dinner, but she kept her life separate, and that was fine."

"So what happened?" She leans forward a little, like she really wants to know.

"Working late one night, I kissed her." I swallow. "She initiated it, but I'd found her attractive for a while."

Madison keeps her emotions to herself, except for a slight wince.

"I'm not saying this to hurt you."

"I know." She straightens and licks her lips. "Please continue. I want to know."

"It wasn't a single incident. We didn't fuck, but we kissed a few other times." I stand and pace. "We've had women try to come between us before. In college, Noah had a girlfriend who thought he spent too much time with us. One of Coop's girlfriends refused to come around us and nagged at him every time he chose us over spending time with her."

The stories are many. And those aren't even the worst of them. Madison's eyes track me.

"There were a couple of girls in college who wanted to experiment. We shared a few. Being with the same woman seemed like the logical step. We spend all our time together. It satisfies my voyeuristic tendencies, and that way women wouldn't try to draw us apart. We aren't just business partners. Those men are my family, and I won't let someone come between us."

I stop and take a breath. Madison just nods like she understands. Dropping into the chair beside her, I run my hand over my hair, holding her gaze steady.

"When I brought up being together with all of us, Rachel drew away like I'd handed her a poisonous snake. The next day, she came into my office and gave me her resignation. That whole next week, she kept asking if it could be just the two of us. When I finally told her it was all or nothing, she left. Walked out and took her stuff."

Madison takes my hand. I take a deep breath and refocus on her.

"I fucked that up. The others found Rachel attractive but were reluctant. They would have done it for me." I squeeze her hand. "I should have never made a move on her."

"How many others have there been?" Her voice is cautious, like she doesn't really want to know.

"We fooled around with the same girls in college a little. Nothing serious. Andrea was the first that we tried with the work arrangement." I lifted my eyes to her. It's only been a week and a half, but she's already becoming part of us. Like she's a piece of our puzzle we didn't even know was missing.

"Thank you for telling me." She kisses me.

One last thing. "I didn't know Rachel worked with Harper or I would have prepared everyone. Including you."

"She talked to me in the bathroom. Said you were perverts." Madison's gaze holds mine.

"What did you say?"

She smiles softly. "That maybe I wanted what you had to offer."

Perfection.

Chapter 30

Working Hard

Blake

"Did you see my jewelry box when you packed my things?" Madison drops into the seat across from me in the library. She's wearing a pair of sleep shorts and a tank top without a bra. Her hair is loose around her shoulders.

My cock hardens, remembering her riding me last night while taking the others in her mouth. Fuck. Her hard limits list is barely a list. I can't wait to find her soft limits and press into them, make her want more.

I lift my hands off the keyboard. My focus is shot for work right now. All the blood has rushed southward. I focus on when I went back to pack her apartment. Her room looked like someone had tossed it. I'm glad she wasn't there to see it.

The police are looking for Valerie and Jeff, but they aren't having any luck yet.

"I think so." Trying to at least answer her question about the jewelry box, I remember finding a small box of earrings and necklaces. Nothing fancy, but things she would wear every day.

It was bad enough they roughed her up, but to know someone went through your private belongings is just one more violation.

She blows a breath out. "I haven't found it yet. My jewelry isn't valuable, so I don't think Valerie would have taken it. But my grandma's charm bracelet was in there."

"If you don't find it, we can go back to the apartment and check. I changed the locks so no one else has access." That doesn't mean those two won't try to break in though. "But only go if you're with one of us."

My gaze drops to her breasts. Her nipples poke at the thin fabric. I glance around, but it looks like it's only the two of us in here.

Dinner was an hour ago, and everyone is doing their own thing. Coop is probably working out. Noah had a project he wanted to work on in his office. And Seth... Who knows where he is.

"Okay." She gives me a little pout. She fidgets with her fingers on the table. "What are you working on?"

I arch an eyebrow. "I *was* working on a report, but seeing you like that has me distracted."

Her gaze drops to my obvious erection in my sweatpants. She grins and squirms in her seat. Her eyes sparkle. "We can't have that."

The corner of my lip twitches. "Want to play, tiger?"

She nods. My cock hardens painfully.

"I have to get my work done, and you need to fix this problem. On your knees under the table."

She slides down to her knees and ducks under the table. I scoot my chair back, so she has room and I can watch her.

"Take out my cock."

She pulls my sweats down and frees my cock. It twitches in anticipation of her touch and that mouth. Fuck, her mouth is heaven. Her hands stroke over me as her eyes meet mine. She licks her lips, and precum leaks out of me at her eagerness.

"Suck my cock while I finish this report. Don't play with yourself, and don't stop unless I tell you to."

Her eyes widen. She nods before taking my tip between her beautiful, full lips. I groan, watching her for a few beats as she licks the precum from my slit. Clearing my throat, I shift my attention to my report.

I type and edit the words as her tongue glides over me. Her warm mouth encloses my cock. Her hands cup my balls lightly as she takes me down her throat while her fist works what she can't fit in. I keep my focus on my work as much as I can.

I'm three pages in when my balls tighten, and she sucks on me, hollowing out her cheeks. Her darkened eyes meet mine. She moans, sending vibrations through me.

I explode and come down her throat. She swallows every drop and licks me clean. When she lifts off my cock, I grab her hair and tilt her face to mine.

"Why did you stop?"

Her eyebrow rises, and her gaze drops to my still semihard cock. "I—"

"Did I tell you to stop?"

She shakes her head and takes my cock in her hand, stroking it. I guide her mouth back to the tip. Her mouth opens to take my cock in again.

I release her hair as she sinks down on me. "You stop when I say to stop. Snap if you understand."

She snaps her fingers and sucks on me, getting me nice and hard again. My hands return to the keyboard, and I make good progress on my report. Her lips and tongue and teeth and hands work my cock until I'm close again. I pause my typing to watch her.

Her pink lips stretch around my cock as she bobs over it. She hums as she takes me deep again. I can't hold back any longer.

When I come, she swallows and keeps her mouth on me. Her fingers massage my balls. I smirk as I return to writing. It takes a little longer before I'm fully hard again. Finishing my report, I save it and close my laptop.

I lean back and watch her, sliding her lips up and down my cock. She's fucking amazing. Her jaw has to be getting sore, but she doesn't stop or complain. I grab her hair and stop her. Her eyes dart up to mine. I ease her down farther on my cock for a second before pulling her off completely.

"Stand." I push the chair back so she can stand in front of me. Her nipples are hard. Her breathing is chaotic, and her pupils are blown with desire. "Take off your shorts and panties."

She does as she's told and stands before me in just her tank.

"Give me your panties."

She hands them to me.

I lift them to my nose and smell. She groans. "These are soaked. Are you wet for me, tiger?"

She nods. Her fingers twitch against her thighs.

"Turn around and put your hands on the table." She turns and sticks her ass out toward me. I stand behind her and knead her ass cheeks, drawing them apart to look at her puckered hole.

Coop works her ass every time he gets a chance. He's already claimed dibs on taking her ass first. His cock would be a hell of a lot easier on her than taking mine for the first time. I want this ass, but I can wait.

Her head drops between her arms as she sways under my touch.

"You stopped without permission, tiger. That earned you three spanks."

She whimpers and nods. "Yes, sir."

"Count them." I draw back my hand and spank her.

"One."

I follow with the second one immediately on the same cheek.

She moans. "Two."

The third spank elicits a groan.

"Three."

I rub my hand over her reddened skin, and she sighs and squirms beneath my touch. Her hips rock again. My hand strays closer to her pussy.

"Do you want me to fuck you?"

She hisses. "Yes, Blake, please."

My cock hardens more. Her pussy glistens she's so wet.

"Did sucking my cock make you wet?"

"Yes." Her legs spread for me, and she keeps swaying like I'm already pounding into her tight pussy. Not yet. I may not take her ass, but I can help with the training.

I dip two of my fingers into her pussy and stroke them in and out, getting them nice and wet. She moans and follows my fingers with her hips mindlessly.

I draw them out and circle her puckered hole with them before easing my two fingers all the way inside her. Her ass is tight. I'm not a small man and my fingers are thick.

"Relax, Madison."

She gasps and her legs shake. "Blake?" Her voice is strained.

"Don't come, tiger, or you'll get spanked again for being a naughty girl."

"Fuck." Her body is flushed with color as I massage inside her ass, helping to loosen the muscles. Her pussy would tighten on my cock if I had it in her, but I want to wait.

My cock aches with the need to be inside her. But she's waited this long to come, she can wait a little longer.

I'm so focused on Madison's tight ass, I barely notice when Seth sits across the table from us. Madison lifts her head to look at him, and he just gives her a smirk. He won't join in, at least not right away. But he'll watch.

Her ass tightens around my fingers. I smirk because I know Seth's attention will help her get off even faster.

"How does that feel, princess?" Seth asks.

"Weird and good," she breathes out.

I keep my fingers buried in her ass and take my cock in my other hand. I rub the tip against her clit, back and forth, getting it nice and wet. She makes these mewling, needy noises that almost make me come right then and there. Her breathing is all chaotic gasps as her hips seek my cock.

"Do you want me to fuck you now?" I slide my tip to her entrance before moving it back to press against her clit.

"Fuck yes," she bites out. Her fingers clench against the table.

"Are you going to come as soon as I get inside that tight pussy, tiger?" I draw my fingers slowly out of her puckered hole until I almost come out before thrusting them back deep inside.

She cries out, and her hole tightens around my fingers. "No, sir."

Stroking the head of my cock between her legs, I press the tip to her entrance. "Don't come, Madison."

She whimpers. I just slip my tip inside her, feeling her pussy pulse on the intrusion, and her hips rock, trying to take me deeper. I hold her hips steady.

"Can you take more?"

"Yes, please, yes." Her fingers curl into fists on the table.

I push in an inch and then draw out and press in an inch again. "Like that?"

Her body is hot and tight and on the edge of exploding. Her breathing shudders in and out of her.

"More, Blake. Please. Need more."

I chuckle as I slide a little deeper before withdrawing and doing it over and over. I want to know how much teasing she can take before she comes.

"Please, Blake. Please, I need it." Her arms and legs shake. Her voice is hoarse and filled with desire.

"If you need it, then take it, tiger." I lift my eyes to Seth. His hand is below the table, stroking his cock, but his eyes are on Madison. I wish I could see her face. The frustration. The need. The ache.

Shoving her hips back against me, she impales herself on my cock with a long moan. Her cunt tightens all around me. The muscles flutter, so close.

"Don't come yet." I keep thrusting my fingers in her ass, but don't move my hips. "If you want it, do the work."

When she rocks forward, my cock almost slips out of her before she pushes back onto me again. Over and over, she fucks my cock. The wet sound of her pussy taking my cock fills the room. I hold myself steady, letting her take her pleasure, but I keep my fingers moving in her ass.

Double penetration will be fantastic with her. A cock in her ass will squeeze her pussy tighter around my cock. Even my fingers in her ass make her tighter.

"Can I come, please?" she grinds out. Her skin is slick with sweat. Her thighs tremble, and her cunt is soaked around me. She's been on the edge for so long.

"Since you asked so nicely." I'm feeling generous.

She slams back harder and faster on me. Her tits sway in her tank top. She's making these noises that fill the entire library. Seth grunts as his fist stills in his lap. I meet his eyes. If I hadn't already come twice, it would have been all over.

I wrap my hand around her hip and press my fingers into her ass harder. Her motions get jerky as her pussy convulses around my cock. She pushes onto me one last time as she cries out. I take my fingers out of her ass to hold her hips.

"My turn." I slam into her repeatedly, making her take every inch of my cock in her tight pussy. She cries out as she tumbles into a second orgasm, tightening almost painfully around me.

Roaring, I explode inside her, filling her slick walls with my cum. She twitches beneath me as we stay pressed together, not moving. I take a deep breath and see Seth grabbing a tissue for himself.

"Wait." I hold up my hand to stop him.

He raises an eyebrow but stops. When I pull my cock out of Madison, she sags against the table.

"Clean up Seth with your tongue."

She lifts her head and goes around the table. Keeping her eyes locked with Seth, she drops to her knees before him and licks his cock, stomach, and hand.

When she finishes, she sits back on her knees. Seth leans forward and captures her mouth in a kiss that looks consuming. My cock pulses, but we've had enough fun for the night.

I circle around behind them and stroke Madison's hair. It's not either of our night with her. I wonder if we can ever wear her out. "Good girl."

Chapter 31

Tied Up

Noah

After a postworkout shower, I head back into the main living area in only my shorts. Technically, we could walk around naked if we wanted, but I'd be stiff every time Madison was in the room. That wouldn't differ greatly from normal, but it would be more noticeable.

Tonight she's all mine and I have plans.

She sits at the island talking with Coop while they eat ice cream. Her hair is twisted into two braids. She wears a thin tank top and sleep shorts. I'm surprised ice cream is the only thing Coop is eating.

When her laughter fills the room, I take in a deep breath. My insides tighten. I'm not jealous of him for making her laugh. Jealousy can't be part of this equation. She's not mine alone.

After the trauma she's been through, I'm just glad she's laughing at all. Her throat is now shades of green and purple, lighter than yesterday. I'm not usually a violent man, but after seeing her in the hospital, seeing the marks that asshole left on her makes me want to find him and end him for daring to touch what is ours.

Her hard limit is choking, completely understandable. I'm not into choking, but there will be times when I want to hold her still, and some of those times will be by the throat. But we'll cross that bridge when we get to it. So many things I want to do with her.

But I'll ease her into my kink.

When she notices me, she grins and holds up her spoon. "You want some ice cream?"

I shake my head and stop next to her at the island. Her soft floral scent fills my nose. "Are you almost ready for bed?"

She nods and her eyes darken. Fuck, this girl is as aroused for us as we are for her. That's a good thing, because I can't seem to get enough of her, and neither can the others.

I hold out my hand to her. She takes it and leans over to kiss Coop on the cheek before she gets off the stool.

"Have a good night, sweetheart." He gives her a wicked smile. Some night, he and I will play with her together, but not tonight. Our play styles work well together. Not that we don't play well with the others, but Coop and I just seem to communicate in the same way when it comes to sex.

I don't release her hand as I lead her to my bedroom. There's a play room that technically belongs to us all, but it's too early to show her that. That's why it wasn't on the official tour. We figured the enormous bed in her room would be enough to start with.

The bedrooms are all similar in size. My walls are a dark gray. I have heavy wood furniture and my king-sized bed has plenty of rails on the headboard and footboard. My sheets are white while my duvet is a blend of darker colors. It's rolled down at the bottom of the bed, out of the way.

"I like your room." Her gaze falls on the leather chair in the corner, next to a wooden chair that almost seems out of place. It serves a purpose.

Not tonight, but soon.

"Strip for me, kitten." I sit in the leather chair. My cock hardened the second I drew in her floral scent. My shorts don't disguise it. Not that I would hide my erection from her.

Madison doesn't act shy. I appreciate that as she peels off her tank and drops her shorts to the floor.

"Where are your panties, kitten?" Curious.

"Blake took them." She blushes slightly.

"Did he?" I tap my fingers thoughtfully against my lips. "Did he fuck you?"

"Yes." Her fingers twitch against her thighs.

"Tell me." I lean forward, clasping my hands between my knees and looking up at her.

She shifts on her feet, and her cheeks and chest turn pink. "He had me on my knees, sucking his cock while he worked."

"Did you swallow his cum?"

Her throat works and she nods. "Twice."

I raise an eyebrow. "And then he fucked you?"

"He bent me over the table. Using his fingers, he fucked my ass, but only penetrated me a little with his cock." Her eyes met mine. "Seth watched while Blake made me do all the work to get myself off. Then he fucked me."

I can picture it. Wish I'd been there for that show, but I have her to myself now. I relax back into my chair and steeple my fingers against my lips while I take in her hardened nipples and quickened breaths.

I examine every inch of her as the quiet in the room surrounds us.

She stands uncertainly in front of me. Waiting for me to tell her what to do. Will there be a time when she takes what she wants? She needs to if she wants to succeed in business and in life. When she finds something she wants, she needs to grab on to it with both hands and refuse to let it go.

"Sit on the bed."

As always, she follows directions beautifully. When will I push her hard enough to fight back? Not truly fight, but resist. Balk. Because sometimes that makes things hotter. The others may like her submissive, but I love her spark, her intelligence.

Sex isn't just about the physical with me. I want someone real like Madison. Clever. Present.

"Lie down."

She does, and I walk to the bed to loom over her. Her breasts rise and fall rapidly with her breath as she watches my every move.

"I'm going to tie your hands to the bedposts. The ties won't be tight, and you'll still be able to move your arms. This time."

Her eyes widen at my last words. "Okay."

I grab a strap that I threaded through a rail above her head and hold out my hand for hers. She gives it to me. This trust she gives us intoxicates me.

"Remember your safe word. Use it if you need to." I tie her wrist, then step back and drop my shorts onto the ground so I'm naked with her.

I climb onto the bed and straddle her waist. I reach for her other hand and tie it to the other end of the strap. Giving it a quick tug, I smile down at her. She's stretched out beneath me.

"Is that it?" Her brow furrows.

"Tonight, yes." I sit above her. My hard cock bobs against my stomach. "Next time we'll try a blindfold. Then maybe progress to tying your feet."

She squirms beneath me and licks her lips. "And then?"

Fuck, I can hear the longing in her voice. "Then we play."

I stroke my hand down her cheek, and she leans into the touch. I trail my hand along her neck, careful not to apply pressure to the bruised skin.

"Tonight, I want you to come when you need to. You don't need my permission."

My fingers graze the sides of her breasts and she inhales sharply. Her nipples are so hard they pucker into tight peaks. I pinch them and she moans.

"Have you ever had your tits fucked?" I keep my tone nonchalant.

She has decent sized tits for it. She shakes her head.

I grin and cup her tits together, imagining my cock sliding between them. "I have other plans for tonight, but I want to fuck your tits another time."

"Yeah?" She arches up into my hands as my thumbs trail over her nipples. Her waist shifts between my thighs, and she tugs gently on her restraints.

"Yes, kitten." I move lower onto her thighs and lean down to take her nipple into my mouth while I squeeze both her breasts.

"Noah," she gasps.

Her hips buck against mine, but I don't move lower. Like I have all the time in the world, I taste her nipples and the surrounding skin, testing the texture with my tongue. Using my open mouth, I cover her breasts in kisses and stop to suck on spots until hickeys form. I play with her breasts, one, then the other, and then alternate faster until she's a writhing mess below me.

I sit up and meet her passion-laden eyes. My fingers continue to stroke and pluck her nipples. "How are you doing, kitten?"

She releases a breath. "Good."

Her hips buck against mine, and her thighs rub together, looking to ease her ache. But I'm not ready to do that yet. When I lick her nipple and blow across it, she whimpers.

Smirking, I do the same to her other nipple before I slide lower. I cover her stomach in my kisses and nips and sucks. The guys might be mad at me for leaving love bites all over our girl, but fuck 'em. The way she arches up to meet my mouth tells me she likes it. Her soft skin is hot beneath my lips and tongue.

She tugs at her restraint, and I lift my head to watch her struggle. I trail my fingertip down her side.

"What's wrong, kitten?" I try to make my voice sound concerned.

"Touch me, Noah," she whimpers. Her blue eyes meet mine.

I kiss her stomach. "I am touching you."

"Noah." Her voice is on edge.

"What do you want, kitten? Maybe I'll give it to you." I crawl up her body until my legs straddle her right beneath her armpits. I hold on to the headboard as I lean over her. My cock brushes over her lips. "Or maybe I'll just take what I want."

She parts her lips to talk, but I slide my cock between them. When her tongue flicks my tip, I groan as a little precum leaks out.

I push farther into her mouth, gently but steadily. She relaxes beneath me as I slide my cock in and out. She licks and sucks when she can. I push a little deeper than I normally do, but she relaxes her throat to take me in.

She's exactly what I want.

"Do you like that, kitten? Do you like when I fuck your mouth?"

She makes a noise of affirmation that buzzes down the length of my cock. I told her she could come when she liked, but what I didn't tell her is I have no intention of getting her there. Oh, I'll lead her right to the edge, but then I'm going to retreat and do it over and over again until she's begging for mercy.

But I'm an equal opportunity edger, so when I get close to coming from her sucking my cock like it's her favorite candy, I pull back and move down her body to her waist. My chest brushes her nipples, and my wet cock lies on her stomach as I devour her mouth.

She meets my tongue with hers, and we make out. Her body rubs on mine, trying to get some friction, but I hold myself just out of reach, chuckling at her frustrated noises.

I trail kisses down her neck, softly. She stills beneath me like she's afraid it'll hurt. When I get to her collarbone and lick along it, she relaxes. I nip and suck along her collarbones. My cock grazes her pubic bone, and my shoulders brush her hard nipples.

Releasing an impatient sigh and whimper, she spreads her legs wide beneath me.

"Noah." Frustration tinges her tone. "Fuck me, please."

I chuckle against her skin and move down to her breasts with my mouth. She has amazing breasts. The perfect size for my mouth and hands and so fucking responsive. The lube in my nightstand is right there. I could get us both slick and fuck her tits until I come all over her pretty neck.

Would it be enough to get her off?

I suck harder on her nipple, and she arches against me, her pussy brushing against my cock. Her breathing stutters as she does it again. It's a light tease of a touch for both of us, barely a whisper.

Releasing her breast with a pop, I move to the other and suck it hard into my mouth. She makes these needy noises in the back of her throat. I'm curious if she can come from having her tits played with, but I'm not willing to let her come just yet.

Another night. Definitely.

I move down to her stomach again, and my cock is now out of her pussy's reach. This time, my kisses trail lower. She holds her breath. I kiss the top of her pubic bone, then explore her hips, sucking on the skin drawn taut over her hipbone. Her hips try to move, to lead me where she wants, but I'm content where I am.

Her breath catches, and she pauses in her noises, when I move toward her center again. I flick my tongue against the top of her pussy before moving to the other hip, sucking and nipping at it. I pause there, searching for control. She makes me want to lose myself inside her, but I want to play more first.

"Noah, please." She arches up against me, but I press my hand down on her hip to hold her still. A guttural noise rips from deep inside her. "I need to come, Noah. I need to come so bad. Please."

"You can come anytime you want, kitten." I grin against her hipbone as I trail kisses back to her center. I blow hot air across her soaking wet pussy.

She sucks in her breath. Her thighs are spread wide in invitation.

"Please," she whispers, lifting her head to meet my eyes. Her eyes are dark pools surrounded by blue. She craves this, but I won't give it to her. Not yet.

I shift lower on the bed and grab her hips to flip her over. I crawl over her, resting my cock on her ass. My chest brushes her shoulder blades. I lean in and whisper in her ear. "Not until I taste all of you."

She groans and lifts her hips to rub her ass against my cock. My cock twitches and aches with the need to come. Precum drips out of me, and it would feel so fucking good to sink into her cunt and get us both off.

Fuck, Madison is exactly what I want. What I need. But there's so much to taste still before either of us will find release.

Chapter 32

Unbound

Madison

Noah is trying to kill me. And if he doesn't succeed, I'm hoping someone else will finish the job. My whole body aches. Every touch is like flames scorching my skin. His lips and hands massage my back, sending tingles coursing through my veins and pooling with all the pent-up need coiled in my pussy.

If my hands were free, I'd get myself off in seconds. I swear, a breath in the right place would set me off. Okay, maybe more than a breath.

He sucks and licks and nips at my shoulder blades. He's covering me in hickeys. I'm not sure if I love it or hate it yet. Part of me wants to be marked by Noah, to show everyone that I'm his. The other part is worried about what the others might think. The worry isn't enough to say my safe word, though.

If I don't come soon, I might need to use it. Because this is sweet agony.

His lips tickle my sides a little, and I recoil from them instinctively.

"Ticklish, kitten?"

"A little." My voice is deeper and huskier because of the damage to my throat, but the breathlessness is all Noah's fault. If he'd just spend some quality time in the right spots, I know I'd be more than satisfied.

He kisses my ass and the muscles tense.

"Relax, kitten."

Easy for him to say. I have lady blue balls.

He kneels between my legs and lifts my hips. I move my knees beneath me so I'm kneeling, sort of. I'm putty in his hands. My arms are flat on the bed, so I'm tits down, ass up. If he'd just slide his cock inside me, I could get off.

Noah's hands part my ass cheeks, and his hot breath caresses my crack. I'm pretty sure, if I don't come soon, I'm going to go insane, that I will trade anything for an orgasm.

He nips and sucks on my ass cheeks, and then he drags his lips over my asshole. My whole being stops. My breath freezes. Did he just... ? He does it again.

"Noah?" My voice is shaky.

He doesn't answer me. Instead, he thrusts his tongue inside my asshole, and I'm right there on the edge again. My pussy throbs as he starts to steadily fuck my ass with his tongue. It's so weird and wonderful.

Instead of recoiling, I'm widening my legs and pressing back against his tongue. Right as I'm about to explode, he backs off.

I bite out a frustrated scream. My hips rock like he's still tongue fucking my ass, but nothing is giving me that sweet friction.

He sits on his heels behind me. I'm breathing heavy. My pussy throbs, empty, and I want to scream my frustration more. I want to flick my own clit and explode. His fingers touch my calves lightly.

Every time I've begged him, he's slowed down again. I don't know what to do to get there. I can't do anything to rub myself into an orgasm.

His warm breath bathes my pussy, and I moan at the sensation.

So fucking sensitive I could fall over the edge, but I need just a touch more than a stiff breeze to get me there.

Taking a deep breath, I wait for the next torture session to begin. The bed dips between my legs and hands grab my hips. His cock thrusts hard and deep inside me. We both groan loudly. Finally.

I widen my stance and arch my back as he draws out of me slowly, tantalizing every overstimulated nerve ending, then he thrusts back in hard and fast. He keeps his slow-then-fast pace until my hips are following him. My fingers clench his sheets as my teeth gnash. I know the second I get close, it's all going to end again.

Keeping my breath steady, I try not to focus everything on what's happening between my thighs, but it's impossible. His cock feels divine, and all my blood is currently pooling in my pussy.

He picks up the pace slightly, and I'm no longer able to even think. All I can do is feel the heavy thrust of his cock in my pussy, the slap of his balls against my lower lips, his fingers digging into my hips.

Just when I think he's going to pull away, he reaches between my legs and pinches my clit. I scream as my orgasm thunders through me, milking his cock hard as my whole being shatters into a million pieces.

He roars as he comes in my throbbing pussy. My core convulses around him, drawing every drop of cum he has into my body until we both slump in a heap. His chest presses against my back. His weight feels so good as my body trembles beneath him.

Between my erratic pulse and frantic breaths, I don't think I'll ever be normal again. He reaches up and unties my hands, rubbing my wrists gently with his thumbs and fingers. He pulls me onto my side. His cock remains inside me as we slowly come back from the cosmos.

"Fuck," I whisper. My throat is a little more hoarse now from the screaming orgasm.

Chuckling, he kisses the back of my neck, sending tingles through me. "Did you like it, kitten?"

"Ask me tomorrow." I wave him off. "I don't know how I feel about it right now besides so fucking tired."

He kisses my neck. "Then sleep, love."

My heart clenches at that term of endearment. It'd be so easy to pretend this is more than it is. With his warmth surrounding me, I slip into sleep.

ME:

Can you come over after work? I can't go out right now.

I glance over my shoulders at the closed doors. It's almost quitting time, and the guys have been busy all day. I've been busy all day. If there was something that could burn down, it was on fire.

And we all ran around putting them out as best we could.

HOPE:

Sure. You're in the apartment now, right?

ME:

Yes. I'll come down to let you up when you're ready.

HOPE:

Exciting. I can't wait.

Neither can I. I obviously enjoy the guys, but part of living my life includes having actual friends. And Hope just started being my friend before last weekend.

I text the guys that Hope will be coming up after work for a while and not to wait for me for dinner. I'm almost glad we were too busy today to do anything.

As much as I love being fucked by them and want them all the time, I'm pretty sure my pussy could use a little rest. Of course, tonight will be spent in Coop's bed, so I'm not planning on getting much of a break.

But I don't actually mind.

Speak of the devil. Coop stops by my desk.

"I feel like I've barely talked to you today." He glances at the closed doors and then takes advantage of me sitting to look down my cleavage. "How have you been?"

"Good. Feeling much better." And I am. Maybe the sex is an excellent cure or just makes me sleep extra hard. Maybe sleeping naked next to a hot male helps me sleep… though I'm getting used to having a cock thrusting into my pussy as an alarm. Again, not complaining. It's better than electronic bells any day.

"I'm thinking about tonight." He drags the tips of his fingers across his lower lip.

"Yeah?" I'm curious if he wants to do something unusual or more prep.

"I have some thoughts." His heated eyes find mine. "You have Hope over early?"

I nod. My hand touches my scarf. "I'm going to tell her what happened."

He bobs his head. "I'll text you if I need you to do anything before coming for me."

"Do you mean coming to you?"

His hand captures my chin and tips my face toward his. "No. I don't."

Heat floods my face as he smirks and disappears into his office.

At least that's one thing that is guaranteed. They will make me come. Sometimes often, sometimes once. Either way is good for me.

I cross my legs and finish up my day. When Hope texts me she's ready, I grab my purse and head to the elevator. The elevator reaches her floor and opens. She grins and her eyes go wide.

"I love the scarf. Is that silk?"

I touch the button for the apartment.

"Yes. Thanks." My fingers go to it to make sure it covers the bruises. "Fair warning. We have to go through the main living area to get to my apartment."

Hope's blue eyes widen. "You share a living space with the guys?"

"Yeah." I touch my scarf. "It's actually nice."

"Wow. I mean, I knew there were perks to the job, one of them being the bosses are hot man candy, but to share a living space..." She fans herself. "I don't think I'd ever take a warm shower."

I laugh, because yeah, it is hot. Especially when Seth bent me over the couch and fucked me, or Coop ate my pussy on the island. But I can't share that with Hope. Not now and not ever because of the NDA.

My heart falls to my stomach. Something that is so important in my life right now has to remain a secret. The elevator stops, and shaking off that thought, I open the door to the apartment.

"Holy shit. Now I'm kicking myself for not applying for the transfer. You get to live here?" Hope's eyes dart around the place. "But if I'd gotten the job, I wouldn't have met you, so I'm over it."

We exchange smiles, and I gesture for her to follow me.

I lead her to my door, and we walk into my living space. I have the bedroom door closed. That bed would cause a lot of questions I'm not ready to answer, and can't answer completely anyway. I'm not sure Hope wouldn't look at me differently if she knew about me having sex with all four of my bosses.

No trace of sexy times shows in my quaint sitting room.

"Oh, this is so nice." Hope settles on the couch and puts her feet on the ottoman. She snuggles into the pillows. "Oh, yeah, I could get used to this."

"Want a drink? I put some wine in the fridge this morning."

"Yes, please."

I pour two glasses and then join her on the couch.

"How's week two going?" Hope takes a sip of her wine.

"It's good. But I wanted to tell you why I haven't been downstairs as much." I set my glass on the end table and turn to her.

She sets her glass down and takes a deep breath. "This seems ominous."

I wring my hands together, hoping I'm trusting the right person. I don't want her to think the guys did this and I'm lying to her to keep them from getting in trouble. "My roommate and her boyfriend assaulted me on Friday night."

"What?" Hope puts her hand over her mouth. She reaches out and puts her hand over mine. "Oh my god, are you okay?"

I unwrap the scarf from my neck. "When I got home that night, I didn't think anything of her being there, but they were looking for money I didn't have."

Hope gasps at the sight of my neck. I set the scarf on the ottoman.

"Her boyfriend choked me, but Blake ended up saving me."

"That's lucky. Why was Blake at your apartment?"

Yeah, not going into that. "He wanted to check up on me after the first week."

"If he hadn't..." Hope leans in and touches my arm.

I nod. It's what haunts my dreams. What if he hadn't? The guys didn't plan to see me until Monday. No one would have expected me until Monday. Those two could have kept me trapped all weekend. *You want to pound her first or watch me take her?* Ice pours through me as I shake off Valerie's words again.

"I'm so glad you're okay." She glances around. "So, the guys moved you in early? See, I knew they're good people. Fuck the haters."

I smile as my insides soften, thinking about my guys. "Yeah, they're good. They didn't want rumors to start about me moving in early or that they were choking me." I shake my head like it's a ludicrous thought. They wouldn't do anything without my consent, and the finger bruises on my throat are not someone trying some new kink on me.

The guys might leave marks but not violent ones. The marks Noah left all over my body last night are all hidden beneath my clothes, so I don't need to explain where I got the love bites.

"I wish we could go celebrate you moving in properly, but I understand now why you wanted to meet here." Hope takes a drink. "Did they catch your roommate?"

I shake my head. "They've gone underground. The police are still after them. They were out on bail, and my assault means they'll be held this time, once they're found."

"Locking you in a tower is probably ideal, then. Fuck." Hope finishes her drink and goes to get the bottle. "You doing okay? Is there anything you need?"

She brings the bottle and tops off my glass.

"No, I've got everything I need here. I just didn't want you to think I was blowing you off. I really want to be friends." Even if I suck at actually making friends.

Hope grins. "You've got me. Okay, you've got this huge TV, and I'm imagining access to every streaming service possible because those guys are loaded. Let's begin your TV education with a little *Witcher*."

Chapter 33

First Time

Madison

I ride the elevator down to the ground floor with Hope.

"We're going to binge the rest of the season on Sunday." She points at me. "I'm not taking no for an answer."

"You don't have to twist my arm. Seriously, how did I not know about this show?"

"Because you lived under a rock." Hope shakes her head as the elevator stops. She grabs me in a tight hug. "I'm so glad you're okay. I'll see you this weekend, if not before."

I squeeze her back. "You've got it."

As she exits, I wave and don't even peek my head out of the elevator before I hit the button to go upstairs. The receptionist is probably long gone, but I don't want to risk her catty looks. It's exciting to have a new friend in Hope. It's nice to be happy for once and not struggling to make ends meet.

But I keep waiting for the other shoe to drop. For the shit to hit the fan. For... whatever other metaphors I can come up with about things falling apart like they always do. Happiness doesn't last long in my world.

Not without a lot of struggles to get there.

I touch my scarf. Maybe this will be it for the struggle, and once I heal, it will be forgotten. The twinge in my gut tells me I'm never going to forget being choked, even long after the bruises heal.

I enter the apartment and it's quiet. The TV isn't on. The dishwasher runs with the guys' dinner dishes. I check the library, but no one is in there, either. Maybe they're still at work?

I consider going up to the office, but they could just as likely be at the gym. I don't know if they go out to bars or have other obligations I won't be a part of. At least our deal includes them only having sex with me, so I don't have to worry about them picking up women.

After changing into pajamas, I return to the living room. I nestle into the corner of the sectional and open a book on my phone. My eyes get heavy.

The next thing I know, someone lifts me into his arms. His clean and crisp scent surrounds me.

"Coop?"

"Shh. Just bringing you to bed."

I snuggle into his warmth. "Where were you guys?"

"We had some last-minute work to get done." That wakes me up.

"Why didn't you let me know? I could have helped."

Chuckling, he carries me into his bedroom and closes the door. "You need time off too, sweetheart. You deserved to have a girls' night with Hope. We got it done."

Without me. I almost pout as he sets me on my feet.

His thumb trails along my lower lip. "We won't make it a habit, okay? If we're working late, we'll let you know."

"Good." I meet his light blue eyes. He better mean that.

His hand cups my jaw as he lowers his mouth to take mine. He still has on his dress shirt and slacks from work today. Rising on my tiptoes, I reach behind his neck and pull out the pins holding his hair in its bun.

His dark hair is silky soft as I shift it through my hands. He deepens the kiss, dancing his tongue against mine. His kisses could last me forever. His hands slide my shorts down and off. Breaking the kiss, he lifts my shirt over my head.

I undo the buttons on his shirt and shove it off his shoulders before working on his pants. Soon we stand in just our underwear, still kissing and exploring each other's skin.

Releasing my mouth, he presses his forehead into mine. "What do you think?"

Think? I blink up at him. I wasn't doing a lot of thinking currently. My breasts are pressed against his chest, his hard cock rests against my stomach, and my pussy is hot and wet and ready.

"About?"

He slides his hands into the sides of my underwear. "I want to try tonight."

He drops to his knee before me as he lowers my panties. My brain just isn't latching onto what he's saying.

"Try?"

"I want to fuck your ass tonight, sweetheart." His blue eyes peer up at me before he leans in and licks my pussy. I gasp as his tongue explores me, fanning the flames of lust even higher.

I thread my fingers into his hair, not really thinking about what he wants to do as he pushes me back to sit on the edge of the bed. He spreads my legs and flicks his tongue over my clit. My fingers grip his hair as he takes his time with his tongue and lips, sucking and thrusting until I'm panting with need.

He doesn't relent, pushing me higher and higher until I tumble over the edge into oblivion. My pussy pulsing, hot and empty.

"Coop." I tug at his hair. I need him inside me.

He grins. "Don't worry. I'll take good care of you tonight."

He stands and goes to his drawer of goodies. Still breathing heavily, I sit on the edge of the bed, watching him sort through things. He drops his boxers to the floor and brings back a handful of toys.

"Will it hurt?" Sometimes the toys hurt a little. I keep my eyes locked with his.

His face softens as he kneels between my legs.

"Not if we get you relaxed and ready." He leans in and kisses my lips softly. His hand holds my breast as his thumb traces my nipple. Something cold and wet presses between my legs. He slides something as wide as his cock into my pussy and pumps it in and out.

"Oh, fuck," I whisper against his lips. My eyes close as those flames rise again.

He releases my lips, and I look down at the blue dildo he's stroking inside me.

"I want you to come again, Madison." He takes my nipple into his mouth and sucks hard on it as he thrusts the dildo into me. "Can you do that for me?"

My lips part and I nod. He grins mischievously and slides lower to flick his tongue over my clit before he sucks on it.

My brain officially leaves the building as a Fourth of July fireworks display goes off inside me. A gush of fluid rushes out of me as I come around the toy and his sucking mouth.

"Good girl." He holds the toy inside me. "Roll over, sweetheart."

My brain is officially fried. I'm a puddle of cells, his to do with what he will as I roll onto my stomach. His fingers are wet with lube as he strokes around my asshole before pushing them inside. He presses into the muscles until they relax, just like before. It's a little tighter with the dildo filling my core.

"Breathe, babe. You're doing exceptional."

My pussy clenches around the dildo. He adds another finger, working them in and out until all I can do is feel. The heat of his skin against mine. The thrust of his fingers along my delicate nerves. He slides a thick toy into my ass with ease, and crying out, I come undone from being so completely filled.

The pulses of my orgasm are almost painful around the toys. Coop removes the dildo from my pussy and leans in to lick, suck, and tongue my clit and pussy. When I rock against his face again, he stops.

He pulls the plug from my asshole and strokes his fingers inside me again.

"I'm going to start with the tip, babe. Not much at all. Just remember to relax. Let me do the work. Okay?"

"Yes." I blow out a breath, needing more, wanting more. His hard cock is wet and hot as he presses gently into my asshole.

"Fuck, that's hot." Coop's voice is low and reverent. "You doing good?"

"Yeah." Surprisingly, I am. I want more.

"If it hurts, we'll stop."

I let out a breath and relax my muscles.

He thrusts a little, easing the tip a little farther inside, and pulls out. The tight ring of muscles stretches every time he pushes deeper. He keeps doing it over and over again until I need so much more.

I raise my hips to push back into him, trying to take him all. I just want to feel him inside me. His warmth, his thickness, sliding against those tantalizing nerves. He pulls all the way out and sits beside me on the bed.

"Come here." His voice is lower and curls around my ear.

I stand between his legs as his eyes take in every inch of me. His hands rest on my hips as he sucks my breast into his mouth, keying me up, teasing my nipple with his tongue. When he looks up at me, I'm beyond hot and bothered.

My thighs press tight against the ache between them, throbbing for more.

He raises his eyes to mine. "This is easier if you can control penetration."

I give him a confused look.

"I'm going to position you. I'll hold your hips to help, but you are going to lower onto my cock." He flicks my nipple with his tongue again, and I gasp. "Ready?"

"Yes, Coop."

He helps me straddle him, and I hold on to his shoulders. I want this. I want him. He grips my hip as he lines his cock up with my asshole. My breath stutters as his tip penetrates me again. It feels so good. I just want to sink down on him, feel him inside me, thrusting like he does with the plugs.

"Relax, babe. Take me in as you can." Coop holds my hips, and I lower myself over him slowly. The first bit is fine, but then I get to the tight ring of muscles.

I hesitate and tighten up instinctually. "I don't know if I can."

"If it doesn't happen today, that's okay." He leans in to lick and suck my nipple. His breath is hot against my breast as he says, "We can try as often as you like, sweetheart. It's worth the wait, and then I'm going to want this ass all the time."

His fingers pull my ass cheeks apart, and I slide a little farther down on him. I gasp at how good it feels. My pussy is dripping wet. My skin buzzes with desire.

He sucks my breast into his mouth, and I ache for more.

"Just imagine Friday. Me thrusting into your ass while Blake fucks your tight pussy, Noah's cock in your mouth while you and Seth stroke his cock with your hands."

Tingles spread through me. I want that so much. Relaxing, I ease down past the burning sensation. There's a little pain, but it goes away.

He kisses my shoulder. "Good girl. Breathe. You're doing so well. We're going to fuck you all the time. Fill you with our cum until it leaks out of you. I'll push it in so you stay full of us."

He slides farther in as I relax on him. His words are heating me up, making me need every inch of him. To feel all these men in me, coming for me. All of them finding pleasure in my body. I want it. I want this.

It's slow, but soon my ass presses against Coop's legs as I take him all the way in. He's inside me. My breath shudders out.

"That's it, sweetheart." He sucks on my shoulder. "So tight, so perfect. You feel so good."

Fuck, I can feel him inside me. Thick and hard, all my nerve endings tingling as his hot skin slides inside me.

"Go slow." He trails kisses up my neck, gentle against the bruised skin. He sucks and kisses along my jawline. "We don't have to rush this."

I lift. My body is on fire, in a good way. My breasts rub against Coop's chest on the way up. When I sink back down on his cock, my lips part from the sensations coursing through me.

Coop's lips find mine, and he helps me rise and fall over him at a slow pace. The sensations build within me, making me burn.

I break our kiss and press my forehead against his. My fingers tangle in his hair as I ride his cock. "Coop."

His voice is breathless when he asks, "What do you need, babe?"

"I need—" My thighs tremble as I get closer to falling over the edge again. My lips part as my head falls back. "So close." I'm moving more, and the slide of him inside my ass makes everything quiver.

One of his hands slides from my hip to my pussy. He rubs my clit for a few seconds before his fingers slide into my slick channel and hook inside, pressing on a spot that makes me shatter.

I come hard and long, my body clutching around his fingers and cock. My mouth opens in a silent scream as I ride him through my orgasm. It spreads through me everywhere. Even my toes curl.

"Fuck, Madison," he groans as he slams me down onto his cock and comes deep inside me, triggering a secondary orgasm, or making the same one last longer. I can't tell anymore. I'm just a mass of sensation and pleasure.

My limbs shake as I wrap my arms around his neck and rest my head against his shoulder. He runs his hands up and down my spine soothingly.

"I don't think I can move," I whisper to his chest, kissing his warm skin.

Coop chuckles darkly. "If we stay like this, I'll be hard again."

My pussy pulses at the thought.

He captures my lips, kissing me hard and deep. Grabbing my hips, he stands. My legs wrap around him as I make a little startled noise into his mouth.

Once we're in the bathroom, he reaches into the shower and

turns on the hot water. Then he backs me against the wall and kisses me hard while he pulls his cock out. I lean my head back against the wall and stare into his eyes in a daze.

"I'd draw a bath, but I'm afraid you'd be asleep within minutes." Coop lightly traces my cheekbone with his thumb.

I give him a sloppy smile. "You're not wrong."

My arms tighten around his neck, and my legs hold on to his hips as he checks the temperature of the water before walking us into the shower. I slide my legs down to stand, and he lowers me to my feet.

The water feels divine, and his skin next to mine makes me want more, but my body is so done. We wash each other's hair, and thoroughly wash each other's bodies.

I lift my gaze to his darkened eyes as I stroke soap over his hard, thick cock.

"Fuck, Madison." He crowds me back into the tile wall and takes my hands, pressing them next to my head. A thrill shoots through me. "Keep them here," he growls.

My breathing is rapid as I wait, needy, watching him step back into the spray. He rinses the soap off, then lifts me and impales my pussy on his cock. Air bursts out of my lungs at the feel of him filling me. There's nothing slow about the way he takes me this time. His hips pump into mine. I reach up to hold on to the showerhead but do my best not to put my weight on it.

His mouth sucks on my shoulder, next to a hickey Noah left yesterday, as Coop grinds into me. It's too much. I can't hold back. I moan loud and long as I come all over his cock, but he doesn't let up. Keeping me on the edge, he reaches between us and pinches my clit.

It shatters me again. I cry out, grabbing on to him as he thrusts one last time inside me, filling me with his hot cum. His cock pulses inside my pussy as my core convulses around him.

He rests his head against my shoulder while I try to recover my breath.

"I can't wait for Friday." He kisses where my neck and shoulder meet, and an aftershock ripples through me.

I can't wait, either.

Chapter 34

Messages

Madison

My body is hot and achy. I wake up breathing heavily with Coop sucking on my clit.

"Coop." I arch against his mouth, but his hand holds my hips down. I swear I feel him smile against my pussy as he thrusts his fingers inside me. I explode into a fast and furious orgasm.

"Good morning, sweetheart." As he rises over me, he grabs my hands and holds them next to my head. His cock notches at my entrance before he easily slides inside.

Aftershocks ripple through me as he thrusts hard and steady. His eyes pin me to the bed, just like his hands do. I wrap my legs around his hips, meeting his every thrust until we come together. My breath catches as my insides tremble. My pussy clenches around his cock as he fills me with his warm cum.

He collapses over me, holding his weight mostly on his arms, but I like the press of his skin against mine. "One of these days, we're going to play hooky from work and fuck all day long."

My core throbs around him. He lifts his head and smirks down at me.

"You like that idea, sweetheart?"

"You fucking me? Always. Skipping work? Not so much." I grin as my breathing steadies. "Thanks for the wake-up call."

"Anytime." He kisses me. "You need me to wake you up, I'm here for it."

He thrusts his still-hard cock inside me before pulling out. When he lifts off me, he spreads my legs wide. His fingers go to work, pressing his cum back inside me. It's still a little weird, but I can't help the little thrill that races through me.

"How's your ass today?" His fingers dip inside my pussy, and I can't resist rocking against his hand.

"A little sore, but fine." My voice is breathless as he drives me higher again.

"Mmm." He licks my clit.

I groan as arousal swirls inside me.

"I love making you come." Coop thrusts his fingers deep and sucks my clit into his mouth. It's like he hits the ignition switch as flames scorch my insides.

"Fuck." The word is soft, as I can't find my breath. I shoot up into another orgasm, burning from the inside out, and then collapse on the bed. Breathless. Muscles that feel like water.

Chuckling, Coop stands. "Come here."

Dragging air into my lungs, I eye him warily but scoot to sit on the edge of the bed.

His hand wraps in my hair, and he tilts my head back. "I haven't taken your mouth yet."

I lick my lips, and his cock hardens completely. Fuck. My insides pulse with aching need yet again. I've never been this insatiable before, but these men drag something from me that I don't want to resist. I meet his eyes.

"Then take it."

Giving me his wicked grin, he lowers my head to his cock. When his tip touches my lips, I part them and flick my tongue out to taste him. Groaning, he thrusts deep inside my mouth, making me gag slightly. He waits until I relax my throat for him. With a smile, he fucks my face, thrusting like he did in my core. Hard and fast. His blue eyes hold mine.

My desire swells with each thrust, and I try to suck and lick when I can. There's something about giving in to him that appeals to something deep inside me. When I reach up and cup his tight balls, he explodes down my throat with a shout. I swallow all of him and lick him clean as he pulls my head back.

His mouth captures mine, and he tastes me. I can taste myself on his tongue.

When he releases my mouth, he leans his forehead against mine. "This will be a never-ending thing. I get you off. You get me off. So I get you off. Not that I'm complaining, but we have work today."

I grin up at him, and he leans in to take my mouth again, pressing me down into the bed. I could forget all about work in this bed. Wrapping my legs around his waist, I drag him down with me. Suddenly, playing hooky seems like an excellent use of both of our time.

"I want to fuck your ass again," he says against my lips.

My body clenches at his words.

He lifts off me and stands. His gaze rakes over my aroused body. My skin is flushed. My nipples hard. My pussy aches.

He groans and finds my pajamas and panties. "I'd offer to shower with you again, but I'd just fuck you more, and if I fuck you again, I'll want to bury my cock so deep in your ass..." Touching his fingers against his lips, he shakes his head. "It's too soon for that."

I sit up and sigh. He's right. Neither of us would have the willpower to not fuck in the shower. And if he wanted my ass, I'd let him have it, knowing I'd shatter on his cock all over again.

He groans and leans down to kiss me. When he pulls back, he heads to the bathroom. "You are addictive, sweetheart."

He closes the door and I whisper, "So are you."

I don't know how to feel about any of this. Is this really just about sex? The soft moments with them weigh on my mind, but so far, it's been a lot of sex, and I'm not complaining. They're definitely making up for my lack of experimenting in college.

It's still early, so the apartment is empty as I walk through to my room. When I enter my bedroom, a beep catches my attention.

Yesterday, I found my old cell phone in one of the boxes. Dead, of course. I found the charger and plugged it in.

I sit on the bed as I lift my phone. There are so many messages.

ROBERT:

I hope you're okay. A guy took you to the hospital.

ROBERT:

When are you coming home?

ROBERT:

Guys came and moved your stuff. Are you moving out?

ROBERT:

Why aren't you answering me? Did I do something wrong?

ROBERT:

I hope you're doing well. Your boss stopped by and asked me some questions. He said they moved you somewhere safe.

ROBERT:

If you need a place to stay, I have a couch. You could use the bed.

ROBERT:

I'm here and worried. Please text.

I sigh. As much as he was creepy, he also watched out for me.

ME:

I'm doing fine. Please don't worry. I don't think I'll be back to the apartment. I can't risk Valerie finding me.

ROBERT:

Okay. Keep in touch.

He answers quickly, but there are more texts to go through. I set the phone aside and head into my bathroom to get ready for work. I can read them while I eat breakfast.

When I'm ready, I grab my old phone and head into the kitchen. I leave it on the island while I get a cup of coffee and start some eggs. The availability of food is still a little novel to me, and I really enjoy being able to have more for breakfast than just a piece of fruit or toast.

When I sit down with my eggs and toast, I grab my phone and start going over the texts from the past few days. There are a bunch of texts from various services and appointments. But as I scroll down, the next number makes my whole body freeze. It's from Valerie.

"Madison?"

I lift my gaze from my phone to Seth's worried eyes. He takes the phone from my hand. He reads the texts, but I don't need to see them to remember. They're burned into my memory already.

VALERIE:

Don't think we're done with you.

VALERIE:

If I'd known you were putting out, Jeff and I would have sampled the goods before.

VALERIE:

You changed the lock, you cunt!

VALERIE:

I'm going to fuck you so hard for fucking with me.

VALERIE:

Don't think those guys can protect you forever.

VALERIE:

We both know they'll toss your slut ass to the curb soon enough. Then you'll be mine to play with.

VALERIE:

If we don't kill you first.

"Fuck." Seth does something on my phone and then slides it into his pocket.

I'm still frozen, like I never got out of my apartment. Like they still have me trapped, crushing my throat. I jerk at the scarf around my neck like it's choking me. I toss it aside and draw in a breath.

Strong arms wrap around me, and my forehead rests against his chest. When my nose fills with sandalwood, my breathing becomes less strained. Seth's hands rub down my back.

"What happened?" Blake's voice is thick with worry.

Seth shifts and holds his arm out to Blake, but he doesn't release me. I assume he's giving him my phone. My lungs burn, and I pant to try to catch my breath. My fingers clutch Seth's shirt as I try to ease the tightness inside my chest and slow my breathing.

"Fuck," Blake breathes out.

"I reported it to the police. I'll drop the phone at the station so they can go over the texts." Seth's hand returns to my back.

"What about this other number?"

My head lifts at Blake's question. He has my phone in his hand and glares at it.

"I didn't go through it all."

Seth tips his face to look into mine. His thumbs come up and wipe at the wetness on my cheeks.

Sitting back, I swipe at my face. When did I start crying?

Blake glances at me and then shakes his head. "We'll talk about it later."

"No." I hold my hand out, trying not to let it tremble. "It's my phone. You aren't cutting me out of this conversation."

"It's an anonymous caller. They included pictures." Blake doesn't hand me the phone. "Someone's been watching you."

My brow furrows. I know I just locked up and cried, but I'm not a delicate flower. I just needed a moment. "Let me see, Blake."

His lips thin, and it seems like he is going to deny me, but then he blows out his breath. "Fine. Finish your breakfast first."

He slides the phone into his pocket. Seth and Blake move around the kitchen, getting coffee and making breakfast. They're doing their best not to make it noticeable that they're worried about me.

I force myself to eat my eggs. Each bite almost chokes me, but I don't care. I'm doing what I have to in order to get the information.

By the time I finish, Noah has come in and given me a kiss on the forehead. Then Coop comes in with a bright grin that falls when he sees me.

"What happened?" he asks, glaring at the others like it's their fault the smile he left there this morning is gone from my face.

"My old phone has texts." I swallow the last bite and sit back. My gaze finds Blake. "Are we going to do this?"

He nods curtly and jerks his head toward the living room. When I head for the couch, the others follow me. Before I can sit down, Coop grabs me and drags me down on his lap. I give him a sharp look, but he ignores it. Noah and Seth sit on either side of Coop, and both put a hand on me.

Noah takes my hand and Seth puts his on my thigh. Their touch and closeness settle me as Blake sits on the ottoman in front of me.

"You don't have to see these, tiger. I don't want to frighten you." Blake's eyes are filled with concern.

I take a deep breath. "It's better to know than to imagine."

My imagination has taken me to some pretty dark places recently, and I don't need it to expand to the unknown.

Blake nods and holds out the phone.

UNKNOWN:

You and me, little one. Soon.

The first picture is from the day I went shopping for new clothes. There's a picture of me looking through panties and bras. One of me trying on shoes. One of a mirror in a changing room, reflecting me stripped down to the underwear I was trying on.

Blake scrolls forward, and there is a picture of me studying in the library from a few months ago. Walking on campus. Blake carrying me out of my apartment, unconscious. One of me sleeping in the hospital bed.

My hand goes over my mouth at that one. The next one is a video.

"We don't have to—" Blake starts.

"Play it." I squeeze Noah's hand. Seth's hand tightens on my thigh.

It sounds like rain in the background until I focus on what the camera is aimed at. It's the linoleum in my bathroom at my apartment. My hand covers my mouth again as I realize that's not rain.

A moan fills the audio. My face burns with embarrassment because every one of these guys can recognize that moan. Coop's arms tighten around me. It's not like they all haven't seen and heard me masturbate, but this wasn't for show.

The angle changes, and suddenly, the camera is looking into the glass shower. I'm naked, pressed against the wall. One hand teases my nipple while the other is buried between my legs. I cry out softly as I come.

The camera swings to the side and suddenly we are back to the view from the ceiling or the corner, I can't tell for sure. But I step out and put a towel around myself as I dry my hair. It keeps watching me as I dry off and put on my underwear, then it stops.

UNKNOWN:

I'm going to enjoy watching the live show, little one.

I don't even realize I'm trembling until I'm curled up in Coop's arms. Seth strokes my back while Noah massages my hand.

"I'm going to kill him." Blake shuts off the phone and sticks it in his pocket.

"We don't know it's a him," Seth points out.

"Someone was in that bathroom with her."

It's too much. My insides churn violently.

I jolt out of their embrace and into the kitchen. My stomach spills out of me like those images, vile, burning, disgusting. A hand grabs my hair away from my face. Another hand strokes down my back. Someone runs the sink, so the filth goes down the drain, but that violation sticks to my skin.

In my bathroom. A camera in my bathroom for who knows how long.

My stomach heaves a few more times before it gives up. I'm pulled up against a hard chest, and a gentle hand wipes my mouth with a washcloth. I meet Seth's eyes. His lips are pressed together.

"Here."

I turn to Noah, take the glass of water, and sip it slowly. Watching me closely, Coop leans against the counter, meaning the arms around me are Blake's.

"You should stay here today." Seth's tone is commanding.

"I can't sit here and do nothing all day." My arms wrap around my middle over Blake's.

I'd rot if left alone with my thoughts. The intrusion into my life. For how long? Months, maybe years. Had it been Valerie taking the video? Did she know about the camera? Or was her privacy violated too?

"I've got some work I can do down here for a while," Noah offers. "I can bring down my spare laptop for Madison to work on."

"All of us have some work that can be done down here." Coop meets Seth's gaze but holds firm. "We can rotate who stays with Madison."

"I can work at my desk." No one listens to me, though.

"Yeah, I have some projects that have been put off." Blake rubs the back of his neck.

"Guys, seriously. I'm fine." I straighten and glance at my scarf. I don't want it around my neck. It feels like his hands at first, before he choked me.

Four sets of eyes land on me, and I squirm a little at the attention.

"I won't fall apart." I take a breath. "Again. I can be a professional. Give me, like, thirty minutes to clean up, and I can work."

I hold my breath as I give them all a look that says I'm fine.

"I'll stay with her until she comes upstairs." Noah steps beside me, and his hand goes to the small of my back. "We'll be there soon."

Seth

We leave Noah and Madison in the apartment and head into the elevator.

"I'll make copies before the police get here." Blake's thumb runs over the screen of the phone almost unconsciously.

"This is fucked up." Coop clenches his fist as we get on the elevator. "Who the fuck does something like that?"

"It could have been the roommate." I try to ignore the tension winding inside me at the look on her face when she read those texts. "Though she doesn't seem like the subtle type."

"No, if she had this shit, she'd have sent it." Blake shakes his head. "We have to protect her."

"What more can we do?" Coop steps out into our office space. "We deal with cybersecurity, but we aren't law enforcement. They'll figure out what this is."

Blake chuckles harshly. "They'll take the threats from Valerie seriously because her and her boyfriend assaulted Madison. But this?" He flicks on the video, and Madison's moan fills the space. "It's intrusive, but there's no threat."

"What about the *soon*?" Coop glares.

"Harmless." It hurts to say it, but it's the truth. I run a hand over the back of my head. "She has a stalker. Maybe she knows about it, but it seemed like new information."

That reaction couldn't be faked. She was mortified and terrified. Whoever this is, they accomplished their goal.

"Fuck." Coop stalks away and back again. "What the fuck do we do?"

"Notify the police." Blake sighs and slips the phone into his pocket. "We watch and wait for the fucker's next move. We keep her safe."

Coop nods.

"She's not like the others." I glance back at the elevator, knowing it will be a little while before she comes up.

"No, she's not." Coop's blue eyes meet mine.

"Maybe she'll be able to figure out who it is." I move toward my office. "Until then, we don't treat her like she's about to break."

Coop shakes his head, and a small smile lights his lips. "She's definitely not breakable."

Blake nods and walks into his office, closing the door.

"Do you think she'll be okay today?" Coop glances at the elevator. "I wouldn't mind occupying her mind with other things all day long."

I shake my head. "We'll keep her close and keep her safe. No one will get to her while she's under our protection."

"Fuck!"

We both turn as Blake comes out of his office.

He's pissed. "You'll never believe what this fucker just sent."

Whatever it takes, we'll keep Madison safe.

Find out what happens next in PRIVATE LISTING: BIND ME.

Meet C.S. Berry

C.S. Berry is a combination of my love for writing and my love for reading. She began as an experiment and took off into something I absolutely adore. It's not often you can do what you love and it works as a career. As for me, I love reading and romance and heroines seriously getting railed. I assume since you've read my books that you do too.

If you want to discuss books or anything with me, come join my Facebook group, C.S. Berry's Spicy Executive Suite. And you can always catch me on Instagram @csberry.

Oh and me, I have a lovely family who aren't allowed to read my books. But are so proud, they keep leaking my pen name. My dog and cats don't care about my writing as long as I sit still long enough for them to snuggle. For more of my books and to join my newsletter, visit my website csberry.com.

XOXOXO,

C.S. Berry

For more stories and updates:
csberry.com
Join my Newsletter on my Website

Made in United States
Troutdale, OR
06/10/2024

20464948R00181